IN HARM'S WAY:
Surviving the
Zombie Apocalypse

SHAWN CHESSER

CONTENTS

ACKNOWLEDGMENTS

For Mo, Raven, and Caden, you three mean the world to me...love you. And thanks for putting up with me clacking away at all hours. I owe everything to my parents for bringing me up the right way. Mom, thanks for reading… although it is not your genre. Dad, aka Mountain Man Dan, thanks for your ear and influence. Cliff Kane, RIP. Daymon, thanks for taking me all over the slopes in Jackson Hole! Thanks to all of the men and women in the military, past and present, especially those of you in harm's way. Thanks to all LE personnel for your service. To the people in the U.K. who have been in touch, thanks for reading! Beta readers, you rock and you know who you are. Thanks George Romero for introducing me to zombies. Steve H. thanks for listening. All of my friends and fellows at S@N, thanks as well. Lastly, thanks to Bill W. and Dr. Bob … you helped make this possible. I am going to sign up for another 24.

My idea for the cover was interpreted and designed by Jason Swarr of Straight 8 Photography. Thank you sir!

Special thanks to Craig DiLouie, Gary Mountjoy, John O'Brien, and Mark Tufo. One way or another all of you have helped me and provided me with invaluable advice.

Once again, extra special thanks to Monique Happy for taking In Harm's Way and giving it some special attention and TLC while polishing its rough edges. Working with you, Mo, has been a seamless experience and nothing but a pleasure. You are the best!

***

Edited by Monique Happy Editorial Services
www.moniquehappy.com

Chapter 1
Outbreak - Day 8
Schriever Air Force Base
Colorado Springs, Colorado

Daymon stomped his feet and heckled the nearest zombies. He wanted to lure all of the creatures in the immediate vicinity to the barrier in front of him.

The creep of panic brought on by his claustrophobia was brewing internally. Even in the pitch black he could sense the twelve foot chain-link topped with coiled razor wire pressing in on him. Since childhood he had had a profound fear of enclosed spaces and fought like a wolverine when cornered. More than one former schoolyard bully could attest to that.

If another human had been present the flash of steel would have been lost on them. Daymon was lightning quick; the largest of the walkers wavered and then folded sideways, crumpling in a heap. Ten inches of pointed tent stake to the eye made sure the corpse would stay down for good. The sharpened steel was the only weapon Daymon could scrounge up and would have to do until he found something more lethal.

The sudden burst of movement drew the walking corpses nearer. They clambered over their brother's unmoving body to get to the living. Cold white fingers probed the honeycomb-shaped openings as their combined weight pressed the fence inward.

"Come and get me," Daymon chided the ghouls in a singsong voice, barely audible over the shuffling of their lifeless feet. Gaunt faces pressed closer, bringing their stench with them. Their demonic guttural moaning commenced. The man in black was afraid of neither the walkers nor what one bite could do to him. He had been dead inside since the day he was discarded, like so much trash, in the dumpster behind the community hospital where his biological mom spit him out.

A small helping of patience was all it took. One by one the foul smelling abominations moved up a space in line. Curiosity didn't motivate them; it was their unstoppable desire to consume his flesh. He lured them near until all but one lay in a heap, victims of the tent stake. An old saying that he once heard popped into his head, *an eye for an eye leaves a room full of blind men.* This whole apocalypse thing was to his liking; he tolerated very few people and loved no one now that the lady that adopted him, the one that actually *deserved* to be called Mom, was gone.

Daymon raked the cold steel back and forth across the chain links. The ensuing *tink-tink-tink* failed to get the remaining zombie's attention. It was a very old specimen, gnarled and hunched over. It had probably been prisoner in an assisted living facility, lonely and waiting to die, before being infected and mercifully released to join the hungry ranks of the walking dead. The man in black watched the monster pan its shriveled head back and forth, like a ravenous lion, smelling the air for prey.

Daymon scaled the first few feet of fence, and when he was within arm's reach of the coiled razor wire, he tugged the burlap potato sacks free from where they had been hanging, like a tail, jammed between the small of his back and his wide leather belt. He had liberated the sacks from behind the twenty-four hour mess tent where some anal individual had left them neatly stacked amongst a myriad of other recyclables. *Old habits died hard. Who the hell do they think they are saving the planet for now?* he mused.

Hanging on perilously with one hand grasping the rusted fence, Daymon lofted the first of the sacks over his head and steered it, as gravity pulled it down, to the spot where he wanted it to land.

From his high perch he witnessed the elderly zombie stagger twenty feet to the south and perform another sniff test on the air. Daymon had a feeling that its other senses were compromised. *Did somebody forget their contacts on Judgment Day?* He quietly snickered.

After fully covering a two foot wide section with all of the burlap potato sacks, he gingerly began to inch his way over while his body weight compressed the coils. At first he didn't feel the scalpel sharp barbs as they bit into his skin. However, he did sense the hot sticky fluid soaking into his thermal undershirt. Dismayed by the sheer volume of his own coppery-smelling blood, he wondered whimsically if he was going to die before he even made it out of the base. Once he was on the ground, outside of the wire, he quickly assessed the damage. The cuts weren't as bad as he had initially suspected and they would stop bleeding eventually. The tough firefighter had been cut to the bone before and survived so he wasn't about to let a few superficial gashes slow him down now.

Daymon triaged his situation as he warily eyed the walker deliberately shuffling along the fence in his direction. The creature would have to be dealt with first and then the wounds to his torso.

He already knew the odds of completing this foolhardy excursion weren't favorable. But the thought of spending another second inside the Air Force base, unarmed, feeling like a neutered dog, was out of the question.

***

An hour before dark, Daymon had taken a long meandering walk around the north and west sides of the base searching for the right spot to scale the fence. The first thing he noticed was that there were very few walkers near the perimeter. The snipers had been engaging the flesh eaters with surgical precision since they began arriving outside the perimeter a week ago. The massive mounds of dead still awaiting burial stood testament to the shooters' lethality. He returned to his billet two hours later, confident he could escape the base; whether he would find what he was looking for once outside the wire was another story.

***

Schriever Security Pod

The airman tasked with monitoring the northeast perimeter cameras during the early morning hours was distracted, to say the least. He was trying to listen in on the action in downtown Springs in one ear and watch the multi-camera feeds on the monitor at the same

3

time. The rooftop snipers were constantly calling for ammunition and relaying body counts. The drama being played out over the radio was enough of a diversion to make the airman miss the melee taking place in the lower corner of the flat panel monitor. The ethereal shadow lunged and hacked at the group of zombies until they were a dark unmoving pile of bodies at the bottom of the screen. He also missed the dark shape leg sweep the last standing zombie and deliver a final fatal blow, pinning the thing's head to the ground.

By the time the sleep-deprived sentry turned his attention to the eight separate camera feeds on the divided LCD screen, Daymon had already melted away into the darkness.

***

Outside the wire

Daymon pulled consistent five minute miles when he ran cross-country for the Teton High Redskins. That was over a decade ago, and in track shoes, not leather boots. The steady breeze caressing his back was calming and helped push him along, more mentally than physically. Late afternoon thunderstorms the day before had softened the ground, lessening the strain on his knees. Large mountain ranges like the Rockies had more of an effect on the weather than most people realized. Nearly every day like clockwork, the angry dark clouds would pull in from the west, form up like soldiers awaiting marching orders, spill over the craggy peaks and violently roll across the high desert. The summer weather was the same back home: both the Wasatch front in Utah, where his mom used to live, and the Tetons in Wyoming, where he spent most of his childhood. After high school Daymon followed his parents to the Salt Lake suburb of South Jordan, where he rented a studio apartment and worked loss prevention at a number of different electronics stores. He quickly found that the work was neither challenging nor rewarding. The city was too vanilla for his liking, and as much as it pained him he decided to move back to Driggs, the poor man's Jackson Hole, and get a job with the BLM fighting forest fires. Before long the lanky young man worked his way out of the heavy fire crews and up the government pay grade, eventually finding his true calling--jumping out of perfectly good airplanes into dangerous situations.

Before the outbreak Daymon was enjoying a one week stand down; late July had seen fewer forest fires than usual so he risked a quick trip to South Jordan to see his "Moms" as he liked to call her. He had left the fire station in Jackson Hole early Saturday morning and was on his way to Salt Lake when he heard the first Department of Homeland Security alert announced on the radio. He vividly remembered the first tingles of caution he sensed when he couldn't get a call through to Chief Kyle at the station. His cell phone wasn't one of the new "smart" models--those kind usually didn't last long when he was jumping out of airplanes or hacking through heavy brush and setting backfires. Cursing his bad luck, he tossed the chunky Ericsson phone into the glove box of the Suburban, chalking the lack of reception up to a cellular dead spot. He skirted Salt Lake by staying on I-80, but only made it as far south as Provo, Utah before being repulsed by the living dead. Grudgingly he made the difficult decision to head back to Jackson Hole, leaving his Mom's whereabouts seemingly forever unknown. It was during the return trip, in the little town of Hannah, Utah, where he met Cade Grayson and they embarked together on the dangerous trek that eventually delivered them to Schriever Air Force Base on the outskirts of Colorado Springs.

***

Two miles outside of the wire

Daymon had spotted the Rocky Mountain Outdoor Store near a boarded up strip mall the night before while riding shotgun in the Wells Fargo armored car. It looked, from a distance, like the entire block and parking lot had been surrounded with chain link fencing. Even though it had been dark and the vehicle he was riding in had been moving at a decent clip, it appeared as if the stores had been spared from looting. The close proximity to Schriever, with its large military presence, was probably its saving grace.

Daymon stopped to surveil his surroundings, getting his bearings while he racked his brain, striving to remember where he had seen the cluster of stores.

After a moment's rest he decided to keep looking and resumed running, picking up the same fast pace. The early morning high desert air had a crisp edge to it, allowing him to see his breath with each hard earned exhale. Daymon was just hitting his stride, long legs propelling him smoothly forward, when the ground under his boots suddenly disappeared. The instantaneous sensation of weightlessness compelled his stomach to take temporary residence in his throat as he plunged into the abyss. The impact that followed was as startling as the realization that the ground had seemingly been yanked out from under him. He sensed something sharp poking his knee through his thick dungarees and his right hand rested on a cold smooth surface with a small amount of give. The makeshift weapon in his other hand had become embedded in something solid.

As Daymon's eyes adjusted to the new environs a pallid face, inches from his, came into sharp focus. The zombie's death mask, stretched tight across its skull, thin waxy lips riding over a picket of ivory incisors, stared blankly back at him. Thankfully, worms squirmed from a gaping, fist-sized cavity in the thing's temple, confirming that it was *really* dead.

Daymon recoiled and removed the tent stake from the thing's shoulder. As he shifted his weight to avoid the inadvertent kiss of death, his hand plunged into something sticky, releasing a burst of noxious gasses. Elbow deep in entrails, he detected a shifting within the sea of carrion. Frantically he scrabbled to his knees, pulling his right arm from the gore. Mercifully it was dark and the true horror of his predicament wasn't fully revealed. Once again he sensed something moving underneath him, whether it was a bunch of zombies or just the result of his added weight was moot, he wanted out.

The Gods taunted him as the moon briefly appeared, shining golden light down the middle of the mass grave that he had unwittingly tumbled into. Hundreds of dead bodies surrounded him, and like the faces in a madman's nightmare, they silently snarled and laughed at his misfortune. Daymon found out the hard way that it was impossible to retch and breathe through his mouth at the same time. Acid-laced bile backed up and sluiced from his mouth and nostrils. Each heave of his body was answered by more subtle movements from just under the surface layer of decaying corpses.

Daymon shakily arose while nervously eyeing the area near his feet. A shiver coursed up his spine and the small hairs on his neck stood at attention when the muffled wanting moans began to resonate from deep inside the grave. Daymon slipped and slogged through the pit of corpses and once he finally made it to the edge, like he had done hundreds of times while skiing in the backcountry, he kicked postholes into the mud wall and slowly made his way up the slippery seventy-five degree incline.

Daymon sat on the edge of the muddy wound that had been gouged into the earth and contemplated his latest brush with death. He knew it was going to happen sooner or later... death was inevitable. The Grim Reaper was going to have to wait though, because Daymon still had a few hundred things left to do on his bucket list. Snapping back to the present, his eyes were drawn to the distant sky show. The sweeping spotlights in downtown Springs, twenty miles to the west, were dwarfed by the backdrop of Pikes Peak and the southern Rockies. The mountains rose to 14,000 feet, jutting like sharks teeth into the inky night sky. *Good idea,* he thought. Even though the noisy transport planes bringing the soldiers back from places around the globe had stopped arriving hourly, the hungry dead kept showing up outside the wire. Utilizing the intense spotlights to draw the monsters away from the base and back into the metro area was ingenious. But just how long it was going to take to kill all of the zombies once they amassed was the sixty-four thousand dollar question.

***

With the ordeal of the pit fresh in his mind, Daymon loped at a slow trot northwest while keeping a wary eye on the ground. He jaywalked diagonally across the street towards a darkened Texaco gas station and happened upon two zombies trapped inside a 1970s Cadillac Eldorado. The car was adorned with the full luxury package, including the faux gold plated spare tire kit on the trunk; it had been a regal car when it was shiny and new, but now the once white interior was streaked with dried blood and a milky film of unidentifiable fluids fouled the insides of the glass. The creatures hadn't seen him yet and he didn't want to give them a reason to moan, so he kept out of sight and quietly snuck around the rear of the gold Caddie. *No way,* he thought to himself when he spied the red and blue Grateful Dead sticker proudly displayed on the car's rear bumper. Don Henley would have been proud, he mused, as the Eagles' lyrics began to resonate in his head.

He moved on with his attention divided between avoiding the zombies in the car and watching the ground in front of him, and nearly ran headlong into a lone walker emerging from behind one of the gas pumps.

Daymon had little warning and was forced to leap over the snarling ghoul. The move brought back memories of his track and field days at Teton High. He stopped abruptly, turned and sized up the pint-sized flesh eater. Somewhere along the line the zombie had lost its foot and most of the fingers on both hands. Daymon had noticed that nearly all of the creatures had similar defensive wounds, suffered when they were still human, trying unsuccessfully to survive the brutally vicious attacks the packs of hungry dead were capable of.

The limping ghoul scraped forward dragging its mangled stump, nubs for hands reaching for him. Daymon thought the thing would be a good candidate for an eye patch considering that the raw protruding leg bone resembled a peg leg and the guttural moaning sounded a little pirate like. *What a way to end up,* he thought to himself.

Calmly, the lanky dreadlocked man stood his ground. Like a bullfighter without a cape, he swiftly sidestepped the gimpy zombie and followed through with a vicious downward blow to the top of the skull. The twice dead corpse slid freely from the blood slickened shank and collided with the ground.

Daymon wiped his only *weapon* off on the zombie's tee shirt and continued on his way. He was only three blocks removed from the encounter at the Texaco when he found what he was looking for. The enormous darkened sign loomed above him. It appeared to Daymon that *C.K.'s Rocky Mountain Outdoor and More* was closed for business... indefinitely. The words on the reader board silently urged everyone passing to *Gear up for bear season!* And the promise of a *Military Discount* adorned the bottom of the sign, likely put there to

deter base personnel from venturing into the big city for their
sporting goods needs.

The temporary fencing here was nearly as tall as the one
ringing the air force base; uneven and sagging in spots, it looked like
it had been hastily erected. Still smarting from his last encounter with
a security fence, he walked the perimeter looking for an easier way in
than over the top.

Daymon noticed several smaller businesses standing adjacent
to the outdoor store. A cellular store, flanked by a sushi restaurant
and a UPS mailing center; all were boarded up and dark. It was your
garden variety retail cluster, minus the ubiquitous Subway or Baja
Fresh fast food store. He had no idea why they took the time to
board up the sushi restaurant. Fifteen minutes with no power and all
you have is bait anyway. He couldn't even fathom what it smelled like
inside after a *week* without refrigeration, and he shuddered at the
thought. As for protecting the Verizon shop from looters--that was
wishful thinking at best. Thanks to the zombie apocalypse all of those
fancy phones were now just useless paperweights. *Welcome to the Dark
Ages,* he thought.

As Daymon walked the fence on the far side of the sporting
goods store, he found the chink in the armor he had been searching
for. With a little jostling he successfully moved the two cinderblock
bases apart enough to allow his narrow frame access to the empty
parking lot. A stiff wind kicked up, delivering the stench of rotten
flesh to his nose. After surveying the surroundings for the source and
finding the lot free of undead, he came to the awful realization that
the odor was from the bodily fluids soaked into his sleeves and pants
legs. His first order of business, he thought, was to find a real
weapon and then a set of clean clothes.

After locating the front doors of the outdoor store, Daymon
quickly traversed the large parking lot with the *Mission Impossible*
theme playing on a loop in his head. *Shit,* he thought, as he spied the
heavy duty chain coiled around the handles like a steel anaconda.
One glance told him the lock wouldn't yield so he chose the path of
least resistance, and prying around the edges with the tent stake,
removed the quarter inch plywood covering the glass. Daymon's first
kick, aimed just below the door handle, buckled the entire window

inward. The subsequent blow from his size eleven boot shattered the spider-webbed pane spraying hundreds of pea-size glass nuggets inside the store. He ducked his head under the bar, contorted the rest of his body to follow, and slowly crossed the debris field, trying to heel and toe it as quietly as possible, although doing so while retaining a modicum of stealth proved to be futile. The glass shards crunching under his boots sounded like small caliber gunshots echoing about the cavernous store.

Daymon sat on his haunches with his back against the wall, letting his eyes adjust to the shadowy interior. Now that he was inside and sitting in one place the stench of death permeating his clothes quickly overwhelmed him, so he stripped naked and heaved the stinking clothing outside.

Daymon stood silently in the dark. *So far, so good.* He heard none of the hissing and moaning he had come to despise since the outbreak. Nothing stirred inside the store and it appeared that his amateur attempt at breaking and entering had gone unnoticed.

Since he had no one watching his back, and certainly didn't want any visitors while searching for supplies, he looked around the store entry for something big to take the place of the missing glass. Daymon wasn't worried about tangling with a few zombies. The walking corpses were fairly predictable, and in small numbers, easy to handle. Humans, on the other hand, were to be avoided. Except for Cade and the old dude, Duncan, most of the people he had encountered since the dead started walking were nothing but opportunists and stone cold killers.

He decided early on that anybody slowing him down, thus lowering his odds for survival, was expendable. Hoss wasn't the first warm blooded biped that Daymon had seen fit to cull from Earth's dwindling herd. He had already left several unlucky bandits littering the roadside in the days since the outbreak.

Between the restroom doors labeled "Buck's" and "Doe's" in a small alcove off of the store entrance stood a six foot tall wooden Indian. The carved piece of brightly painted art weighed upwards of two hundred pounds, and with some effort Daymon was able to move the statue into place, effectively blocking the opening.

IN HARM'S WAY: SURVIVING THE ZOMBIE APOCALYPSE

The big Chief eclipsed the scant amount of moonlight
filtering in from outside, causing Daymon to change his priorities. A
new weapon and change of clothes would have to wait, what he
needed now was a working flashlight. The nude dreadlocked man
cautiously crept further into the store, painfully aware of his *exposed*
situation. All around him it looked as if a small amount of looting
had taken place. The glass cases ringing the walls, usually reserved to
display the high end pistols and collectible knives, were still intact but
all of their shelves had been picked clean.

The low slung checkout counter seemed a logical place to
start. The cash drawer was open with a note, written on a crisp sheet
torn from a yellow legal pad, sitting where the bill tray would have
been. Daymon plucked a Mini Maglite dangling from a display and
cast the beam on the paper.

C.K.

*I got here early Sunday morning. Some people were waiting for the store
to open. (Not looting like on TV... strange.) I only recognized a couple of them
but they all had guns. I wasn't threatened but I could tell they were desperate. I
know that if I didn't let them in they would've made me. So much for friendly
Coloradans... They bought all of the guns and ammo in the store plus camping
gear and some other stuff. The itemized bill and credit card imprints are in the
office in the top desk drawer. By now you probably realize they left me in one
piece... hope this thing gets under control. Schriever AFB is locked down. I took
half of the secret stash before bugging out. Going to check on my parents in
Sulphur Springs.*

*P.S. As you see the fence guys you called showed up sometime
Saturday... get your money back the shitty fence didn't keep anyone out! Take
care of yourself. Thanks for everything! Lewis.*

Daymon snorted after reading the last sentence, and thought
to himself, *at least the fence kept the zombies out.*

He panned the flashlight left to right across the knotty pine
walls adorned with multiple trophy kills: pheasant, turkey, geese, and
duck, all in a permanent state of flight. He was feeling the chill in the
air as he walked the aisles, but still he passed up the display of bright
orange coveralls. *Not gonna cut it,* he thought. Finally Daymon found
the Carhartt work clothes, in all the usual drab colors, stacked chest
high and tucked behind the day glo hunting garb. Using his mouth to

11

hold the flashlight, he wasted no time rifling through the piles with both hands.

Once again dressed in full black, courtesy of whoever C.K. was, Daymon crept towards the back of the store. He passed the narrow beam of light across a display of camping gear searching for a stuff sack or soft internal frame backpack to load his loot into. The maroon and gold Kelty propped up beside a White Stag dome tent caught his eye. To show off its full capacity, the backpack was already stuffed full of pre-packaged freeze dried food, an MSR stove, a sleeping bag, and a rolled up Therm-a-Rest mattress, most of which Daymon had no use for. He emptied the bag of everything except for some of the food.

Not everyone liked to hunt bear with a high powered rifle. In Daymon's opinion there wasn't much sport involved and therefore not enough adrenaline in the equation for him. Judging by the reader board in front of the store, he reasoned that there must be a department that catered to bow hunters such as him.

Stealthily he slipped through the jungle of clearance priced clothing, his head on a swivel and the flashlight held high. Unexpectedly a pale form materialized from the shadows. Daymon's senses were already ratcheted up, and he reacted without thinking. The tent stake flashed and pierced the mannequin's Styrofoam head with a dry squeak. *Fuck!* He caught the dummy by the wrist before it could fall and make a racket. *Want to dance?* Then he lowered his partner to the floor and removed the survival knife strapped to the high riding pair of hip waders and clipped it onto his belt.

Before proceeding deeper into the bowels of the outdoor supercenter, Daymon paused and remained still, listening for any telltale movement or sound that would indicate he wasn't alone. *Nothing. The store's all mine,* he thought, as he passed through the white water recreation section. Racks of colorful kayaks and canoes formed a plastic canyon that funneled him face to stomach with a six foot Black Bear. The big mammal stood upright on a two foot tall pedestal. The taxidermist had done a superb job of bringing it back from the dead. Bared canines glistened, forever longing for its next victim. The obsidian eyes twinkled in the flashlight beam and seemed to follow him as he stepped around the ursine.

Daymon had once encountered a specimen its size in the wild, but unfortunately the cagey bear proved difficult to track and managed to elude the hunt. The following season, in the High Uinta Mountains of Utah, he proudly bagged a smaller black with only a compound bow.

This stuffed bear would have been menacing had the ridiculous placard not been hanging around its thick neck. The sign read *Everything you need to hunt me... and Bear repellant.* At least there wasn't a smiley face on the sign, Daymon thought. What a way for an Alpha predator to end up--shilling bear spray in an outdoor-n-more.

Like a kid in a candy store, Daymon salivated over the selection of crossbows spread out before him. Fitted with optics and bristling with extra bolts, the Excalibur Equinox called to him. The thousand dollar camouflage beauty would have been a luxury purchase a little out of his price range in the old world. *Put it on my AmEx,* he thought as the corner of his mouth curled, revealing a sly toothy smile. After arming himself with the crossbow, Daymon continued through the store. He traded the tent stake for a pair of eighteen inch machetes, both identical to the one he was relieved of upon entering Schriever AFB. The best binoculars money could no longer buy went into the Kelty, along with a pair of two-way radios. Loaded for bear, the ex-BLM firefighter donned the backpack and beat feet.

After leaving the sporting goods store, Daymon crossed the street and jogged around the Cadillac, once again giving it a wide berth. He could see that the ghouls were still inside, rocking the boat on its springs. With the flashlight beam sweeping the ground, he carefully skirted the mass grave that had almost become his final resting place. Nothing moved and all was quiet as he picked up his pace, racing the clock to get back over the fence before first light.

The corpses were still where they fell and the burlap sacks remained, fluttering in the light breeze, still stuck to the pointed barbs where he had placed them. Without realizing what he was doing, he ran his hand over his shirt, tracing the painful gashes on his chest. Clearly the thought of going back over the sharp wire was a little disconcerting to him.

Daymon tossed the Kelty backpack in a high arc, trying to keep it from getting snagged. It fell back to earth on the opposite side of the fence with a dull thud. Then he strapped the crossbow on his back and climbed over himself. Once on the other side and clear of the camera's watchful eye, he pulled up his shirt, inspecting his body for fresh wounds. There were none, but the ones suffered earlier were beginning to fester and had become hot to the touch. He wasn't surprised. There was no telling what kind of shit he may have contracted in the pit of the dead.

Chapter 2
Outbreak - Day 8
Schriever Air Force Base
Colorado Springs, Colorado

Brook awoke as the first tendrils of muted pre-dawn light probed the interior of her family's quarters. Cade's chest rhythmically rose and fell under the threadbare sheet. He appeared at peace, blissfully content. She lay next to her man until he stirred. Cade's eyes opened slowly and scanned the room, taking inventory of his surroundings. Once he was awake and became fully aware that Brook was in the bed next to him, a sleepy smile cracked his usually stony demeanor.

"I was playing voyeur," Brook confessed. "You were sleeping like a baby."

"The operative word is *were*. What time is it honey?"

"It's nearly five," Brook said, her empathetic expression making an apology unnecessary. "Did you make a decision?" She gestured at the thick folder sitting under the bunk bed. Top Secret, spelled out in bold red letters, was prominently displayed across its otherwise plain russet exterior.

"Not without your input," Cade said, stroking her arm. He stole a long look at her beautiful face, intently trying to memorize every crease and soft curve. He couldn't help but notice how her brown eyes had changed. They were no longer soft and all encompassing; instead they were focused yet distant. In the short span of a week Brook had changed forever. Cade didn't need to hear it from her mouth to know she would be reliving, for the rest of her days, those painful seconds, minutes, and hours spent running, surviving, and protecting Raven.

"My gut tells me whatever is in that folder is more important than what I might want you to do. Major Nash wouldn't have asked you back on board unless it was an act of desperation."

"Nash isn't on point this time... this comes straight from the *President herself*," Cade said.

"If that's the case, Cade Grayson, then you have no choice. I'm telling you to go... get it done and come back to me and Raven." Her eyes were moist but she somehow managed to hold the tears in check. "To be brutally honest, I wish I were going instead of you. This waiting in one place is killing me. I know those things are still out there and I've seen up close and personal what they are capable of."

"You and Raven will be safer in here. Carl should be back on his feet in a day or two. I want you to stick close to him while I'm gone. And keep close tabs on our daughter." Cade's voice was even, almost monotone when relaying very important information to Brook or Raven. To anyone listening in, the way he spoke to her would have sounded condescending as hell. Brook knew he was just being direct and thorough with his delivery. "If the base is compromised and you aren't lucky enough to get on a helo like you were back at Bragg, then go west overland through Manitou Springs. I trained with the Unit a number of years ago near Lake George. We brushed up on rappelling and mountaineering at the Gunderson's horse ranch. Real nice folks... John and Lucy are their names. Go there and I'll find you."

Brook collapsed atop her husband and clutched him in a viselike embrace, afraid to let go. She allowed herself a few precious moments of peace and just lay there, holding him. Finally she sighed and sat up, brushing her hair back from her face. Cade squeezed her hand gently and locked eyes with the love of his life.

"Mom... where are you going?" Raven's sleepy disembodied voice asked from the dark side of the bunk.

"I'm going to check on your uncle. Go back to sleep. You and Dad can go to the mess hall in a couple of hours."

"I can't go back to sleep... they'll be waiting for me."

"Tell me about your nightmare sweetie," Cade urged. He knew full well that confronting her subconscious fears and putting them into words would take the power out of them.

"I keep having the same one. I'm at the dark store... peeing in the parking lot..." Raven's face tightened and her brow furrowed as she looked at her mom. "Those things pouring from the store... ." Her lower lip quivered.

Cade noticed a silent message pass between his wife and daughter.

"That was my fault Bird..." Brook said. Her eyes brimmed with tears. "We should have never stopped there." Brook shuddered, thinking how close they had come to being eaten.

"The monsters get us. We die every time... *horribly*. I'm not staying in bed. I'm going with you Mom," Raven said forcefully.

"You're safe now honey. Mom and I will protect you," said Cade.

Raven crawled off the bunk and grabbed her jeans. Pausing with one leg in and one out, she peered at her dad, trying to decide if she should keep playing dumb. "Dad?"

"Yes honey?"

"I wasn't sleeping. I was listening to you guys... If you need to go and help the President...*don't worry*, while you're gone nothing will befall Mom when I am on the job."

"I've heard that somewhere before. Correct me if I am wrong, but so far you're batting a thousand," Cade said, giving his daughter a little wink.

He lay in bed propped up on one elbow while Brook and Raven got ready to leave. He took note of how Brook carried herself, the way she grabbed her rifle, holding it naturally, like it was a part of her. Reassured, he watched his family leave and then rolled over, looking forward to an encore to his best sleep in days.

***

Brook decided to change her morning routine around a bit and let Carl get some extra rest. She was more than happy to put off her least favorite part of being a nurse until later.

Raven followed on her mom's heels trying her best to keep pace. After a series of twists and turns moving along the internal corridors dissecting Schriever AFB, Brook stopped in front of a door marked "Authorized Personnel Only" and rapped sharply on the metal door.

"What are we doing here Mom?"

"Practice patience, sweetie. You'll see when we get there."

The door cracked open a sliver. "Give me a minute," a baritone male voice said before shutting the door.

Precisely forty-three seconds elapsed before the fully dressed and squared away Colonel Cornelius Shrill reopened the door. "Top of the morning ma'am," he nodded his bald head in Brook's direction and then bent down to Raven's level, "and a good morning to you young lady."

"Hi." Raven offered a hesitant little wave to the imposing figure.

"Good to see *you* again and it comes rather unexpected at that," Shrill said as he arched one eyebrow and shot Brook a quizzical look. "To what do I owe the pleasure?"

"Colonel, I'm sorry we're here so early but sleep seems to be rather elusive these days. I was hoping you could do me a favor. I wouldn't normally be this forward... but considering the times what I need from you is very pertinent," Brook explained.

"You helped me. No, I take that back. You helped everyone inside of this base by stepping out of your comfort zone and going up into that tower, picking up a rifle--and using it *very* effectively, I might add, against the Z's." Shrill gazed down at Raven whose eyes were bugging out of her head. "And then there's the whole sneaking into a helicopter full of Rangers and going along on the hospital assault thing," Shrill said, finishing with a barely perceptible wink at the petite woman.

Brook was almost speechless and more than a little bit embarrassed from the accolades that Shrill had just heaped on her. "Colonel, all I need is a small caliber rifle and some ammunition. I want to teach my daughter how to shoot so she can protect herself *when* the need arises. I didn't know who to ask... and since you're the base commander..."

Shrill cut her off before she could finish. "Your husband is going on an important operation today... is that why?"

"No Sir. She's eleven and in these times eleven might as well be twenty. There are so many things I need to teach her..." Brook sighed. "She won't always have her Dad and me to protect her and I just want the little peace of mind knowing that she at least has a grasp of the basics. That's all."

"Let's go see what we can beg, borrow or steal from the armorer," the Colonel said with a little gleam in his eye.

***

Just inside of the East fence

"Hold it firm against your shoulder and look down the sights," Brook said as she hovered behind Raven. "Do you see how the two pieces of metal line up?"

"Yeah... sort of," Raven answered. "Should I shoot now?"

"Yes. Once you're sure the target is in your sights... gently *squeeeeze* the trigger," Brook instructed her daughter.

POW!

The report from the Ruger 10/22 wasn't as loud as the other gunfire she had been exposed to, yet she still jumped. "Gross..." Raven exclaimed, remembering to engage the safety before putting the gun down. Then she covered her face with both dainty hands and commenced pacing back and forth.

"Raven, get back on the horse... you can do it. Pick up the rifle. There's a round in the chamber so wait until the target is in the sights and follow the same routine... but this time aim a little higher."

Raven retrieved the gun. "Do I have to?" she asked even as she was aligning the rifle with her shoulder.

Brook didn't answer.

Unfazed by the wound, the creature still clutched the fence with both alabaster hands, working thin bony fingers against the wire. Raven's shot had entered the male zombie in the neck area, where black fluid from a dime-sized hole steadily seeped onto its soiled tee shirt. She had been aiming for the thing's nose, but this time she shifted her bead to the walker's forehead.

POW!

The zombie's right eye disappeared as the lead from the small .22 entered and then tumbled around inside of its skull, destroying the brain in the process, and causing the twice-dead creature to collapse on the ground.

"Put the safety on and keep your eyes open," Brook ordered. She hefted the M4, double checked that the selector was on single shot, and then closed the distance to the fence. While steadily firing, Brook swept the carbine left to right, methodically dropping the amassed walkers with accurate head shots. She stopped advancing only when the magazine was empty and the bolt locked open. "They're not human anymore... don't you forget it," Brook said with an icy tone to her voice.

"Want me to finish the last two?" Raven asked.

"I want you to *enjoy* finishing the last two." *There goes the Parent of the Year Award,* Brook thought while she watched Raven concentrate on the task at hand.

After six shots mixed in with a fair amount of hesitation, the remaining walkers were felled by the diminutive eleven-year-old.

Raven turned around and gazed into her mom's tired eyes. "Mom, you need a hot bubble bath."

Calgon isn't taking me away anytime soon, Brook thought, resigned to the fact that they would never be allowed to let their guard down if they were going to survive the apocalypse. And after what she just put Raven through she wondered which direction Saint Peter was going to send her when she met him at the Pearly Gates.

Chapter 3
Outbreak - Day 8
Apartment 904
Viscount Arms Condominiums
Downtown Denver

Wilson pried the blinds open and peered between the dusty horizontal slats. During the last thirty-six hours the zombies had begun exhibiting a strange new routine. On the street below the dead had returned in greater numbers. The shambling creatures clumsily caromed off of each other in their attempt to keep pace with the lead elements of the pack. At first Wilson had enjoyed watching the "running of the bulls" as he had taken to calling the spectacle. Even though the monsters weren't a herd of snorting, frothing bovines thundering through downtown Denver, that's precisely what they sounded like.

***

The previous day Wilson had left his sister alone in their apartment and embarked on a fact-finding mission to the penthouse one floor above. The Viscount Arms was only a ten-story building in a city of skyscrapers; the title penthouse had been applied loosely. Ted, one of the residents on the ninth floor, had informed Wilson that the penthouse owners were staying elsewhere while their unit was being renovated. Fully aware that the wall of windows on all four sides of the penthouse would afford him the best vantage point, Wilson ventured upstairs to observe the zombies and their new behaviors.

Kicking in the door had been the easy part--sitting alone with his thoughts and worry was nearly unbearable. Wilson had to wait two hours before the zombies finally returned. Although he was no expert in estimating the number of bodies in a crowd, what he saw scared the shit out of him--it appeared that in only twelve hours the throng of dead had doubled in size. He was so shaken by their sheer numbers his legs went numb, forcing him to sit down. The young man cradled his face with open palms, took a deep mind cleansing breath, and thought his options through. Every scenario he war gamed in his head boiled down to one outcome. Wilson harbored a sinking feeling that it would only be a matter of time before the crowd of dead would return in such massive numbers, he and the others would become encircled and forever trapped. He feared that if they didn't leave soon, the ten-story Viscount Arms would become their very own Alamo.

***

Apartment 904

Wilson and Sasha gawked as the shambling corpses crashed and slammed into every abandoned car lining South Proctor Boulevard. With each impact below, hollow thuds echoed up to the ninth story window. Wilson noticed that sound carried all too well in the dead city as another sharp crack, like two cars colliding, resounded from the street below. "Scratch her back bumper," Wilson said. He was witnessing the slow and steady disintegration of his very first car.

"I told you to use Mom's reserved parking spot while she's not here," Sasha said, never afraid to give her two cents' worth to anyone that would listen. Even though the siblings were very close, her know-it-all attitude rankled Wilson. Acting out of pure superstition, he had intentionally left their mom's spot vacant. He hoped doing so would ensure her return. Now, unfortunately, he was the only person around for *Miss Perfect* to correct.

Their mom was a flight attendant for Southwest Airlines and had been working on a flight to the East Coast the day the outbreak began. When the DHS and FEMA stepped in and started taking measures to control the spread of the new virus, her plane had been grounded, along with thousands of other aircraft around the country.

Their mom's last call came from a pay phone at Dulles International and she seemed upbeat about the forced layover, even telling Wilson it would give her the time to finally see the Smithsonian and actually be able to enjoy it. At the end of their conversation she told Wilson that Southwest had put her up in the Washington Dulles Marriott until the TSA could sort things out.

Because Wilson had been the last to see her as she drove off and the last to talk to her on the phone, he carried a heavy cargo of guilt.

The siblings watched CNN, reluctant to take even a bathroom break, while news reports trickled in from around the world on that first day. They couldn't turn off the television. The footage of undead creatures lurching along Pennsylvania Avenue was horrifying and inconceivable. They sat wide eyed, holding each other for comfort, as the nation's capitol, the very place their mother had been stranded, was overrun by living dead. Hours prior to nightfall the news channels broadcast word that President Odero, his family and most of his cabinet were being evacuated from the White House to an undisclosed, safe and secure location. It was apparent then that the city belonged to the dead. Wilson and Sasha hadn't heard from their mom since.

Wilson, being the older of the two, didn't have the heart to tell his sister what his intuition was telling him. Deep down, he knew they would never see Mom again. With the raw current of sadness and loss still coursing through every cell in his body, he thought back to the previous Saturday. He had watched from the very same window as his mom's Volvo exited the basement garage and zippered into the river of traffic heading south to Denver International Airport.

Before Wilson had left the condo to live an eighteen-year-old bachelor's lifestyle, the odds of Mom leaving them alone overnight were slim to none. Wilson, now twenty years old, had recently returned to the nest. Because of the economy and his shitty job, he found that paying all of his bills *and* eating was not possible. And with the hours his boss expected him to work to earn his salary, a second job was impossible to hold down. He still hadn't gotten used to the newfound trust he had apparently earned since coming home but being the "man" of the house had its privileges; Sasha had to listen to him for once. That feeling of empowerment was short-lived and turned into a ten ton yoke of responsibility the second their mom went missing and the dead started to walk.

Wilson snapped out of his daydream as yet another walker abused his prized Ford Mustang. He clasped his hands behind his neck and witnessed the last wholly intact piece of glass on the passenger side implode, the sharp report adding to the dissonance on the street.

"Get your bag Sis... We're leaving as soon as the tail end of the herd passes."

"I'm ready," the redheaded teenager said, hefting three trendy leather bags.

Wilson put his favorite photo, the one with Sasha, him and their mom together posing in front of a Christmas tree, inside his purple and black Colorado Rockies bag and slung it over his shoulder. He retrieved the baseball bat he had propped up next to the door, then cautiously eased the door inward and peered down the hallway. The first thing to catch his eye was the dried up lake of blood that had saturated the once beige carpet. The sight instantly reminded him of the violence he had been part and parcel to when the two zombies had emerged from their condominium-turned-crypt. The couples' blood still stained the barrel of his prized Todd Helton-autographed Louisville Slugger. No matter how hard he tried, Wilson couldn't purge the ugly sound of wood on skull from his memory.

As they passed 905, the deceased couple's door, he couldn't help but envision Angela and Saul's bloated bodies festering in their front room where he had deposited them. The memory of their undead two-year-old, arms flailing, desperately trying to attack him through the baby gate would haunt him forever. As if on cue, her little body slammed into the gate. The sound of her ongoing struggle resonated through the door and into the hall. Wilson winced, eager to put the reminders of yesterday's events out of sight and earshot.

"Stay close to me and do *exactly* as I say," Wilson admonished his sister, who was a few steps behind and struggling to keep up. Even with the death chamber fresh on his mind, he still had to suppress a smile as she tottered along. Her favorite Louis Vuitton purse dangled from one arm, while two fake Coach handbags swung awkwardly, like leather pendulums, from the opposite arm. Her fully loaded swap meet treasures made her walk like Charlie Chaplin, which Wilson found a bit amusing.

After pausing outside of number 907, listening for anything to indicate that things weren't all right inside, Wilson summoned his courage and knocked rapidly.

"Who is it?" a muffled voice inquired from the other side of the door.

"It's Wilson." *Use your peephole, genius.*

Ted opened the door after recognizing the familiar voice. "Come in guys." The big bear of a man ushered them inside and promptly apologized for his partner's scruffy appearance.

The two middle-aged men, whom Wilson and Sasha hadn't met until after the apocalypse, were lucky to have been home, both sick with the flu, when the world went nuts. They had remained indoors, watching the mayhem unfold through their picture window and on television. William sat on the couch shivering even though he had layered himself with two fleece sweat suits. The thick fabric made him appear as bulked up as his partner.

"Ready to go?" Wilson asked, making a mental note to stay away from the sickly man.

"As ready as we'll ever be," Ted said, emerging from a back room hefting two full daypacks and wielding a wicked-looking black shotgun.

"I want to stay here," William said, dabbing his handkerchief across his brow.

Ted spoke slowly, enunciating every syllable. "If we do not leave now we may never get the chance again." He loved William to death, but he knew exactly what the lifelong martyr was about to say.

Before responding, William blew his nose and looked at Ted with glassy bloodshot eyes. "Just leave without me. The condition I'm in... I'll just slow us down and get *everybody* killed."

"We are out of what you *need* in here. We have to act now... or never." The big man pointed at the closed curtains and the world outside. "We'll find a pharmacy--maybe a Rite Aid or something as soon as we get out of the city." Ted put the bags and the gun down, planted his hands on his hips, and waited for a response.

William blew his nose, silently glaring at his partner.

"Let's get the others," Wilson said to Sasha in his best listen to me and do what I say voice. Being a manager at Fast Burger didn't pay much, but it had taught him to be assertive when he had to. Time was dwindling and he was going with or without these two. *Hopefully with,* he silently reminded himself, *because there is strength in numbers.*

***

Ted asked Wilson and Sasha to go on ahead so he could have a moment of privacy with his partner. Since he had always worn the pants in the house, Ted was used to making most of the big decisions and it took him all of three minutes to browbeat William into submission.

Ted and William caught up with Wilson and Sasha in front of 909. Wilson had stopped there to see if the other four people were still going along with them to Colorado Springs.

Wilson had run into the thirty-something couple a few weeks earlier while he was working out in the building's meagerly appointed gym. At the time he thought Megan was pretty hot for an older woman, and James seemed like a nice enough guy. James and Megan were sharing their condo with Lance and Cheryl, who also appeared to be somewhere in their thirties. They had arrived at the Viscount Arms two days after the Omega outbreak, with nothing but a couple of golf clubs for protection and the clothes on their backs. Before the outbreak Lance and James had worked for the same IT firm and regularly played golf together. Cheryl and Megan met at their husbands' company Christmas party, clicked immediately, and had been best friends ever since. Lance and Cheryl considered themselves extremely lucky, somehow covering the three blocks from their loft to the Viscount, on foot and unscathed.

***

IN HARM'S WAY: SURVIVING THE ZOMBIE APOCALYPSE

One day earlier
Viscount Arms Penthouse

The eight remaining residents of the Viscount Arms condominiums met amidst the construction debris in the vacant penthouse to plan their escape.

Wilson raided his mom's nearly bare pantry to provide the canned food feast. Their candlelight dinner was relegated to room temperature Dinty Moore beef stew, canned peas, and a loaf of week-old bread that was just starting to spot with mold.

The two bottles of Chianti which Ted brought to the informal meeting were received well and soon passed around.

Since the day Wilson moved back into the nest, Sasha considered it her job to test his authority, especially when their mom wasn't around. Wilson quietly watched his sister as she boldly poured herself a small glass of the light bodied Italian wine. He was still learning when and where to pick his battles; therefore, considering the state of the world around them, he turned a blind eye and allowed his sister to win this particular skirmish.

While the small group of survivors "dined," the undead herd made yet another appearance down below on Proctor Boulevard.

Everyone stopped what they were doing simultaneously, forks and glasses frozen in midair and failing to deliver their cargo. The clink of dropped silverware and the sounds of seats being pushed back echoed about the empty space as the group hurried to the windows to take a look.

Wilson, having already seen enough of the horde, waited until everyone had returned from the windows and taken their seats before he addressed them. He had to speak in his "manager's" voice in order to be heard over the commotion outside. Once Wilson had everyone's attention, he quickly spelled out how he and Sasha planned to escape from Denver. His thinking was that Colorado Springs would be safer than anywhere else in the state, mainly because of the large military presence in and around the city. He detailed how they were going to get out of the building and onto the freeway heading south. When he was finished, he made it clear that he couldn't think of anywhere else to go and welcomed their input or questions.

Arms went up immediately and the picking apart of his plan commenced.

"I'm a little confused," Megan said, adding a tilt to her head.

To Wilson her tone of voice made her statement sound more like, *you're full of shit, kid.*

"So we're in our cars and then we wait for the tail... that's what you called it, right?" Megan asked.

Wilson wavered a moment, thinking it through, before he answered her question. "When the main group passes by, on the way to wherever the hell they go, there are always a couple of hundred stragglers. Compared to the size of the main body... I call that a tail." *Who is this chick,* Wilson asked himself, *Greta Van Susteren?* He felt like he was being cross-examined. Gone were the days when his biggest worry was a bad secret shopper sent from the corporate office. Wilson didn't want to lead these people. He just wanted to wake up, go to work, and, in the worst case scenario, maybe have to dress down one of the high school-aged employees because of a dirty Fast Burger uniform.

The others silently watched the exchange.

"There's no power in the building... or the city, for that matter, and I'm assuming our pass cards won't work at the gate. How do you propose we get out of the lot?" Megan asked, glaring at Wilson over the dancing flame.

"Good point," Lance added.

Wilson began to feel pinpricks of pain from the seat of his pants. His butt had fallen asleep from sitting, much too long, on the plastic five gallon paint bucket masquerading as a chair. He straightened his back and shifted his weight, trying to coax the blood to flow back where it belonged and let silence dominate the room while he tried to collect his thoughts. Wilson made eye contact with the people sitting around the "table" before he delivered his rebuttal. His mom had taught him that looking a person directly in the eye while speaking to them was the best way to get their attention, especially when he wanted to be taken seriously. "I've already explored that *minor* detail. I think we'd all agree that power is usually the first thing to fail during a fire, *and* that it would be awful to find a few crispy tenants trapped behind that snazzy electric gate. I found the quick release levers; they are about chest high, one on each side." He held his hand horizontally across his sternum. "It's a safety feature designed to release the gate, and let it roll up, when the power is out." *Touché, Megan.* Wilson smiled inside.

Megan remained silent while her girlfriend came to her aid. "Who's going to pull the pins then?" the pretty blonde pressed.

Wilson swallowed, realizing he couldn't remember the woman's name. "If you're not *driving* one of the vehicles... then *you* are pulling the pins. Congratulations... you get to be the heroine."

William interrupted. "When do we leav...?" His question was choked off by a fit of violent coughing.

"When the dead let us," Wilson replied solemnly, eyes downcast.

Ted offered William a tissue and rubbed his back through the two tracksuits. Ted's lips brushed his partner's ear as he shared some quiet reassuring words.

By the time the group was finished talking, the candles had burned down to inch high nubs. The wax pooled and hardened on the slab door they had used as a makeshift table. It had taken the "running of the bulls" three hours to squeeze by the Viscount and another thirty minutes before they were out of earshot.

"When the sun comes up tomorrow we are going to be packed and ready. As soon as those things come by, Sasha and I are leaving." Wilson scanned the others' faces, searching for any doubting Thomases. "If any of you want to come along you need to be ready."

Ted raised his hand as if Wilson were his teacher.

Wilson cocked his head, smiled, and called on his Paul Bunyan-looking neighbor. "Yes?"

"What makes you think they are coming back?" Ted asked, his voice tinged with doubt.

"I've been coming up here for the last five days trying to get a sense of what's going on outside. Initially the creatures were very predictable--all they did was hunt for people like us to eat. During the last two or three days their movements morphed into what we are seeing now." Wilson gestured to his old telescope and tripod standing next to the north facing windows. "Even though I can see farther with the telescope, the taller buildings make it difficult to see any of the surrounding streets. So far, I haven't been able to determine what route they follow or where they go, but the one thing I am certain of, day by day, is that their numbers have been growing *considerably* larger."

James was silent for a tick while he processed the bad news. "If we go along, my truck isn't big enough for all four of us," James said, looking at Cheryl and Lance.

"What does Megan usually drive?" Ted asked.

"Our other car is a Civic. It usually has more gas in it than my truck. Lance and Cheryl can drive that I guess," James answered slowly.

"If I can't figure out which vehicle belonged to the people in 905, Sasha and I will need a ride," Wilson added.

"You and your sister can come in our car," William offered.

"We might take you up on that, but we'll cross that bridge when we get to it." Wilson didn't want to have to explain how he got the couple's car keys, let alone that he had killed Saul and Angela and didn't have the balls to put their toddler down. Sarah's pale mottled face and tiny snapping teeth haunted him every time he closed his eyes.

Wilson had taken the keys from the front pocket of Saul's bloody jeans moments after he brained him. His next door neighbors were the first of the infected that he had seen up close and the first ones he had been forced to kill. Days later he was still trying to wrap his mind around how he had summoned the courage to do what he did... to do what was necessary to survive.

"We had better turn in," Wilson said. "Tomorrow is going to be a big day." Then he said a silent prayer, asking for some sleep without little Sarah starring in any of his nightmares.

Chapter 4
Outbreak - Day 8
Schriever Air Force Base
Colorado Springs, Colorado

Cade Grayson stirred underneath the thin sheet. Army-issued sandpaper never felt so good. Compared to the previous six nights, this one might as well have been spent at the Ritz Carlton, or Sandals in Jamaica. He slept soundly, all the way through, without a cameo appearance or even the perceived smell of one stinking corpse--real or imagined--invading the sanctuary of some much needed REM sleep.

Cade was in the company of his wife Brook and daughter Raven for the first time in many days, surely the impetus allowing the weary operator to shut down so completely. He stretched and yawned, Brook's scent gracing the covers blessing him with a Zen-like calm.

A series of loud raps on the outside door wiped away any escapist thoughts, bringing Cade back to reality.

"Who is it?" he yelled, hoping he would be able to shoo him or her away without opening the door.

"Airman Davis, I'm here to see Captain Grayson."

Cade rubbed his eyes and plowed his fingers through a bad case of bed head. It was going to be tough to stand before the green E-2 with a straight face--especially after the ruse he had pulled on the naive young man less than twenty-four hours ago. Also, being called Captain was going to take a while to get used to. He'd never had any aspirations of climbing rank and serving as a paper warrior in the Pentagon. All Cade Grayson wished to do was serve his country honorably and follow orders. He couldn't bring himself to believe that he had said yes to President Valerie Clay. She knew exactly how to angle her request, she simply appealed to his patriotism to get him to come back to the Unit.

Cade replayed the President's words in his head. "I need you... in fact, what's left of your country needs you." The last part was all she needed to say to reel the former-Delta operator back into the fold. Cade shook his head, erased the hangdog look from his face, and invited the visitor in.

The E-2 offered a crisp salute to the man he had earlier assumed held a much higher rank than captain.

"What can I do for you, Airman Davis?"

"May I have permission to speak freely, Sir?"

"Shoot," Cade said, trying to decide if he should apologize to the young man or leave it alone.

"You were a *civilian* and you passed yourself off as someone you weren't. Major Nash won't let me live it down... she thinks it's *funny* but I don't. Why did you lead me on?"

The operator admired the kid's candor and instantly regretted taking advantage of him. "Consider it a free lesson. Never assume anything; a lot of good Americans have lost their lives since the world went to shit assuming that their already dead family member would *never* take a bite out of them. Assuming that the situation would improve and the government was going to save them. Assuming that help would ride in on a white steed named FEMA and save their ass. I'm only elaborating because I was already contemplating making amends to you. I had a very good reason to use you to fetch those men for me." The temperature seemed to drop in the room as Cade held his steely gaze on the shorter airman. Then, in an easy tone while offering his hand, he uttered two words that he rarely had to use: "I'm sorry."

The airman quickly pumped Cade's hand. "Apology accepted. There's a briefing scheduled shortly. The President, Colonel Shrill, Major Nash, and General Desantos will all be in attendance." Davis

32

glanced at the Timex on his wrist. "I have orders to make sure you're present and there are only ten minutes before you *have* to be there."

Cade retrieved the folder stamped Top Secret, donned his cover, and followed his escort out the door.

The E-2 moved with a purpose. Cade had a hunch the airman's sense of urgency was directly related to the classified dossier that Major Nash had dropped into his lap the day before. The implications spelled out within only strengthened the decision he had made. *Welcome back to the teams... sucker!* Cade admonished himself.

He stayed on Airman Davis' heels, easily matching the shorter man's stride. The two wove their way through the internal corridors crisscrossing the expansive base, traversed a once manicured swath of now knee high grass and entered the nondescript two story structure that housed the 50th Space Command.

Chapter 5
Outbreak - Day 8
Viscount Arms Parking Garage
Denver, Colorado

Wilson had no idea which SUV had belonged to his dead neighbors; to him they all looked alike. "Do any of you know which vehicle belongs to Angela and Saul... the couple that lives in 905?" All he received were blank looks and heads wagging side to side. He examined the thick microchip embedded key and turned it over in his palm. There were no markings to indicate what kind of vehicle it belonged to.

"Why don't you just hit the panic button?" Sasha said, pulling a Lucy van Pelt and doling out her five cents' worth of advice.

"I don't even want to take the chance and accidently set off the alarm with this thing," Wilson answered. "The blaring horn, even if it sounded for only a second, would let *them* know we're in here." Then he addressed the others crowding around him, "Be very quiet..." He held up the alarm fob for all to see. *"Do not sound the car alarm... use only the key to unlock your cars."*

Wilson canvassed the garage, testing the key in every vehicle. It seemed like everyone in Colorado drove an SUV, and the Viscount garage was full of them. He had checked all but three of the SUV type vehicles: a Kia Sportage, a Jeep Liberty, and a huge Black Suburban remained. Wilson knew beggars couldn't be choosers, but he was hoping for something bigger than the Kia or Jeep to run the gauntlet, so he bypassed them and approached the bigger SUV. He held his breath and tentatively slid the key into the door handle. His silent prayer had been answered; the shiny black Chevy Suburban had indeed belonged to the yuppies. Wilson climbed in and sat in the driver seat, waiting for his sister to load her "luggage" before starting the rig. The SUV was enormous inside and out. *I hope Saul left us a full tank of gas,* he thought before he started the big vehicle.

Wilson kissed the photo of his mom and gently placed it in his shirt pocket next to his heart. Then he started the SUV and listened to the engine's throaty rumble. Out of habit he reached up to adjust the rearview mirror, but quickly recoiled the moment he eyed the pink baby shoe swaying back and forth. Then he noticed the Graco car seat; it looked lonely, lost in the expanse of the vacant back seat. He said a quick prayer for the little girl upstairs. A tear traced his cheek as he realized Sarah would never again feel her parents' warm loving embrace. So much life had been lost because of the scourge sweeping the United States. He dried his face and let his eyes linger on his little sister. Wilson strengthened his resolve by telling himself there was no way on earth that he was going to let a fucking microbe do any more damage to his family.

Like racehorses at the Kentucky Derby, the survivors' four vehicles idled, waiting for the gate to rise so they could escape from Denver.

Wilson hadn't been joking when he said the passengers would be expected to disengage the garage door. "Pull the pins, ladies!" he hollered.

Megan and her friend, Wilson still couldn't recall her name, pulled the release pins, and started the metal gate on its upward journey.

Wilson tried hard to ignore the baby shoe and focused only on the rear view mirror as he watched Megan get back into the Toyota Tacoma driven by her husband. Behind them, what's-her-name rejoined her boyfriend in the white compact car.

Ted was in the driver's seat of his blue Subaru Forester. William, sick and useless, was sprawled in the reclined front seat.

The black Suburban rocked subtly on its suspension as Sasha swayed anxiously on the edge of her seat. Wilson chewed his fingernails and watched the gate slowly disappear into the ceiling.

When it finally cleared the middle of the windshield he tromped the accelerator. The roof rack atop the three-quarter ton Suburban scraped the gate as it raced up the incline to street level and took flight. Wilson didn't know that the horsepower-to-handling ratio of the Suburban was extremely lopsided, suffering excessively on the maneuverability side of the equation; furthermore, he had never driven anything with more balls than his six cylinder lipstick-red Mustang which his friends called a girlie car.

"Slow down, slow down, slow down..." Sasha chanted. She had a death grip on the grab handle near her head, and when the zombies came into view she stopped the mantra and began to hyperventilate.

The big rig left the ground for a second or two, attained a cruising altitude of six inches, and then landed slightly sideways, slapping three of the walkers to the pavement. Yellowed puss and gray brain matter streaked the truck from the b-pillar all the way back to the taillights. Wilson, gripped by panic, stabbed the brake pedal. The SUV's anti-lock device pushed back against his foot, further confusing him. The crunch of bone, gristle, and muscle resonated through the floorboards as the fallen creatures were ground into the road. The slimy, brownish-gray mess spit out by the Goodyear radials bore a strong resemblance to liver pâté.

After the truck lurched to a near stop, Wilson quickly inventoried his situation: only a handful of walkers occupied the road in front of the slow rolling Suburban, and one lone female zombie clawed at the passenger window, smearing more viscous fluids along the tempered glass.

Sasha shrieked and lunged towards Wilson, nearly crawling into his lap.

"Calm down. I can't hear myself think!" Wilson shouted to be heard over her hysterics. "We have to wait for the others... we *need* to stick together!" His eyes darted between the open road ahead, the garage, the girl zombie loping alongside, and the condensed cityscape reflected in the rearview mirror.

After a few agonizingly drawn out seconds the Tacoma 4x4 nosed out of the garage and little by little inched across the sidewalk, followed by the white car, with the Subaru bringing up the rear.

Wilson gingerly pressed the gas pedal, urging the rig forward. One more glance in the rearview confirmed that all three vehicles were lined up behind him. "Oh shit!"

"What's wrong now?" Sasha asked nervously. Her eyes were riveted on the zombie limping alongside trying to keep pace with the creeping Suburban. Every so often its brittle fingernails would skitter and tink on the glass, causing the short hairs on Sasha's arms to stand at rigid attention.

"They're back and it's too soon. No... no... no!" Wilson wailed, shaking his head vehemently and slamming his hands on the wheel as if his disagreement could change the reality of their situation. With Marty Feldman eyes and mouth agape, he froze in mid breath and his chest convulsed violently. The dry throaty rasp that came out when he coughed sounded like a dog fighting to expunge a hairball. Sasha gasped and pinched her nose tight, trying to deny the noxious air entry into her lungs. The odor preceding the zombie horde was an invisible wall of eye-watering stench like nothing they had ever inhaled before.

"Drive, Wilson, it's staring at me," Sasha said with a nasally-sounding twang. Her hands palsied as she clumsily unbuckled her seatbelt. The lithe teenager scrambled over the center console and squeezed her small frame into the back seat, where she cowered on the floor trying to escape death's gaze.

***

"Good Lord, that smells awful," William exclaimed. He hitched his shirt over his nose and tried to breathe only through his mouth.

"William, lock your door!" Ted screamed over the din of the approaching zombies. Then he cursed the slow moving car blocking the road in front. "Fucking piss or get off the pot," he muttered. "The first chance I get, I'm going to pass those two," he warned William. Self-preservation was first and foremost on his agenda.

"Take this." William thrust the shotgun, pistol grip first, in Ted's direction.

"What do you expect *me* to do with it?" Ted asked. His grip on the steering wheel was white knuckle tight; there was no way he could pry a hand off to accept the offering.

37

"I don't like guns... they scare me," William whined.

"Do they scare you more than those rotting corpses?" Ted arched an eyebrow. "Listen. I can drive... or I can shoot. I *cannot* do both at the same time. As much as I'd like to think so... I'm not Mad Max." Ted sensed that William was losing it. He pried his attention from the steadily encroaching mob while he addressed his partner. "It's time to put on your big boy pants." Ted patted the shotgun on the ribbed pump. "You just pull on *this* to chamber a shell, point the gun, *not in my direction though,* and shoot. Rinse and repeat."

William examined the weapon with a skeptical eye. After a moment of careful consideration he turned it around and took hold of the pistol grip, then tentatively pulled the slide chambering a round. The resulting metallic clack made him jump.

***

Wilson wheeled the truck in between stalled cars and around a large cement planter that had been fractured into several jagged pieces. Brilliant red and yellow pansies lay trampled, their colorful petals scattered amongst the spilled black soil. A multitude of dirty footprints leading down the street drew his attention to his battered Mustang. The old girl's rear bumper lay directly in the Suburban's path. Without thinking twice he rolled over the top of the obstacle.

"We're almost to the freeway Sash. Check and see if Ted's car is still behind Megan's friends."

Sasha looked through the smoked rear windows. "James' truck is too big, I can't see anything beyond it," she replied anxiously.

"Once we get up this elevated onramp you should be able to see everything behind us. Hopefully it'll be safe enough for us to wait and let them catch up. First things first. I have to get this boat between those cars; it's going to be a tight squeeze. If you hear a crunch... don't worry... it's a rental." Wilson's attempt at humor flew miles over his sister's head.

The sign above the freeway entrance read *"I-70 South, Denver International, and Colorado Springs. Right Lanes Only."*

Wilson eyed the onramp, lamenting the tiny sliver of a lane he was going to have to negotiate in order to access the much wider four lane tollway. He stole a glance in the side mirror. Ted's blue Subaru popped into view. Two of the wheels hopped the curb and it sped up, quickly overtaking the two middle vehicles. To Wilson, it looked like a slow motion NASCAR move as Ted tucked his Subaru into a tight drafting position between the Suburban and James' Tacoma. Wilson noticed the reason for Ted's aggressive driving. The zombies had caught up to the slow moving caravan and now the walkers were about to overtake the white Honda.

Megan's friends are toast, Wilson thought as he watched the little car spurt ahead. For a moment it appeared that Lance was going to escape the walkers.

"Straighten it out..." Wilson found himself backseat driving. "Watch out for the..."

Lance was driving with only half an eye on the road. He was so spooked by the number of dead in pursuit that he lost control and veered into a row of abandoned cars. After a moment of gnashing body panels the Honda ground to a halt. In the blink of an eye the car containing Cheryl and Lance was fully enveloped by the dead.

***

"James, stop, you've got to pull over!" Megan screamed hysterically.

James stopped the truck so that he could safely risk a quick look.

The phalanx of zombies choked the street from sidewalk to sidewalk. James stared in wide-eyed disbelief at the lurching tide of bodies filling Proctor Boulevard as far as the eye could see. The small car was completely engulfed. There were intermittent flashes of white, the only evidence that the Honda had been there at all.

"Oh my God..." James said, one hand nervously clutching and simultaneously kneading his ball cap.

They watched the horde pull Lance, kicking and flailing, through the car's broken window. There were so many zombies clutching for a piece of him that he was propelled over the top of them. It was the first and last time he had ever crowd surfed, and in seconds the grasping hands pulled him under the carrion sea.

"They are dead and we have to go now!" James bellowed, never taking his eyes off of the advancing throng.

While the pack's attention was focused solely on consuming Lance, Cheryl crawled out of her window and wormed her way onto the sedan's roof.

James took his foot off of the brake and let the Tacoma roll forward.

"*Wait*," Megan yelped. "Cheryl is on top of the car." Pleading with James, she placed her hand on the steering wheel. "We have to go back and try to save her."

No sooner had the words slipped from Megan's mouth than the ghouls wrapped their clawing hands around her friend's ankles. Cheryl involuntarily performed the splits. A half-second later her legs were ripped from her body and carted off in different directions. Cheryl's trunk pitched forward; like a warm rain, her blood pulsated from the meaty stumps onto the excited zombies.

Megan gnawed on her fist as she watched her friend disappearing into the crush of rotten bodies. She was near enough to the grotesque scene that she could read her dying friend's lips: Cheryl mouthed the words, "Help me," over and over until she slipped from view.

"Cheryl!" Megan screamed. There was no answer--Cheryl was lost forever. The crimson blood trails painting the top of the white car were the only evidence that the carnage had taken place. After the undulating mass greedily devoured the two warm bodies, they flowed around the white Honda, made a small course correction, and surged towards the meat in the silver truck.

***

James' booming voice snapped his wife back to the present. "They're both dead and if we don't get going... we're next!"

It was difficult, but Megan forced herself to look away from the feeding frenzy, turn in her seat, and focus on the road ahead. Her stomach instantly went into free-fall when she realized the other two vehicles were already a block away.

James glanced into his side mirror. The monsters were now within arm's reach of the truck's tailgate and closing. He jumped on the accelerator, coaxing a little chirp from the rear wheels, and wrenched the steering wheel to avoid the piece of Wilson's Mustang lying in the middle of Proctor Boulevard. The maneuver made the left front tire roll over the jagged shards of the shattered cement planter. The resulting gash in the sidewall was the beginning of the end. The shrill hiss of escaping air was drowned out by the raspy calls of the dead. James, unaware that the beefy tire was seconds from being entirely flat, noticed the steering becoming sluggish and soon it became nearly impossible to make the truck go where he wanted it to.

Megan watched as her husband fought to keep the truck moving in a straight line. "What's wrong?" she inquired frantically.

James ignored her and engaged the four wheel drive. He hoped to get enough traction from the three good tires so he could power steer the truck and catch up with the others. Unfortunately for them, the four wheel drive didn't help. No matter which way he steered, the truck insisted on going in the opposite direction. Instantly the gravity of their situation became obvious. There wasn't enough time to change the tire--the truck was fucked and so were they. "Get out now!" James screamed at Megan.

The sight of his friends being ripped apart was burned into his brain and he didn't want to suffer the same fate. Running for their lives on foot was their only option. James threw his door open and leaped out of the truck, directly into a zombie's waiting arms. He looked over his shoulder and screamed at Megan, begging her to run. Like most agnostics facing death, James said a quick foxhole prayer and hoped there *was* a God listening. The weight of the clawing creatures pulled him to the ground, while greedy hands tore into his stomach and played a game of tug-o-war with his entrails.

Megan gaped as her husband was eaten alive. Her hands shook so violently the simple act of unlatching her seatbelt had suddenly become a monumental task. After taking a couple of calming breaths she finally managed to free herself and hastily kicked open her door. The momentum carried her out of the truck and into the road where she landed, catlike, on her hands and knees. On the periphery of her vision she perceived the shuffling feet of approaching zombies. In a moment of absurd clarity, she caught a glimpse of a pair of shredded feet complete with chipped fire engine red nail polish and ornate silver toe rings, and suddenly remembered she had missed her pedicure appointment yesterday. The shaken woman tried to stand so she could run, but her trembling limbs wouldn't cooperate. Megan became aware of the monster's jagged teeth a second before they ripped a blood-spewing chasm into her neck. The army of moaning zombies yanked her to the asphalt and tore into her squirming body, their gnarled fingers stripping off long ribbons of skin and flesh. Like a mother's loving embrace, Megan sensed an all-encompassing warmth wash over her body. Despite the penetrating daggers of pain, she was oddly at peace. At last the muting dam of fear finally broke; Megan drew her final breath and exhaled a blood curdling shriek.

***

Wilson watched the melee with cold detachment. The violence didn't seem real, it was almost like he was at a drive in theater watching a George Romero movie and soon the credits would start rolling and life would return to normal.

After the zombies finished feeding, they resumed their relentless march up the onramp.

A series of clown car beeps made Wilson jump.

As she climbed back into the front seat, Sasha stated the obvious. "That was our gay neighbors trying to tell us something. You should probably drive or they're going to end up like the others."

Silently, Wilson cursed his neighbors for owning an SUV the size of a school bus. On the upside, in small numbers, the zombies had little chance of stopping the truck, but the utter lack of maneuverability was already a major issue on the clogged tollway near the big city.

After successfully negotiating the onramp to I-25, Wilson found the road so crowded that he could only drive the behemoth a scant five to ten miles per hour. The Subaru, with Ted and William safely ensconced inside, was small enough to follow in his wake as he steered the Suburban like an icebreaker through the sea of cars. The multicolored scratches and dents, combined with the gore-smeared exterior of the slab sided vehicle, would be a testament to how utterly terrifying their flight from Denver had been.

Wilson contemplated taking a side road and waiting to see if the walkers would bypass them and continue their march down I-25, but thought better of it after seeing the corpses of the unfortunate people killed by the infected while they waited in their cars stuck in the miles-long traffic jam. Nearly every one of the stalled cars had unmoving half-eaten corpses or putrid sunbaked grabbers trapped inside. The scenes of carnage chilled Wilson to the bone; he had to warn Sasha to close her eyes more times than he cared to count. She finally listened to him and retreated to the back seat after seeing one too many of the graphic displays of death. Wilson was grateful that he no longer had to divide his attention between driving and babysitting, because threading the truck between the stalled cars while trying to avoid the hungry walkers took all of the concentration that he could muster.

Chapter 6
Outbreak - Day 8
Schriever Air Force Base
Colorado Springs, Colorado

Duncan's fist was clenched, but the intended knock went
undelivered as the thin aluminum and glass door whipped inward. A
bony hand darted out, grabbed a fistful of the aviator's ACUs, and
pulled him the rest of the way inside the darkened room. As quickly
as it opened, the exterior door slammed closed behind his back and
Duncan found himself standing in the dark anteroom face to Adam's
apple with the enigma named Daymon.

"Knock-knock," Duncan drawled. He fancied himself a
comedian, and in his book even a bad joke could soften anyone up.

"Who's there?" Daymon forced a sterile thin smile and
released his grip on Duncan's uniform, then backed away, slowly
lowering the machete to his side.

Duncan's eyes narrowed and his characteristic mischievous
grin appeared. "*Boo!*"

Daymon, still riding an adrenaline high, hadn't been able to
sleep since he had slinked back onto the base. Still, he played along,
but only because the southern boy had grown on him. "Boo who?"
he asked flatly.

"Don't cry, everything will be OK." Duncan recoiled
theatrically, clearly expecting a negative reaction from the bigger man.

"I'm too tired for your wannabe comedian shit... and why are
you here so *goddamn* early?" Daymon laced his hands behind his neck

and stretched, popping every vertebra in the process. His black tee shirt hiked up, revealing the numerous blazing red furrows scribed vertically up his abdomen.

"I was trying to disarm you with my wit to keep from being cleaved in two... I've seen your work. *Plus* I have good news." Duncan produced a wan half-smile, wondering why Daymon was behaving like a surly teenager. "Don't kill the messenger," he continued, poking himself in the chest with his thumb. "Because you're going to need him to fly you home." The aviator loitered in the shadowy doorway, waiting for his words to register with the dreadlocked man.

Daymon yawned and pinched the bridge of his nose, mining the sleep from his eyes. "I ain't going back to Utah, my Moms is dead and gone. And I sure as hell don't want to go and find out she got bit and is one of them now." He shook his head rapidly side to side, his dreads whipping his cheeks. "Nope... not gonna go back," his voice choked off as he looked back into his billet.

"I'm not a vampire, it's safe to invite me all the way inside," Duncan drawled. He wanted to lend an ear in case Daymon needed to talk about his loss. Also, he couldn't help noticing the fresh wounds, and he was somewhat concerned. The last thing he needed was a zombie strapped into his helo raising hell all the way to Eden.

"Can you take me to Driggs? I used to live there before Moms and Pops moved to the Salt Lake 'burbs."

"It depends. Where exactly is Driggs?" Duncan eyed the bulging backpack and high tech crossbow lying partially concealed under the low slung bunk.

"It's on the west side of the Teton pass in Idaho. Driggs is where all of the po' folks live. The money stays on the other side of the pass in Jackson," Daymon replied, his words muffled as he struggled to pull another shirt on over his dreads.

"Cade told me he was greasing the skids and trying to get me a bird. You wouldn't know by the way he carries himself, no swagger, no bullshit buffoonery, but he's seen a lot of shit and been right smack dab in the middle of it. He's a good man... he'll come through." Duncan said, weighing whether he should ask Daymon about the goody bag on the floor, but what he really wanted to know was how the man received his new injuries. Duncan quickly decided that later would be a better time to try and pry out the details behind Daymon's apparent tangle with Freddy Krueger. "How bout we get some chow? *I'm buying,*" Duncan joked.

"Sure thing old man." Daymon gestured toward the door with a regal flourish. "Age before beauty."

Duncan was out the door first. *Age is only a number,* he thought.

Chapter 7
Outbreak - Day 8
Schriever AFB - 50th Space Wing Command
Colorado Springs, Colorado

Airman Davis opened the door for Captain Cade Grayson. With a barely perceptible tilt of his head, the newly promoted captain ordered the airman to fall in behind him. The men entered the room, filled in the two spots nearest the door and stood with their backs against the wall, waiting for the briefing to commence.

General Mike Desantos made eye contact with Cade, crowded Colonel Shrill over a few inches, and nodded toward the newly created opening.

Message received. Leaving Airman Davis behind, Cade made his way, as inconspicuously as possible, to his mentor's side.

Mike Desantos offered his right hand to his dear friend and teammate, pressing a folded piece of paper into his palm. Cade quickly unfolded the half sheet of legal pad and covertly scrutinized the scribbled words.

Cade stared laser beams at Davis until the airman finally glanced over. He then motioned with his head to have the young airman join him.

After threading his way through a sea of rank much higher than his, E-2 Davis stood at attention and saluted the very intimidating row of officers.

Cade had been watching the major as she cued up some type of media on the immense wall-mounted monitor before he turned his attention to the E-2. "Airman Davis."

"Sir?"

"Have you met General Desantos?" Cade asked.

"Sir, no Sir," Davis replied nervously.

"At ease, Airman Davis," Desantos ordered. "How do you know Wyatt here?"

"Wyatt?" Davis furrowed his brow. "I don't follow, Sir."

"It's his nickname from the teams. The boy is quick with a pistol," the General said.

A hush fell over the room indicating Major Nash was about to begin the briefing.

Cade pressed the folded paper into the airman's hand and whispered into his ear, "Find Duncan and give this to him."

"Sir, yes Sir." Airman Davis snapped off a quick salute and with a sense of déjà vu tickling the back of his mind he went about his new mission.

Major Freda Nash stood front and center, on an elevated stage, and began speaking to the assembled group of uniformed men and women. Although the feisty Major was small in stature, she still commanded attention as if she were Goliath himself.

The Major had a soft spot for Cade. Their service to the country had constantly brought them back into each other's orbit. They had worked together off and on over the years and each held a strong mutual admiration for the other. If Freda had noticed Cade enter the room, she didn't let on.

She communicated only the facts, rapid-fire, targeting points of utmost importance on the LCD with her laser pointer. The beam danced over a still image, portraying in full color a very large metropolitan area which Cade failed to recognize. It was obvious even from the vantage point from which the picture had been captured that there were tens of thousands of infected bodies choking every square inch of asphalt.

"You are looking at downtown Denver, and as you can see, the dead are getting restless." Major Nash paused and adjusted the collar on her three-button dress blues. It was a premeditated tactic

48

designed to allow all eyes in the room a moment to assess the image displayed before them. Nash looked out upon the stunned faces and started the paused frame into motion. "The esteemed Doctor Fuentes, formerly of the Center for Disease Control in Atlanta, has already analyzed this drone footage and made a chilling observation. He thinks the dead have overhunted the city..."

A murmur, like the buzzing of flies on a corpse, rippled through the standing congregation of need-to-know types.

Nash continued. "Groups of walkers, or Z's as our boys have taken to calling them, are starting to migrate. The Z's have been leaking out of Denver, in small groups, from all points of the compass... until yesterday afternoon."

The still shot on the screen suddenly leapt back into motion and zoomed in. It became apparent to everyone in the room that the tens of thousands of walking dead were marching between the tall buildings, all in the same direction, like one single organism reacting to some external stimuli.

From the bottom corner of the frame a brilliant flare of refracted sunlight grabbed the drone operator's attention; the image enlarged yet again and began tracking the slow moving SUV.

To Cade's trained eye, it looked like a small convoy of civilian vehicles fleeing the river of jostling creatures. The lead vehicle, a black Suburban, broke free of the crowd, threading a course between the stalls and pile ups. The next two vehicles, a blue wagon and a shiny silver truck, trailed closely behind the point SUV. The final vehicle, a smaller white car, was being driven erratically and quickly fell behind. Inexplicably the white car swerved into a line of parked vehicles on the passenger's side and stopped moving altogether.

The tsunami of walking dead flowed around the car, sealing off any avenue of escape.

Even though fate had already run its course, Cade silently rooted for anybody that was trapped inside the little car and finished with a silent solemn prayer.

The camera zoomed in one more stop as the pale figures enveloped the stalled vehicle. The screen filled with the writhing biomass as the monsters fought to pry the meat from within. The creatures pulled a man out of the driver's side of the car. He kicked and flailed, fighting the inevitable. The body went limp, appeared to hover for a second and then disappeared beneath the multitudes of dead.

Once more the image paused. "I don't want to show you any more of the footage. I think you all know the outcome. The zombie attack on the couple in that car was so graphic and violent the UAV operator had to hand the bird off to someone else." Nash cleared her throat and continued. "The people in the silver truck, unfortunately, suffered the same fate..."

General Mike Desantos, his face breaking out in every shade of red, interrupted Nash midsentence. "Major, is there a reason why the operator of that Reaper or Predator... whatever type of drone it was... didn't empty the weapon pylons, and finish those poor souls *quickly* before the Z's got to them? They were *Americans*. Living, warm blooded *Americans... and they deserved no less*."

"I spoke with the drone operator and he shared your sentiment. The Reaper was Winchester. All of the Hellfires were expended yesterday on another operation. It made no sense to waste the fuel sending the drone back to Nevada so we vectored it here. It's still useful as a viewing platform... but the bird's got no claws," Major Nash solemnly answered.

Cade exhaled audibly. Like a punch to the gut, it dawned on him why the drone was unarmed. He had been present the previous day in this very room and watched as every missile onboard was fired into the Nazi compound in Idaho, killing Ganz and his group of marauding bandits. Now, armed with this knowledge, witnessing the deaths of these survivors was even harder to swallow.

"Thank you Major Nash, carry on," General Desantos said, visibly reining in his temper.

The Major made the scene on the monitor disappear and, with a few clicks on her remote, replaced it with an ominous view taken from a very high altitude. "As you see on the right corner of the screen, the lead vehicles eluded the dead and successfully escaped from South Denver." Major Nash directed the red laser dot and slowly circled two ant-sized vehicles: one black and one blue. "That's the *good* news... but *only* if you were the folks in these vehicles." The red dot continued to circle the two minuscule specks.

IN HARM'S WAY: SURVIVING THE ZOMBIE APOCALYPSE

Everyone in attendance stood rooted, transfixed on both the Major and the frozen image on the monitor while they waited for the other shoe to drop. Except for the softly purring computer cooling fans, the Space Command operations room was blanketed with an anxious brooding silence.

"Now... for the *bad* news. Hold on to your covers ladies and gentlemen." The image zoomed in, slowly revealing an estimated three hundred thousand living dead pouring out of Denver. They appeared to be following in the same general direction as the vehicles driven by the lucky escapees. "The Z's are moving south. They are in a natural funnel, the Rockies on one side and the high desert on the other, and the funnel delivers them here... right on our doorstep. Unless we act decisively, Colorado Springs is in danger of being overrun."

The room remained quiet. Major Nash had expected a different reaction. *Perhaps they're all in shock,* she thought, *or quite possibly, they're making the necessary mental preparations for the fight to come.* In the Major's mind she was confident it was the latter. With all of the compounding events taking place they were all in harm's way.

"The dead only cover a mile or two an hour, and rest assured we are tracking them with every asset at our disposal. As of now the Z's are still seventy miles away from downtown Springs... but the dead are second on the threat list. The more immediate threat to Springs and the rest of the United States will be neutralized in the coming hours. God willing."

Cade shared a conspiratorial nod with Desantos.

Major Nash turned off the monitor and continued speaking. "Captain Gaines is overseeing our Z eradication efforts in and around Springs. He will be up here momentarily with an update." Before the petite Major turned over the podium to Captain Gaines, she adjusted the microphone, extending it a full twelve inches above her head.

Gaines strode confidently to the front of the room, saluted the Major, and then stood rigidly, head on a swivel as he surveyed the crowd.

"Thank you Major. I'm going to keep this short because I understand President Clay will be having an audience with a select

51

few of you when I am finished. The ingenuity of our young men and women continues to amaze even this jaded middle-aged soldier. The searchlights that went operational in downtown Springs last night were the brilliant idea of one young airman. Bear with me... it's a short but sweet story. I had just returned from an overflight mission north of Springs, and the helo lands and this airman comes running up and waves me down. He's all excited and says to me that he worked at Winslow BMW downtown, and they used to use some very large million candlepower searchlights to attract customers to the lot for special sales and such. But I digress..." Gaines put his hands up over his shiny bald head, opening and closing them, pantomiming a fireworks display. "What he said next seemed so simple that I was *not* a believer at first. His exact words were, and I quote: "If people with the ability to reason had been compelled to investigate the pretty bright lights--then I have a hunch the Z's won't be able to resist." The Captain took a sip from his bottled water. The distant sound of an approaching transport plane ambushed the silent moment.

"Airman Monsour's idea to lure the dead wherever we want them has so far been working as imagined. However, there are some logistical logjams that we are trying to breach. We are nearly out of ammunition and about to deploy our backup slingshots..." This brought a couple of snickers from the shooters in the room, Cade included.

The Captain let his joke ride for a moment and sipped his water before continuing. "Our 10th Special Forces group from Fort Carson recently spearheaded a resupply mission with remnants of the 4th Infantry Division. Their objective: the Hawthorne Army Depot in the middle of nowhere Nevada. They completed phase one of the mission with no casualties. Preliminary reports indicate that they located the ammunition that they were tasked with retrieving. In addition, they are returning with survivors, both civilian contractors and also the Marines that had been guarding the depot. The C-130s are wheels up, and en route, as of this moment."

The outside door opened and four stoic Secret Service men filtered into the room. President Valerie Clay entered next, followed by four more rough looking men making up the rest of her security bubble.

The air went out of the room. After a brief shifting of bodies, the crowd straightened up and every right arm in the room saluted simultaneously.

President Valerie Clay reciprocated to the best of her ability, returning a crisp salute of her own.

"Madam President, do you want the podium?" Gaines asked.

"No sir. Carry on," urged the President.

"Thank you, Madame. Lastly, there is very encouraging news to report on the Omega front. A team of Tier-One operators led by General Desantos successfully evacuated key personnel from the CDC along with all of the files documenting their ongoing research of the Omega virus. The doctor now has an operational lab at his disposal. I won't go into detail, but we filled out the equipment list Doctor Fuentes provided us, thanks to the vacant genome research facility ten miles from here that, unbeknownst to them, so graciously donated their entire lab. Credit goes to the 4th ID for that successful mission."

A chorus of hooahs resounded from about the room.

"Madame President, the podium is yours." Captain Gaines replaced his beret and readjusted the microphone for President Valerie Clay.

After the President took the podium and proffered a few off-the-cuff words of encouragement directed at everyone in attendance, she ended the general briefing and waited for the room to empty. President Clay then dismissed her security detail, leaving only General Desantos, Major Nash, Colonel Shrill, Captain Gaines, Cade and a handful of other shooters behind for the combat operations briefing.

SHAWN CHESSER

Chapter 8
Outbreak - Day 8
Schriever AFB Infirmary
Colorado Springs, Colorado

Cade gently opened the door and entered as quietly as possible for a man wearing combat boots. Brook looked like an archeologist working on a dig, perched on a stool, hunched over with her face hovering just inches above Carl's prostrate body. She was fully immersed in the task at hand. Cade felt guilty for intruding but he had little choice.

Brook looked up from what she was doing. Her eyes smiled when she noticed it was her man standing a few feet away from her. "I'm finished removing the old dressings and now I begin cleaning up Carl's back," she said, thinking out loud.

"How bad were his wounds?" Cade asked in a hushed tone as he crept closer to the bed.

"In addition to the broken ankle, I think you only got to see his mangled face yesterday. He was peppered with a back blast of buckshot. I performed field surgery on him outside of Bragg with dime store tweezers. His modeling career is shot, but he'll be prettier than the zombie that tore into his back. The wounds in his back were deep and got terribly infected." Brook carefully placed the scalpel on the tray, then buried her head in Cade's chest. "That effing monster ripped foot long strips of flesh from his back, and to add insult to his injury Carl contracted a flesh-eating virus that put him into the coma and nearly killed him."

Cade palmed Brook's head with both hands, savoring her scent, and then kissed her fully on the lips.

An emotional dam broke inside of Brook. Her tiny frame heaved in silence, the sobs absorbed by Cade's crisp ACUs.

"You two get a room." Carl's voice came from underneath the table. "Here I am, down here."

Cade went to one knee and hiked up the overhanging bed sheet. Carl's jaundiced eyes peered out from his puffed up pizza face. He was lying on a massage table, stomach down, arms at his side, his ravaged face cradled in the cut out hole.

"Want me to hold a book for you?" Cade joked.

"No... but can you scratch my nose, bro?"

"*Do not* touch his face. The open sores are still very susceptible to infection," Brook warned with her stern nurse's voice.

"Cade?"

"Yes Carl?" Cade answered, eagerly awaiting whatever smartass comment Carl was incubating.

"Will you scratch my ass then?" Carl started to laugh before an intense wave of pain extinguished the humor.

"Wash it first," Cade shot back.

"Boys. Stifle it." Brook shook the scalpel menacingly at her husband. "Is there something that can't wait until later? I'm trying to excise some dead flesh here."

Cade screwed his face up when he was reminded of the spoiled hamburger smell wafting from Carl's wounds. Then he looked under the table. "Big brother, I owe you for getting my family here. Thanks a million."

"No need for thanks here. Brook pulled more than her fair share of the weight. I didn't know my lil sis had it in her," Carl said admiringly.

Cade suddenly realized he hadn't seen his daughter in a while. "Honey, where is Raven?"

"She's with her second mom and no doubt playing with Mike Junior," Brook answered. She quickly contemplated mentioning Raven's target practice session but decided it could wait.

"Sweetie, give Raven my love. I have to leave five minutes ago. Desantos is probably kitted out and on the flight line by now,"

Cade said, forcing the lump from his throat. The prospect of never seeing Brook or Raven again entered his mind and lingered for a millisecond before he squashed it.

Brook's mouth tightened. "*Hoo-ah*... I'm a military wife *again*. Stiff upper lip and all that jazz."

Cade lovingly placed a hand on Brook's abdomen and locked his steely eyes with her big browns. "Stay frosty. If things go sideways... it will happen very quickly." He considered revisiting the egress plan he and Brook had agreed on, but opted not to. Based on what Carl had just said--and bolstered by the secondhand stuff he had heard through the grapevine about Brook's exploits--Cade decided she was mission capable and didn't need to be micromanaged.

Before Cade was two steps out the door he had begun his ritual of visualization, and in his mind he was already running the mission over and over again.

Chapter 9
Outbreak - Day 8
Schriever Air Force Base
Colorado Springs, Colorado

"Great minds still run on the same track, I see," General Desantos said to Cade as he patted the black SCAR-L dangling from its single point tactical sling.

"I asked the armorer what kit you left with... monkey see, monkey do," Cade said with a smile. He gave his own SCAR carbine an affectionate rub. "He told me the long guns are already on the birds. Pray tell, do we have an MSR along for the ride?" Cade had a soft spot for the Remington tack driver. When chambered for the .338 Lapua round it was a versatile sniper rifle that packed a big punch, a great choice if you wanted to reach out and touch someone. The design allowed for quick takedown. And in a pinch, the rifle could be used for CQB (close quarters battle).

"Wyatt... I made you. Therefore I know you. There are two Remington rifles coming along for the ride." The usually stone-faced Desantos smiled, his white teeth making a rare appearance. Cade thought he looked like a movie star waiting for the director to yell action. All he needed was a cigar and he could have been easily mistaken for Hannibal from the A-Team television show.

"With all due respect, Cowboy, Beeson introduced me to the art of sniping. You introduced me to the teams... for which I will be forever grateful." Cade looked over his shoulders to make sure they were alone. "I've been meaning to say something to you. I cannot thank you enough for what you did for Brook, Raven and my brother-in-law. If you hadn't intervened, I have a feeling they wouldn't have made it here from Bragg."

"Don't sell the girls short. Annie told me Brook was her rock throughout the entire ordeal." He paused for a moment and broke eye contact with Cade. *"Good women* picked us, young man," Desantos said, looking to the distant horizon. *"Good women."*

***

Desantos drove the four-person golf cart the same way he attacked life: fast and furious. Cade gripped the chicken bar with one hand and the black SCAR with the other. Sergeant First Class "Low-Rider" Lopez and Sergeant Darwin Maddox took up the seats in back. Desantos cut the corner like Al Unser at the Indy 500. Tires squawked as the cart listed on two wheels, forcing the operators to brace themselves to keep from tumbling out onto the tarmac. The General let loose with a loud, out of character rebel yell.

A bevy of flat black helos came into view from behind the southeastern hangars. Cade hadn't been to this part of the base since he first arrived in Springs with Duncan, Daymon and the young stutter-prone soldier from Camp Williams. On approach he expected, hoped is a better word, to see a bustling triage center full of incoming survivors. However, that wasn't the case here. He noticed there had been a new addition. Next to the induction center a larger tent was erected inside the jumbo hangar. The nylon roof and walls ruffled gently; there was a natural rhythm to the movement, almost like the structure was alive.

"General, what's in the big tent? Cade asked.

The cart chirped to a halt. Lopez and Maddox hopped out and began offloading their gear.

"That's a state of the art laboratory for the good doctors from the CDC. He and his lady colleague have the best equipment the U.S. Army could pilfer for them. Word is they are working on an aggressive antidote that when taken would boost a person's immune system against Omega as well as an antiserum to be used immediately following infection. This is need to know, the Alpha patient is in that tent," Desantos said in a hushed tone. "That thing was a mess, Doctor Fuentes was experimenting on him when we came knocking.

The worst part: we had to bring the thing back kicking and moaning."

Lopez, who had been eavesdropping, interrupted. "Easy for you to say General. You didn't carry that *demonio* up fourteen flights of stairs."

"Still sore Lopez?" Desantos joked.

"No, but I had to burn my stinking uniform afterward," Lopez shot back.

"Someone call Batman... he's missing some toys," Cade said to the rest of the team. He had just noticed the two sleek Gen-3 helicopters sitting on the flight line in the shadows of the hulking, dual rotor, CH-47D Chinooks. Cade had ridden in one of its predecessors, known as Stealth Hawks, but never in a Ghost Hawk also affectionately called "Jedi Rides" by the Night Stalkers that piloted them. It was the ultimate, super secret, stealth helo that the 160th SOAR would never comment on, let alone admit existed. And here they were, waiting to take him into battle. *Oh well, no one to keep them secret from now,* Cade thought.

The ship's angular lines married with soft edges made the rotor wing craft look like something out of the distant future. The Ghost Hawks were painted a matte black that Darth Vader would envy.

"Shotgun," said Lopez.

"Just get in and strap in, Low-Rider," General Desantos ordered.

"We're Oscar Mike in five. Saddle up," Chief Warrant Officer Ari Silver ordered. Ari was the most decorated aviator in the 160th SOAR, and had piloted the Black Hawk that carried Desantos and his D-Boys to the CDC on their recovery mission.

"You heard him, move it. We wouldn't want to keep the Night Stalkers waiting, now would we?" General Desantos had to raise his voice to be heard as the turbines came to life, belting out a high frequency whine. Although the Ghosts were *extremely* quiet, the engines, combined with the whoosh of the carbon fiber rotor spinning a few feet above their heads, made the flight line a noisy place to communicate.

Cade mounted the closest Ghost Hawk and quickly donned a flight helmet. He strapped into the seat across from Desantos, on the port side of the cabin. Lopez and Maddox sat side by side, their backs against the bulkhead, where they could see the horizon through the cockpit.

The CIA man named Tice took a seat opposite from the door gunner. Nash had introduced the Delta team to the operative shortly before the mission briefing. He wore the same desert tan camo as the operators, but his ACUs were devoid of rank, branch, or unit insignia. Cade's first impression of the man was typical spook. The CIA specialist was cold, aloof and seemed to think he was better than his peers. Cade didn't give a shit what the man thought of himself as long as he completed his part of the mission with a modicum of competence. Lastly, the crew chief Hicks entered the helo and took his seat near the mini-gun.

Cade listened in on the chatter between the SOAR aviators.

"Limo *is* a word, Durant. I don't want to hear about it," Ari said.

"It's not a word. It's an abbreviation of a word," Durant answered.

Cade wore a confused look on his face.

Desantos noticed the expression and tried to explain the unusual banter between the pilot and co-pilot. "They're quoting from the movie Black Hawk Down. It's a ritual they perform before every mission. Our co-pilot Durant was not *the* Durant that went down in Mogadishu in Super Six-Four. Ari started doing it awhile back just to bust his balls."

Cade shrugged his shoulders. *To each his own,* he thought. Lord knows he used to have rituals. He contemplated asking Desantos more about Tice before remembering that discretion is *usually* the better part of valor.

The helicopter leapt off the tarmac, catching the operators unaware.

"Hoo-ah," Cade said into the mic. He marveled at the helicopter's incredible power on takeoff, without the earsplitting, bone-rattling rawness of the standard H-60 Black Hawk.

"This is Jedi One-One. Form up right echelon. Tanker rendezvous in six-zero-mikes," Ari said into his boom mic.

A chorus of affirmatives replied back from the other Ghost Hawk and the two Chinooks.

Cade smiled inwardly at the call sign, closed his eyes, and ran the mission through his mind for the umpteenth time.

Chapter 10
Outbreak - Day 8
Western Side of the Rocky Mountains

The Traveler parked his dusty truck on the shoulder near the backside of the small rise in the road. He climbed out of the Ford, popped his back and neck, and then did a couple of quick squats to get the blood flowing into his lower extremities. The man had driven all night, stopping only to clear wrecks from the road when he couldn't negotiate the oversized four-wheel drive pickup around them.

***

He had been breaking and entering across two states looking for supplies and trading up for better rides along the way, and he had grown attached to the truck he was driving now. The shiny Black Ford F-650 had been hidden inside a six car garage underneath an enormous mountain chalet in a little town on the western side of the Rocky Mountains. The only thing that stood between him and the truck was the undead owner.

The man had been a real narcissist; his face adorned nearly every wall throughout the entire house. In most of the photos he was wearing a Denver Nuggets uniform and either dunking or passing a basketball. What a mess the seven foot tall, three hundred pound decomposing corpse had made of the inside of the mansion, ambling around and tearing the place apart. The way the Traveler looked at it, the ex-hoopster didn't need the truck, nor would he ever need the rest of the exotic cars and off-road toys parked in his slick garage.

Two rounds from the .45 caliber Kimber and the pink slip was his. The rig had an extra aftermarket fuel tank, six inch lift and the biggest off-road tires he had ever seen on a street legal vehicle.

***

The Traveler estimated he had fifty yards to traverse between the truck and the top of the hill, with only a sagging barbed wire fence and foot high grass for cover. To keep a low profile and remain unseen, he moved in a combat crouch and followed the shallow culvert paralleling the road. The Traveler's head and eyes were constantly on the move, taking in his surroundings and watching his six. When the hill began to crest, he dropped to his knees and elbows and low crawled the last thirty feet.

Carefully he parted the damp stalks of alfalfa, creating a suitable spot for surveillance. The man settled into the grass, flipped his ball cap around with the brim facing backwards, and brought the binoculars to his face.

The rest area was nestled in a shallow depression just off of the two-lane black top. A gray cinderblock bathroom stood in the middle of a sea of lush green lawn peppered with picnic tables. Multiple empty parking spots angled in towards the structure. Swaying slightly with the breeze, mature Ponderosa pines and Box Elder ringed the site. Four vehicles were parked in formation in the center of the grassy area. The entire rest stop was ringed by a neatly maintained circular drive allowing easy access to and from the rural highway.

His thickly calloused fingers worked the focus ring, bringing the distant vehicles into sharp detail. They were arranged in a crude square, bumper to bumper, forming a sort of corral. The former owners obviously parked them that way to provide a barrier to keep stray walkers out of their little camp. A pair of tents stood in the midst of the circled vehicles. Both were empty, their unzipped flaps fluttering in the wind. Hanging on a line strung between two of the pines, assorted articles of clothing ruffled and popped with each new gust. He panned the scene from left to right, pausing on a tangle of unmoving bodies. A man, woman and child, their eyes frozen open in death, stared back at him. A flash of red drew his attention. Trapped behind the steering wheel of a mud-spattered SUV, a lone zombie tap danced on the brake pedal, reliving some tucked away scrap of memory. The Traveler stood up, twisted the ball cap around, and loped back to his truck.

He drove over the crest and down the hill and parked his truck near the exit. Leaving the nose pointed towards the road, he stepped from the cab and slowly circled the parked vehicles on foot, methodically checking each one. When he rounded the back of the SUV, its brake lights suddenly erupted in a flashing orgasm of red. The Traveler got a chill when he realized that the monster had been watching in the rear view mirror and lying in wait. Not wanting to get near the grab zone, he gave the Jeep a wide berth and approached the dead family. Each one of them had the betraying defensive bite wounds indicative of a zombie attack. The woman and boy were locked in a loving embrace. Both of them had been headshot, and, judging by the powder burns and the amount of blood present, they were still alive when they were put down. The man was missing the rear half of his skull. Gelatinous lumps of his brain littered the grass in an arc that spread ten feet behind him. *What a way to go,* the Traveler thought as he searched for the suicide weapon. The Saturday Night Special was half buried in the grass, next to the dead man. He inspected the weapon, quickly decided it wasn't worth keeping, and tossed it to the ground.

Next he siphoned enough gas from the abandoned vehicles to fill all three of his five gallon plastic jugs. Then he approached the mud spattered Jeep Commander, grinning as he screwed the can onto the business end of his .22 semi-auto pistol. He liked shooting walkers; it was almost a form of therapy. He tapped the silencer on the driver's side glass. "License and registration please." He laughed out loud at his own joke.

The zombie raged and moaned, straining against the seatbelt, all the while banging its head against the top edge of the half open window.

The Traveler moved in for a closer look. A half-eaten dead woman was lying face down in the zombie's lap. "You've got to be kidding me. Road head for the undead." *Good name for a band,* he thought to himself.

The stunted man moved back two steps and leveled his pistol at the driving ghoul. The creature stopped thrashing and focused its milky orbs on the gun. The Traveler hesitated. He had a creeping feeling the former human was exhibiting some semblance of awareness, almost like it knew it was about to be released from its hell on earth. *Bullshit,* the Traveler thought as he put three rapid-fire shots into the monster's head.

Chapter 11
Outbreak - Day 8
Over Casper, Wyoming - 300 Nautical Miles
North by Northwest of Colorado Springs

"Jedi flight, this is Oilcan Five-Five. Maintain heading and airspeed. We are on your six and open for business in five mikes."

"Roger that, Oilcan Five-Five. This is Jedi One-One, be advised you have four thirsty birds."

Ari Silver held the Ghost Hawk steady while the USAF HC-130J Hercules overtook the helos and matched their speed and heading. He watched the refueling probe retract from the tanker's wing-mounted pod and slowly reel out towards the front of his ship. Ari pushed a series of icons on the glass cockpit to release the refueling probe from its internal bay. A soft clunk, followed by a flashing green star on the touchscreen, assured him that he was go for refueling. "Jedi One-One ready to engage."

"Copy that Jedi One-One. Be sure to pick up a Slim Jim when you pay the lady."

Ari broke protocol and replied informally, "Don't you know what they put in those things?"

The Herc pilot replied, "Lips and assholes."

"That is correct, Oilcan Five-Five. I owe you a beer when we get back to Schriever."

"Copy that," said the Herc pilot.

The other three helos went through the same routine to top off. The first of the flight's three scheduled aerial refueling rendezvous went off without a hitch.

"90 mikes out," Ari informed everyone onboard.

"How on earth did you get ahold of these birds?" Cade asked Desantos.

"They just showed up on our doorstep. After we popped Bin Laden, the Pakis shut down *all* of our hot ground ops; after that, there weren't any missions that required an invisible insertion or extraction," Desantos explained.

"I thought they used the H-60 Stealth Hawks for the Bin Laden raid. And correct me if I'm wrong--didn't we lose one of them?" Cade asked.

"Affirmative. We had these two Ghosts flying over watch... ready to take out any reactionary forces. But when the Stealth Hawk crashed--instead of relying on the Ghosts to destroy the downed ship and risk losing one of them--we opted to use C4 to finish the job. Theory was, if the Pakis couldn't see 'em... and couldn't hear em, and the birds leave no hits or EMR (electromagnetic radiation) trace on the radar, were we even there? Turns out the Pakis had no idea we were there until we were gone." Once again reliving that history making mission in his head, Desantos' kid-like grin filled up the space under his smoked visor.

"Plausible deniability... very nice." Cade looked out the side glass. Down below, a petro-chemical tank farm belched flames. The tops of the gigantic holding vessels had already burned through, and like a glacier calving icebergs, the sides of the steel tanks were sloughing off. A massive blight on the earth started near the molten metal from the tanks and stretched as far as the eye could see, thousands of blackened acres rendered useless from the fire and settling soot. Cade was witness to the final death throes of one of man's many industrial accomplishments as the side effects of Omega took the world one step closer to the Stone Age. *The entire country is falling apart,* he thought, *and the only thing we can do is wait for the dead to rot and then try to pick up the pieces.*

Cade snapped out of his melancholy moment when Desantos resumed his story. "The Jedi rides had been wrapped up nice and tidy and were supposed to be rotated back to Fort Campbell, but when Omega hit we had more pressing matters to attend to. They finally made the trip back from the 'Stan onboard two C5 Galaxies that eventually ended up here at Springs."

"Why didn't they return home to the 160th at Campbell?" Cade asked.

"All of our large military installations are no longer responding. They are either abandoned or overrun by the dead. Thanks to President Odero ordering the rapid troop withdrawal from both theatres of war, Colorado Springs dodged the bullet, because if it wasn't for the added combat troops, the walking dead would have already stormed our gates," Desantos replied.

"You saw how many walkers were streaming out of Denver... *this had better work* or eventually Springs is going to suffer the same fate as Bragg," Cade said pessimistically.

The spook twisted in his seat and peered at Cade from behind his mirrored Oakleys. "I'll do *my* job and you Delta boys do yours, and we'll all be OK," he stated matter-of-factly.

***

Cutting through the sky with their wheels and guns retracted, the Ghost Hawks appeared to have been honed from solid slabs of black obsidian. They passed over the truck stop low and slow; the high tech helos were so stealthy that the zombies below didn't react until they had already been overflown and blasted by rotor wash.

Ari put the Ghost into a slow lazy orbit so the operators could recon their objective. Jedi One-Two split off and escorted the Chinooks to their landing zone, out of sight but close enough to help the instant they were called on.

Durant, in Jedi One-One, brought up a live streaming feed from the Predator drone which was flying a racetrack pattern 20,000 feet over the approaching convoy, ten nautical miles from the Ghost Hawk's position.

"Durant... split the incoming feed to the aft monitors," Ari said.

The LCD screens in the troop compartment powered up, glowing brilliant blue at first and then the feed was visible in full HD.

Cade watched the slow moving six-vehicle convoy for a moment before making his battle assessment. "The lead vehicle is a surplus Humvee." The flat black truck had a turret-mounted large machine gun on top. "The two tractor trailers in the two and three slots hold the cargo. The vehicle in the five slot is an Oshkosh heavy fuel tanker." The low slung truck, painted desert tan and stenciled with military markings, could be mistaken for nothing else. "The trailing Humvee is identical to the lead. I estimate a total of sixteen personnel... unless there are guards inside of the trailers." Cade finished his observations and waited for a second opinion.

"I concur," General Desantos stated.

"I estimate, at their rate of travel, you have forty... maybe forty-five minutes before the convoy crests the hill," Ari added, pointing at the hillock in the distance. "It looks like Major Nash's Intel was right on the money. Where do you want me to set her down?"

Desantos pointed out the truck plaza below. "Good a place as any."

Cade silently nodded in agreement.

"Durant... how far out are the targets?" Desantos asked.

"Eight klicks," came the co-pilot's reply.

"Ari, I need you to get me as close to that brown semi-truck as you can," Desantos ordered.

"Yes sir, port side, or starboard?" Ari queried.

"Can you put us on top of the trailer without fast ropes?" Desantos asked.

"Roger that," Ari replied.

The semi-truck, with the UPS logo emblazoned along the side of the trailer, was parked far enough away from the fueling island that the roof covering the pumps wouldn't be a danger to the spinning rotor blades.

Ari nosed the Ghost Hawk down and dove toward the parking lot, flared at the last second and hovered a few feet over the tractor trailer.

"Wheels down," Ari said into his boom mic.

The helo's internally stowed landing gear rotated down with a barely perceptible whirr followed by a solid clunk as the wheels locked into place.

The crew chief, Sergeant Hicks, hauled open the door on the starboard side of the ship, letting eddies of wind invade the interior of the hovering Ghost. Thanks to Ari's precision flying the helo's landing gear hovered less than a foot above the UPS trailer's roof. Desantos went out first; he hopped onto the roof and went down to one knee, waiting for Cade to join him. Once both operators were on the truck, Ari pulled the helo into the same orbit as before, staying below two hundred feet so that Hicks could provide covering fire with the door gun if necessary.

Durant's voice sounded in both Desantos' and Cade's ear buds. He used the call sign that the ground element had been assigned for the mission. "Archer, be advised you have multiple Z's, one-zero-zero meters on your nine o'clock... vectoring to your position."

"Archer Actual here, copy that. Keep us updated but hold fire," Desantos ordered.

"Cowboy, I'm checking the cab for hostiles," Cade said. He padded along the top of the trailer and dropped onto the roof of the tractor, hung his head over and peered through the flat windshield. The front part of the cab was empty, but from his upside down vantage point he couldn't see past the curtain shrouding the entry to the sleeper cab. Cade drew his Glock and tapped the muzzle on the glass. Nothing stirred inside.

"Seven-zero meters," Durant warned over the net.

"Wyatt, let's get a move on," Desantos said calmly as he watched the dead close on them with a steady determined pace.

"Going in," Cade replied as he shattered the driver's side window with the butt of his pistol. He unlocked the door and was inside in seconds. The interior of the truck was oppressively hot and smelled like beer farts and Copenhagen. *Anything was better than the smell of death,* Cade told himself as he parted the blackout curtains with the barrel of his Glock. Fast-food wrappers and Hustler magazines littered the rumpled bedding in the sleeper compartment. "Clear,"

Cade bellowed as he opened the passenger door a crack so Desantos could come inside.

"Four-zero meters," Durant advised from his post in the circling helo.

Desantos scanned the length of the trailer in case there were zombies waiting to take a chunk out of him. After determining the passenger side was momentarily devoid of walking dead, he gently lowered his body over the edge, hung by his fingertips, and dropped to the asphalt.

"Coming in," he warned, before climbing into the Kenworth.

Cade's head was lost under the steering wheel and he clutched a nest of colored wires in his gloved hands. *What a sight*, Desantos thought as the door clicked shut behind him.

Thirty seconds after Cade gained entry, the Kenworth rumbled to life, belching blue diesel exhaust.

"I think you missed your true calling, young man," Desantos joked.

"I know how to *jack* the newer stuff. I used to poach the Bagram motor pool to keep our gun trucks up and running," Cade confessed as he manhandled the transmission into gear. "Let's keep that between you and I... OK Boss?"

"Copy that," Desantos muttered with a slight smirk twisting his lips.

Once the two operators disappeared into the truck, the crew in the orbiting Ghost Hawk could only wait and watch the hungry Z's creep closer.

"One-zero meters and closing." Concern wormed its way into Durant's voice.

Cade was heavy footed on the accelerator and revved the diesel engine a little too much before engaging the clutch. He hadn't driven a truck this size in quite a while and shifting, let alone finding the sweet spot on an eighteen wheeler's transmission, was like trying to solve a Rubik's Cube in the dark: nearly impossible. The big brown truck convulsed and shuddered, fighting the weight of the fully loaded trailer. Like a juiced Impala in a rap video, the tractor's front end launched off of the ground and bounced a few times. Sooty diesel exhaust belched from the stacks in protest to the amateur behind the wheel. After three tries Cade found second gear and the ride smoothed out.

"Not like the minivan at home?" Desantos chided.

"I'd rather be caught riding a moped," Cade shot back as he fought the synchros looking for third gear.

"Try to wedge this thing between the guardrails... and make it look real," said Desantos, pointing at the desired location in the roadway.

Cade took the advice to heart. The truck was rolling along at a fifteen-mile-per hour crawl with a tail of zombies bouncing along, heads bobbing, arms reaching longingly for the big brown semi, when he abruptly swerved the Kenworth into a parked station wagon. The impact caused the Kenworth to shudder yet it kept moving forward.

"Next time... warn me before you do that," Desantos implored.

"Sorry," Cade answered sheepishly.

The trapped Taurus wagon complained with the sound of screeching sheet metal and breaking glass. The formerly white guard rail received a gold racing stripe as the fifteen-ton truck ground the car against it. Cade wrenched the wheel left, disengaging the truck from the mangled station wagon. The manufactured collision left the car looking like a crushed soda can.

"Collision warning," Cade said two heartbeats before he plowed the semi's massive chrome bumper into the opposing guardrail. Twenty feet of the hardened steel barrier peeled off like a velvet ribbon, piercing the truck's radiator. With Old Faithful gushing under the hood, the diesel engine coughed once and ceased running. The eighteen-wheeler was in perfect position: blocking all four lanes of the rural highway.

"Be advised, there are multiple Z's on your location. Permission to engage?" Durant pleaded.

"Negative. Hold your fire," Desantos said. He didn't want to leave spent brass and recently killed zombies lying all over the place and tip off the bad guys before he and his men could spring the trap. The freshly spilled radiator fluid might draw *some* attention but there was nothing they could do about that now.

After Desantos checked for stray walkers, he exited the cab via the passenger side door and climbed onto the hood of the truck where he waited to give Cade a hand up.

While Desantos was making his exit, Cade reached under the dash and un-hotwired the truck to the extent that it couldn't be started again. Then he accepted Desantos' extended hand and clambered after him onto the top of the trailer.

"Archer Actual, ready for exfil," Desantos called to Ari who was circling above in Jedi One-One.

The moment that Ari saw the operators making their way along the top of the big rig, he broke the racetrack orbit and deftly maneuvered the silent helicopter into position to extract the two men.

"Copy that, Archer Actual, I'm one step ahead of you."

Instinctually the two Delta operators made themselves smaller as twenty-six feet of spinning carbon fiber cut the air inches above their heads.

Hicks helped the two Delta operators reenter the helo and closed the door behind them. "Archer is aboard," he informed the aircrew.

The second the crew chief gave the green light, Ari rotated the bird while still in a steady hover and nosed the Ghost Hawk forward to deliver the operators to the predetermined over watch area four hundred meters to the south.

Chapter 12
Outbreak - Day 8
I-25-South of Denver

Sasha worried about her brother. He hadn't said one word since witnessing the four people dissected alive. She couldn't blame him for dealing with the trauma in his own way, but she had a feeling that he was just stuffing his emotions and it was her job, as his sister, to get him to come out of his shell. "Quit beating yourself up, Wilson. There was nothing that you could have done back there to save them."

Wilson continued driving, eyes focused ahead, seemingly oblivious of his sister's unsolicited advice.

Sasha stewed in thorny silence for five minutes before she sharpened her ice pick and went back to work. "OK. Then why don't you tell me what you think you *did* that was so wrong," Sasha pried. She was secretly proud of herself for turning the questioning around. It was a tactic she had seen some old lawyer named Perry Mason employ on an ancient black and white television show.

"I wasn't thinking about what happened to those dumb asses back there. That was on them--not me. I'm sure every second of that shit will come back crystal clear the next time I try to sleep... if there is a next time. In case you weren't paying attention... Wait a minute, you *weren't* paying attention because you were in the back seat hiding," he finished scathingly.

The redheaded teenager sensed the tables turning on her as she nervously fiddled with her seatbelt. "Yeah, so what's your point?"

"After those things finished eating half of our group, they plowed right up the I-25 onramp, behind us, and they're back there right now. They *are* following us, in lockstep... every last one of them," Wilson stated coldly. "And eventually they're going to find us, no matter where we are. Even if we make it to Colorado Springs. So *now you know* what I was thinking about before you tried your shrink routine on me."

"Wilson, don't worry, those things aren't exactly speed demons. They have no chance of catching up to us unless we break down or something."

Wilson glared, "Don't jinx us. Haven't you been looking at what's out there?" He abruptly stopped the Suburban, leaving a couple of black skid marks.

Although unplanned, Ted did the same but nearly drove the smaller Forester under the SUV's bumper.

The former Fast Burger manager grabbed his autographed Louisville Slugger and stepped out onto I-25. Wilson strode boldly toward the nearest car and peered inside. *Shit.* It was empty. Next he approached an older American sedan. The two zombies in the four door Caprice, now aware of Wilson's presence, began moaning and thrashing around.

"*Wilson, get back in here!*" Sasha shrieked.

Watching the proceedings from inside the Forester, the two men were suddenly at a loss for words.

The safety glass was no match for the baseball bat. The undead driver stared oblivious and unblinking as hundreds of glass meteors blasted its face. The creature's maw hung open, longing for a bite of meat, when the bat struck home.

"That's for Mom. I hate you fuckers... leave us alone!" Wilson went berserk. He pounded the seated ghoul until the monster's brains leaked out into its lap. Then, wholly focused on the second zombie, he walked around the car and inexplicably opened the door.

Sasha covered her face and watched the carnage through the cracks between her fingers. "No. No. No. Come back here... please," she pled in a panicked whisper.

Without the door for support, the zombie listed and fell out head first.

Wilson waited, bat in hand, while the putrefied corpse struggled to stand.

The monster emitted a plaintive sound, like a lost calf calling its mom, and lurched towards the angry bat-wielding redhead.

Without warning, a thunderous explosion roared beside Wilson's right ear. He ducked instinctively. The zombie, probably a retiree in life, was launched backwards into the air. A wet slap sounded as the back of his head hit terra firma first.

Ted stood in the roadway with a smoking gun at his side. "*Enough*. You're putting us all at risk... at least think about your sister." He motioned at the open driver's door and the small trembling form on the seat. Sasha was curled up tightly into a little ball; the only thing identifying her was the shock of scarlet hair poking out.

Every window in the dead couples' Caprice suffered the wrath of Wilson's bat before he was ready to return to the SUV, spent and out of breath.

Ted nudged the walker with his shoe, just to be certain it was dead. Although he hadn't seen a zombie playing possum, he didn't take any chances. His stomach started to gurgle at the sight of his fresh kill. The tracksuit-wearing oldster had taken the shotgun blast full in the face and then keeled over backwards, depositing his brains across the oil stained roadway.

Ted noticed that the shotgun blast had drawn unwanted attention to them. "Time to go, slugger," he gently prodded Wilson.

"I'm sorry... won't happen again," Wilson croaked. He was suddenly very thirsty, hungry, and tired. It was like someone else had been dictating his actions. He climbed back into the idling SUV, asking himself: *Who was that.*

Wilson closed the door and placed his hand on Sasha's shoulder, causing her to jump. "I lost it. That wasn't really me back there Sash..."

Sasha cut him off before he could finish making amends. "Just drive," she ordered brusquely.

Chapter 13
Outbreak - Day 8
Schriever Air Force Base
Colorado Springs, Colorado

Duncan filled his cup with the thick, spoon disintegrating, black acid the U.S. Air Force passed off as coffee. He placed the Styrofoam cup under his nose, inhaled, and winced. The steaming liquid smelled worse than it looked. What he needed, he thought, was some of those NoDoz caffeine pills. He was wondering how to drink the swill without being subjected to its odor or flavor when a voice from behind called his name.

"Duncan Winters?"

"Yes... the one and only," he drawled, not knowing who he was answering to. Duncan tried to extricate his legs from under the cafeteria-style bench so he could stand up and face the voice.

"Stay seated, it's just me, Airman Davis, we met yesterday..." he moved to the other side of the table and sat facing Duncan. "Captain Grayson sent me to find you... *again*."

It took Duncan a second for his old brain to put two and two together before the name Grayson rang a bell. "You mean Cade? Cade Grayson?"

"He asked me to deliver this to you." Davis slid the folded piece of yellow paper across the table.

"What does it say?"

"I don't make a habit of reading my superior's correspondence," the E-2 stated matter-of-factly.

Two aluminum trays slapped the tan tabletop. "Lunch is served," Daymon said as he slid a tray with peas and something brown in front of Duncan.

"Shit on a Shingle. Where have you been the last thirty-five years, I've missed you so," Duncan said, tongue firmly planted in cheek.

"Who's Mister High and Tight here?" Daymon asked, obviously referring to Davis' regulation military haircut.

"Daymon, meet Airman Davis, he's the bearer of some really good news. We were just issued a helo. Don't ask me what model of helicopter, that's in the hands of..." Duncan consulted the note, "a First Sergeant Whipper."

"Pleased to meet you," Davis said as he got up to leave. "Safe flight, gentlemen."

Duncan nodded in acknowledgment.

Daymon offered a thin smile and turned his attention to the plate of sludge. "What did you call this?" He speared the mystery meat, turned the fork over, sniffed once and dropped it, food, and all, back onto the aluminum tray.

"Shit on a Shingle," Duncan answered. His southern drawl made it sound like a delicacy.

Daymon held up what appeared to be a piece of green toast. "What exactly is it?"

Duncan was hoping he could break it to Daymon *after* he had taken a few bites, but the picky kid wasn't eating. "It's whatever leftover meat the cooks throw into whatever leftover gravy they have laying around. And then they slop that *shit* on top of the shingle, which is usually any leftover bread lying around that's getting ready to turn green. And by the looks of your "shingle" it was already green."

"I ain't eating that shit."

"You mean to tell me that *you*... Mister Lived in the Country most of his life, Sir He Who Hunts a Lot--has never eaten Shit on a Shingle?" Duncan said incredulously.

"No, I haven't. I was a Bureau of Land Management firefighter--*not* a Gomer Pyle like you. The only army food that I've eaten is one of those awful MREs," Daymon stated.

"Finish up; we have a date with First Sergeant Whipper. We may be wheels up sooner than you think," Duncan said, giving the dreadlocked man a little wink. Duncan already had his ever-present go bag with him and was raring to go. Daymon, however, still had to retrieve his personal belongings from his billet.

Daymon pushed his untouched plate of food away and stood up. "Give me a second, there's something I need to get."

"Make it quick. I want to get in the air before anyone has second thoughts about letting a geriatric and a hothead take one of their choppers and then tries to have us grounded."

Daymon went back behind the chow hall and grabbed two burlap potato sacks from the same neat stack that was there the night before. They were just the right size to conceal his crossbow and haul the rest of his gear to the chopper.

***

Duncan flagged down a passing Cushman shuttle and gently persuaded the young airman that they needed to requisition it to take them to First Sergeant Whipper's office; the signed note from General Desantos sealed the deal.

Daymon heaved his two bags of "potatoes" into the stretched golf cart and strategically chose a seat behind the driver. His early morning covert excursion had left him little time for sleep. On top of that, he had a feeling he might be coming down with a bug, and after taking a dip in the dead pool he hoped it wasn't the Omega bug.

Duncan talked the airman's ear off as they traversed the base, passing a number of massive hangars. All manner of fixed wing aircraft were parked inside or arranged in clusters on the edge of the tarmac, some in various stages of maintenance. Apparently Whipper's office was somewhere between Timbuktu and Madagascar. They had been travelling so long even Duncan had grown tired of talking--a very rare occurrence.

They stopped in front of an oversized hangar filled with a mishmash of civilian aircraft.

The sensation of the cart stopping woke Daymon. "Looks like a junkyard... are we here to see someone about a chopper or is Fred Sanford gonna *drive* us to Idaho?" he quipped.

Wow, the kid has seen Sanford and Son, Duncan thought. *Impressive.*

"The First Sergeant's office is through that yellow door," the airman informed Duncan. Then he asked, "Do you need me to wait around for you?"

"Thank you son... but no, it's the end of the line for us," Duncan drawled.

The airman nodded an affirmative, turned a one-eighty in the Cushman, and went about his way.

"After you, *Sir*," Daymon said, deferring to the older man. In reality he wanted nothing to do with procuring their transportation-- whatever that entailed.

"I don't like your tone of voice, *young man.* Did it ever occur to you that this old fart might be able to kick your scrawny ass?" Duncan said, only half joking, as the "odd couple" walked towards Whipper's office.

Although he had a zinger locked and loaded, Daymon wisely held his tongue.

Duncan rapped on the pockmarked yellow door.

"*Who is it?*" a gruff voice sounded through the closed door.

"Name's Duncan... Duncan Winters," he said, his mouth nearly kissing the metal door. "I'm looking for First Sergeant Whipper."

The door opened inward before Duncan could stand straight. He appeared to be bowing to the rotund man clad in grease-stained coveralls.

"And how might I be blessed to make your acquaintance Mr. Winters...and friend?" the man said as he craned his head to inspect Daymon, who was trying to remain inconspicuous despite his exotic appearance and the half a foot height advantage he had over Duncan.

"You're Whipper?" Duncan said, slightly taken aback. He had never seen such a high ranking grease monkey before.

The mechanic displayed his stained hands. "I was still of the Whipper clan the last time I checked. So the uniform isn't appropriate for my rank, huh?" the first sergeant asked drily.

IN HARM'S WAY: SURVIVING THE ZOMBIE APOCALYPSE

"Just caught me by surprise, that's all." Duncan handed over the hand written requisition order and added, "General Desantos sent me."

Whipper snatched the piece of paper and scrunched up his hawkish nose, which was perched crookedly on his ruddy face, bracketed by closely spaced pale blue eyes. A half-moon of wispy white hair reached for the sky. *The Fred Sanford assumption wasn't far off,* Duncan thought, trying not to pass judgment but failing horribly.

Daymon watched silently as the funny looking fella scrutinized the piece of legal paper.

After a few seconds of reading, the first sergeant looked Duncan and Daymon up and down. After seeming to come to some sort of decision, he gestured toward the door. "Follow me," he said.

As they walked, Whipper explained why he was in the trenches getting his hands dirty. Most of the men and women that were responsible for keeping the birds mission ready lived in Colorado Springs. There were a few airmen on base that Saturday, and only a very small percentage of the personnel living off base returned after the bug hit and the lock downs were ordered.

"Human nature, I guess," Whipper said. "If I would have been in their shoes... can't honestly say that I wouldn't have done the same dang thing."

The first sergeant led them through the open hangar. They emerged on the other side amidst the cluster of multi-colored civilian aircraft. "There she is."

The navy blue helicopter was spattered with evidence of a prolonged Z attack. Silver smears resembling slug tracks criss-crossed the lower half of the fuselage and greasy handprints clouded the cockpit glass. The helo bore the markings of the U.S. Department of Homeland Security, complete with a gold stripe painted front to back.

"What happened to the aircrew?" Duncan asked.

"I can't be certain. There were six people aboard: four DHS agents, the pilot, and his co-pilot. At least one of the Department of Homeland Security agents was infected. A slow burn... he made it here still breathing like one of us, but I assume he turned in

81

quarantine. The rest of the men are probably helping out here on base... *not running away from responsibility."*

Duncan ignored the obvious jab. "Thanks Sergeant. We'll take her." He paused in thought for a tick. "How are the rotors? What I'm getting at, judging by the dead people juice all over the fuselage, it has obviously been through the wringer... were there any blade strikes that you are aware of? Believe it or not, I've had to ride one of these to the ground recently and my back is still feeling the effects."

Daymon had somewhat successfully buried the helicopter crash in his subconscious until Duncan had to go ahead and rehash it. Daymon broke his silence and nervously asked, "Is this thing going to get us to Idaho?"

"Take it or leave it, gentlemen. As you can see," Whipper raised his soiled hands, palms upturned, "I've got my hands full keeping the transports and tankers in the air. Schriever is getting low on food and the soldiers taking care of the Z's downtown need all of the resupply drops that we can give 'em. Those missions need aircraft that have been properly attended to. So to answer your question honestly... I don't know. I really *do not* want to allocate the amount of fuel that you're going to need ... but orders are orders." The Sergeant balled up the handwritten note bearing the General's orders and tossed it on the tarmac, watched the wind propel it bouncing and tumbling down the runway, and then turned and walked away without saying another word.

"What an a-hole," Daymon whispered.

"I can see where he's coming from and I can't blame the guy," Duncan said as he walked around the ship, visually inspecting the moving parts--especially the all-important rotor blades, being very careful not to touch the dried human detritus clinging to it.

Daymon asked, "Will this one stay in the air?"

"Good to go," Duncan said as he hauled himself into the pilot's seat.

Daymon shot the old aviator a worried look and entered the cockpit as well. *What are the odds of us going down again?* he asked himself as a thousand pounds of apprehension and an equal amount of worry weighed down on his shoulders.

The inside of the Black Hawk showed no signs of the violence wrought on the outside. Without the litters and medical lifesaving gear, the cabin of the DHS Border Patrol helo was more spacious than the National Guard Medevac bird Duncan had crash landed smack dab in the middle of I-25 the day before.

Daymon stowed all of their gear and weapons in the passenger area and retrieved two flight helmets before returning to the co-pilot's seat.

Duncan inspected his new bird. The cockpit of the Border Patrol helicopter was slightly different than the military Black Hawk he had gotten used to. He was relieved to find that the flight controls were identical and the switches and gauges were in roughly the same place. The Black Hawk definitely wasn't a U.S. military bird but it did have external fuel tanks attached under the stubby wings, and without them Duncan knew the bird didn't have the range to deliver them to Idaho let alone all of the way to his little brother's compound in Eden.

After taking a few moments to get acquainted with the dials and gauges Duncan started the engine. "So far so good," he said winking at his "co-pilot." The helicopter strained and shimmied as the engine collected rpms. When he spooled the turbines up to near maximum power the rotors suddenly bit into the air. "Hold on to your cookies," Duncan said, poking fun at the nervous ashen-faced passenger to his left.

"Here we go again. I'm stuck with Mister Stand-Up Comedian himself." Daymon took a few deep breaths to calm his stomach from the effects of the hurried take off. "You know this just doesn't seem the same without the other Gomer Pyle here to order me around."

"Don't worry, I'll boss you around in his stead," Duncan assured the big crybaby.

Daymon looked at the aviator from behind his purloined sunglasses. "I respect the dude... but I still resent the other "Gomer" for putting his gun in my face."

"Cut the other "Gomer" a break. In all reality Cade is more "Mitch Rapp" than your garden variety soldier, *which I am proud to call myself*, and I know there are things he's done, in total anonymity, that you and I have benefitted from in spades. And I *guaran-god-damn-tee* you," Duncan butchered every syllable, "that kid will never toot his own horn about it. There ain't no Freedom of Information Act anymore Daymon, and only a select handful of people will ever be privy to the things he has done above and beyond the call of duty." Duncan flicked some switches and made a slight course adjustment and then continued. "I've got a good feel for people and assessing the content of their character. Cade's a man of his word. And in the week plus that I've known him he hasn't let me down. Honoring one's word--that became a lost art in the final ten or fifteen years of *normal.* Shit, just plain old *honor* about disappeared--that's one thing you can't instill or train someone to practice once they're already set in their ways. Cade's one of those guys, like an old Blue Tick hound, once you're friends... it's for life. Don't muck it up... allies like him don't come around very often."

"I started to warm to the man--*after* he put the Glock away. To be honest with you, old man, I've been cursed with a long memory. I'm like a country squirrel--I never forget where I stash my nuts," Daymon said, his usually emotionless face exhibiting a wan smile.

Unfortunately, Duncan's twisted sense of humor kicked in. In his mind's eye he could see the man in the co-pilot seat trying to find a safe place to hide the family jewels. He chuckled at the visual.

Daymon pondered the southern gentleman's words of wisdom while the ground chopped by. "He came through with this bird--got to give him that. I feel dumb even asking." He raised his hands in a sign of surrender. "Who the eff is *Mitch Rapp*?"

Duncan rummaged in his go bag, extracted a thick novel, and tossed it to Daymon. "You'll meet Mitch Rapp in there, read it when you find some time."

The helicopter shuddered. Some kind of warning chime began to sound in both men's helmets.

Daymon glanced up at the multitude of flashing colored lights. He could have sworn they were telling him to "*kiss his ass goodbye*" in Morse code. *One helicopter crash is one too many in a man's lifetime,* he thought. Then it dawned on him that he didn't even know Morse code.

Duncan tapped one of the gauges and, coincidence or not, the chiming along with the blinking lights ceased.

"Tell me son, how are you feeling--still a little green? Any old football injuries bugging you?" Duncan inquired, totally ignoring the helicopter's hiccup with a cavalier, *out of sight out of mind,* attitude. He was prying to see if Daymon would talk about his wounds.

"I'm feeling green now that I know this thing is probably held together with baling wire and boogers. What... uh... are the chances of us *surviving* another crash landing?" Daymon asked, evidently concerned because his voice was now an octave higher.

Duncan raised a fist, and one at a time, he slowly extended three fingers. Then after a slight mental pause, he stuck out a fourth digit. "The chances are good, son. That Black Hawk was the fourth helicopter to fall off of my ass, so I think it's safe to say that you've got a ways to go before Mister Death on his pale white horse comes a calling."

"Remember, I was on *Black Hawk Down* the other night," Daymon said. "Fill me in on your first three helicopter mishaps."

"They were all anomalies: Huey number one, enemy fire... lucky shot if you ask me. Number two got shot out from under me. It was inevitable... I took that slick into a hot LZ to extract some Op Phoenix boys. Put it this way, I got to fight Victor Charlie, on the ground, with those brave men. Thankfully the VC lost our scent and all of us made it to another extraction point alive."

"And number three?"

"Definitely *not* my fault! Mechanical failure led to an autorotation in enemy territory and I got to eat dinner at a remote fire base in the central highlands of Vietnam."

"Thanks, that totally puts me at ease," Daymon retorted sarcastically.

"Don't mention it," Duncan drawled.

Daymon closed his eyes. It was his way of dealing with reality. "Wake me if you need anything... but if we're in imminent danger of crash landing... don't bother."

"Copy that," Duncan said.

Chapter 14
Outbreak - Day 8
Sentinel Butte, North Dakota

It had been thirty minutes since Ari delivered Cade and
Maddox to the superheated piece of rock they were now stretched
out on. Cade ignored the sun beating down on his back as he
watched the red ant pick at the exposed flesh between his sleeve and
gloved hand. He marveled at its persistence as it worked diligently,
rending a tiny piece of his flesh to take back to its queen. Soon
another hunter ambled up, sniffed around, and repeated what the
first insect did. This went on for a few minutes. The pain was
tolerable--Cade had suffered much, much worse. The ants did serve
to break up the monotony of waiting for the target to come to him.
He couldn't help noticing the way the ants kept coming back for
more meat. It reminded him of the same insatiable desire for living
flesh he had seen the dead exhibit.

Sergeant Maddox shifted his body slightly. *Maybe he was feeding
the ants too,* Cade thought. Maddox was spotting for Cade. They knew
each other by reputation but had only been on a couple of operations
together.

Two clicks sounded in their earpieces just seconds before the
engine noise resonated from the lee side of the steep rise in the
highway stretching away from them. Cade clicked his mic two times,
letting the other shooter know he was good to go.

Both men hunkered down, flanked by two fingers of rock in
between which Cade had arranged clumps of sage and grasses to fill

in the center gap. He had picked the spot because of its elevation and the oblique angle to the kill zone. The hide was neither perpendicular nor parallel to the road. The suppressor affixed to the barrel of the Remington MSR pierced the foliage, pointing in the direction of the UPS eighteen wheeler blocking the road. Although Cade was sweating his ass off in the ACUs, and a drink of water sounded good, he didn't want to risk any movement that might give away his position, so he resisted the urge to take a pull of water from his Camelback.

The engine noises grew louder and lower in pitch. It was evident the five-vehicle convoy was climbing the rise and about to crest the top of the hill.

Cade trained the crosshairs on the gash of blue sky where the vehicles were about to emerge. The blacktop at the road's apex appeared to ripple; the shimmering heat waves made it look like a de-cloaking Romulan Warbird was about to materialize. The fact that he was a closet Trekkie was *the* only thing Cade would never admit to anyone.

After a minute of laboring uphill, the first Hummer emerged through the thermal vortex. The helmeted gunner swept his weapon slowly side to side, covering both shoulders of the road. Cade noted that the front bumper and flat sides of the black vehicle were smeared with shiny residue, most likely accumulated from many bouts with the living dead.

Cade momentarily scanned the area with his naked eye. Closer in, the zombies in the vicinity of the road block perked up and started marching towards the noises. As the big rigs in the middle of the convoy came into view and started descending the hill, they used their engines' compression to combat the steep decline and keep their brakes from overheating. The steady drawn out *brrraapp* from the semi trucks' belching exhaust instantly got the attention of the remaining walkers in and around the sprawling Truck Plaza.

Cade could see the Hummer driver's face through the high powered scope. He appeared to be engaged in an animated conversation with the man in the passenger seat, who was also jabbering and talking with his hands. The crosshairs were parked on the driver's forehead. Cade wished he could read lips a little better;

however, he could make out a few of the words, *zombie*, *motherfucker* and *shit* were some of them. It wasn't enough to draw any solid conclusions from, but he had a feeling the crew of the first truck had had enough of the walking dead for one lifetime.

The two Ghost Hawks hovered in a standoff formation to the west where the sun would mask their approach, giving them one more unfair advantage if they needed to join the fight. Desantos and Lopez were in Jedi One-One. Captain Ronnie Gaines and another shooter from the 10th SF Group were onboard the other Ghost. Desantos' orders for Cade and the other shooter, a 10th Special Forces soldier named Dillard, were to hold their fire until he gave the go signal with three mic clicks.

The convoy slowed and came to a complete stop.

Cade and Maddox waited patiently on the ridge, ready to unleash hell.

Chapter 15
Outbreak - Day 8
20 Miles South of Denver

"*Mom!*"

"Caroline honey, remember we *have* to be quiet. The bogeyman is still out there," Karla said in a near stage whisper.

The kindergartener had grown tired of her mom constantly telling her to be quiet and forcing her and her brother to *always* be still. An adult would have had a hard time, let alone a precocious five year old. She parted the curtains in her upstairs room in order to take another look and yelled, "*Mom... bring the noculars!*"

"Shhh. I don't want to have to tell you again. The next time you raise your voice you will be getting a spanking," Karla lied. The truth was, the young mom had never laid a hand on any of her three kids and she hoped that it would never be necessary... especially now, considering the state of the world they were surviving in.

The two-story house vibrated slightly.

"No jumping on the bed Caroline."

"I'm not, Momma."

"Then tell Donnie to knock it off or I'm coming up there when Sadie is done feeding."

"*Mom... bring up the noculars!*"

God, grant me the serenity... Karla put her breast away and started up the stairs with her three-month-old Sadie held snugly in her arms.

Seven-year-old Donnie suddenly appeared and followed his mom upstairs with the binoculars in hand.

Caroline pressed her face against the aquarium glass as ripples began to form, moving outward in concentric circles on the surface of the blue green water. "Don't worry Fin, I won't let them eat you," she said to her pet goldfish as she hugged his five-gallon home.

After summiting the top of the stairs, Karla asked with a whisper, "What were you *yelling* about young missy?" Since the outbreak her one hard and fast rule was to keep quiet--at all times. Noise always attracted walkers, and thankfully it had been a full day since any of them had shown interest in their house. The last one had stood for hours with its marbled face pressed against the kitchen window, peering inside with unblinking lifeless eyes until something else--an enticing sound or other survivors on the move--finally caught its attention and it shambled away.

Using her best inside voice Caroline said, "There's something outside... and I need the noculars to see it."

"*Ohhh*, you mean *binoculars*."

"That's what I said," Caroline answered with a smile, obviously very pleased with herself.

"Here you go Mom."

Karla nearly jumped out of her skin. She had assumed that Donnie was already upstairs with Caroline. "Don't ever do that again... Don," she hissed as Sadie began to whimper. Then she felt something heavy tapping her on the thigh. She looked down. Donnie had the 'noculars' and was playing woodpecker on her leg with them.

"Sorry Mom," he whispered apologetically.

"What are you all excited about Caroline?" Karla said as she opened the curtains a little wider so that she could look out as well.

Caroline pointed for her mom's benefit. "There..."

The gasp that escaped Karla's mouth came from deep within her lungs, sounding like a drowning person's final breath. She didn't need anything save for her own two eyes to tell her it was time to leave the Garner homestead. Less than a mile away, hundreds of the shambling living dead stretched shoulder to shoulder from one side of the tollway all the way across eight lanes and the median and then up the far embankment. The majority of the horde seemed to be marching straight down the middle of I-25, rearranging the stalled cars and trucks along the way like they were small pieces of driftwood caught in an encroaching surf. Karla could barely believe her eyes as the mass pushed a multi-ton fire engine to the wayside. The gray cloud of dust and grass seed being kicked up by the phalanx of walking dead roiled into the air, and because of the haze Karla couldn't discern how far back the main column ended... if it did at all.

"Donnie, I need you to fetch your Spiderman backpack and wait by the front door," Karla said, trying to remain calm. "Caroline... follow your brother... and *do not* go outside yet." She stole another worried look at the terrifying slow-moving procession. As far north as she could see, the creatures on the periphery appeared to be moving much faster than the main army. The small groups of twos and threes were getting closer; a few of them were nearing her property line.

Karla's husband John initially lobbied for the family to flee to Colorado Springs two days after the outbreak. Karla argued that traveling with three kids, one of them an infant, would be suicide. She even agreed with the people on television insisting they stay put and wait for help to arrive. Furthermore, she didn't want to leave the home that she had grown up in--there were too many good memories between the four walls and many more yet to be added. Karla wanted her kids to grow up in the shadows of the Rockies--in the same house that had been in the family for generations. Karla's great-grandfather erected the two-story clapboard house on the hillock next to I-25, a hundred years before there was an I-25.

Now Karla regretted that self-centered decision to her very core. With a sudden burst of frantic energy she ran down the stairs two at a time. Sadie wailed. Donnie and Caroline cowered by the door, watery eyes watching their mom's every move.

The keys to the Tahoe were on the peg where John had left them. God, how she hated to drive the thing... let alone schlep the kids in and out of the gas-guzzling SUV. When her husband left to forage for food last Thursday he drove her minivan. *I can load more into the side door by myself and I won't be fumbling around with the rear hatch or having to open and close the back doors,* he told Karla then. She froze for a second, thinking of her gentle giant while a salty tear traced her cheek.

The out-of-place sound of the good china rattling in the hutch snapped Karla back to reality. Although she couldn't feel the floor vibrating through the carpet, she could sense that the walkers were nearly on top of them.

"When I say go... *look at me Caroline*. When I say go, you two go... run for Daddy's car like it was the ice cream truck and today is free ice cream day."

Caroline perked up. "I want a fudgsicle," she said, looking dreamily away.

"Donnie... listen carefully. Since Daddy isn't here right now, your job is to make sure your sister gets in first and then you jump in after. *Very important... lock the door when both of you are inside...* OK?"

The seven-year-old and current man of the house puffed out his chest and said, "I got it Mom."

Karla's lower lip quivered and her hands shook as she fumbled with the straps on the infant carrier. If they were too tight Sadie would scream bloody murder but if they were too loose the three-month-old might Houdini her way out. Sadie playfully batted at her mom's fingers, blissfully oblivious to the approaching wall of gnashing teeth. The young mom halfheartedly reciprocated. The last thing that Karla wanted to do was break down in front of the kids; it took every last ounce of her willpower to hold it together.

After cracking the door and stealing a quick peek Karla decided that it was now or never. The alarm chirped. "*Ice cream!*" Karla bellowed.

Both kids bolted across the threshold like it was Christmas morning and Santa had left their presents on the lawn.

Karla was right behind her kids, running awkwardly, trying to compensate for the weight of Sadie and the infant carrier. "*Get in! Get in! Go... go... hurry up Donnie!*" She sprinted to the driver's door, ripped it open and flung Sadie, none too gently, across the front seats. Karla was desperately trying to multitask: one hand worked to get the key in the ignition while the other blindly grasped at thin air trying to find the handle. Before she could pull the door shut several hundred pounds of rotting corpses crashed into the door, causing it to violently close on her left side and shattering her wrist in the process.

There wasn't enough adrenaline in Karla's body to block out the intense pain and she couldn't stop herself from screaming.

Donnie fought with the door handle for a few seconds with his little sister seemingly super glued to his back. Once the door was open a crack, Donnie grabbed Caroline by the seat of her pants and with all of the strength that he could muster, propelled her across the floorboard to her car seat. Donnie glanced through the window only to see snarling faces staring back at him, and yelled at Caroline to buckle in.

Karla exhaled a sigh of relief when she noticed in the rearview that Caroline was safely in the car seat. Donnie, on the other hand, was still in limbo--half in and half out of the rear door--when the first zombie latched on to his tiny blue and red backpack.

"Help me Momma," Donnie whimpered as the cold gnarled hands ripped his small form away from the rest of his family.

Karla stopped screaming and tried to get herself together. Her right hand stopped shaking long enough to allow her to turn the key and start her husband's SUV. She looked up and realized that her firstborn was nowhere to be seen.

"Donnie..." she called out plaintively as she put the Tahoe in reverse.

Caroline had just finished clicking herself in; she met eyes with her mom in the mirror and said, "The bogeyman took him."

Karla whipped her head around searching for her son. She couldn't risk getting out to look for him and leave the two girls in the vehicle, so she reversed out of the driveway. The rear passenger door flew open, obscuring her side mirror.

Sadie began to fuss and cry, only adding to the background noise of shuffling feet.

"Mommy... I see Donnie... he's playing tag with the bogeyman."

Out of the corner of her eye, the sight of her son running in circles with two of the creatures in pursuit caused her heart to skip several beats. One of the flesh eaters still clutched her boy's pack in its pale hands. Karla aimed the bumper for the walker and blasted the horn, praying that Donnie would jump out of the way. Donnie reacted--the creatures did not. The impact flung both of the zombies and Donnie's backpack into Karla's mature Rhododendron bushes. They looked like a couple of drunks at closing time as they tried to extricate themselves from the plant's sticky clutches.

Karla frantically laid on the horn then yelled at the top of her lungs, "*Donnie... get in here now!*" Then she looked toward the house in disbelief with her mouth hanging open. There were no words to convey what she was seeing. The procession of dead had changed course a few degrees and the rotting walkers were now pouring around both flanks of her home. As she watched, the old house moved in her direction and, with a puff of dust accumulated over the last hundred years, careened off of its foundation.

An imaginary fist grabbed Karla's heart as she watched Donnie disappear under the crush of death. Then the walkers lunged into the open door and began devouring Caroline. Mercifully the five-year-old didn't scream for long. A feeling of utter helplessness washed over the sobbing mother as she shielded Sadie with her body, waiting to die.

Chapter 16
Outbreak - Day 8
Flight from Denver

Like Sonic the Hedgehog, the cobalt blue Subaru blasted by the black SUV, passing it on the left.

From his elevated perch Wilson snatched a passing glimpse of William slumped in the passenger seat, his slack face looking every bit as pale as one of the zombies. "Where in the hell does he think he's going?" said Wilson.

"It looks like he's leaving the tollway," Sasha replied from the back seat.

After weaving between a grouping of abandoned cars, Ted exited Interstate 25 and drove the wrong way up the on ramp and turned east onto a car-cluttered surface street.

By the time Wilson threaded the Suburban between the throng of cars, three new colors of paint had been added to the side of the less than compact SUV, and more than five minutes had elapsed since he had last seen the Subaru.

"Sis, get up front with me. I need your eyes."

"Are there any of those things out there?" Sasha asked, her voice wavering.

"Just get up here and deal!" Wilson barked. He really hated having to be the bad guy and didn't want to be too hard on his sister considering the stress she had already been subjected to, but he knew he had no choice.

Sasha crawled forward and retook her spot in the passenger seat.

"You look down the side streets and I'll worry about what's ahead."

"OK," Sasha answered, resigned to the fact that she was going to have to face her fears sooner or later.

Wilson had made the trip between Denver and Colorado Springs many times, yet he still couldn't recall the names of the little burghs scattered frequently along the route and this one was no exception. The streets were littered with newspapers and trash, and broken glass sparkled in the sun. They were only two blocks removed from the tollway and Wilson had already been forced to swerve the SUV around numerous walking dead. Every one of the rotten creatures they passed acted in the same manner: instant recognition of the moving vehicle, followed by clumsy swipes in their general direction as they drove by and then the inevitable throng of moaning zombies following in the truck's wake.

Wilson massaged the wheel with both hands and said, "I'm only going two or three more blocks, and if we don't see Ted or William or their car, then I'm turning around."

The usual chain fast food restaurants and cross-competing gas stations dominating the real estate near Interstate 25 quickly gave way to a host of smaller storefronts. Wilson noted the time on the dashboard clock. "It'll be getting dark around nine so that doesn't leave us much time to screw around on this side trip."

"I wasn't paying attention to the road signs... do you have any idea how much further Colorado Springs is?" Sasha asked. The truth of the matter was that she hadn't seen anything at all. She had been curled up in the back seat with her eyes screwed shut since her frightening face-to-face encounter with the walking corpse on Prospect Street in Denver, and deep down lurked a sinking feeling telling her that they still had quite a ways to go.

After looking at the odometer and consulting his mental abacus, Wilson confirmed what Sasha already knew. "We're only twenty-five miles from Denver and we've been on the road for *three* hours," he said disgustedly.

"You didn't answer my question, *Wilson*," Sasha said, hoping to God that her hunch would be proven wrong.

"Colorado Springs is roughly forty miles from here... and I'd be willing to bet this little town is named Castle Rock," Wilson added as he gestured toward the storefronts. It was an easy guess--nearly every business on the street had "Castle Rock" incorporated into their name, not to mention the natural rock formation looming east of town which resembled a squat, windowless, medieval keep.

Fully deflated, Sasha asked if they were going to make it to Colorado Springs before dark.

"I need to concentrate on driving... you need to keep your eyes peeled for our *friends*."

They had driven six blocks from the overpass before Sasha finally spotted the blue car. The Subaru was parked haphazardly half a block down a side street.

Wilson had stopped in towns like this before and he was sure that if this were a normal summer weekend the small business core would be bustling with people. It hosted a couple of antique shops, a Java Junkie Coffee, a greasy spoon diner called Henny Penny's--its faded facade and old school neon signage displaying a chicken motif--and lastly, the Castle Rock Rexall Drugstore that Ted's Subaru was currently double parked in front of. Except for the three zombies lurching towards the drugstore, the two-lane street was deserted.

Wilson stepped on the accelerator, aiming the SUV at the biggest ghoul.

"What are you doing *Wilson*?" Sasha barked as she fumbled for a handhold.

"I'm thinking that the bumper on this thing will do more damage than my baseball bat," he replied, suddenly aware how sore his shoulders and back were from beating the shit out of the dead guy and his Caprice.

As they drove by the drugstore Sasha strained to see inside. The front windows were cluttered with displays and behind them the interior of the store was dark and gloomy.

The zombie nearest to the Subaru was the freshest one Wilson had seen since Denver. The dead woman wore a tattered tube top and white capris; her summery outfit was thoroughly soiled.

Streamers of skin and sinew, evidence of a recent kill, dangled from between her teeth and she appeared to have been painted crimson red from the chin down with someone else's drying blood.

Wilson aimed the massive grill at the stumbling zombie and looked down at the speedometer as it pushed past forty miles per hour. When he looked up again he saw the creature's baby blues peeking over the tall hood; he involuntarily scrunched his eyes shut as the violent impact knocked the zombie off its feet and sent the broken body flailing through the air. Tube Top came to rest face up, impaled on the wrought iron fence encircling the front of a colorfully painted toy store. She looked like a fish out of water as she kicked and flopped, futilely trying to stand up.

"One down, two to go," Wilson said grimly.

"How do you know there aren't more of them inside the stores?"

"For Ted's and William's sake... I hope there aren't. Hey Sis... did you notice anybody in the car when we drove by?"

"I was trying to see inside the windows but it was dark and we were moving... please tell me you're not going in there. Don't you *fucking* leave me all alone again *Wilson*."

The way his sister spit out his name felt like a dagger plunging into his heart. If Sasha could bottle that rage and use it on the walkers, he thought, she'd be a lethal weapon.

"If I go in you're coming with me," Wilson said, locking eyes with Sasha and trying his best to reassure her. "Besides, I've got Mr. Louisville."

Wilson steered the SUV on a collision course with a very large specimen. The bloody butcher apron was still cinched tightly around the portly zombie's waist, the perfect accessory for the apocalypse. Fred the butcher carried a cleaver in one meaty hand and a dainty gray arm in the other. Judging by the shiny white ball joint and bouncing tendrils of ragged flesh, the arm hadn't been cleaved off cleanly but instead had been wrenched free with brute strength.

***

The Traveler was a meticulous, detail-oriented man. Type A would be an understatement; he always had to know what he was getting himself into before he dove in.

The steep road that delivered him from the mansion on the west slope of the Rockies, where he obtained his latest vehicle, spit him out near the row of log cabin-style homes on the east slope of the craggy mountains. Pikes Peak, forty miles to the south, looked stunted and lonely. The view to the north was hazy and distorted. It looked like there was a dust storm on the horizon.

The Traveler entered the first home he happened across; it was empty of people, living or dead. He gathered the absentee owners didn't have much of a voyeuristic streak even though the house had a panoramic view of the valley that opened up below as there wasn't a telescope to be found, so he relied on the next best thing, his trusty Bushnells. He glassed the land north to south. Only ten minutes into his recon he spotted two vehicles moving south on the freeway, weaving in between the stalls and pileups, and maintaining a steady controlled pace. Suddenly, with a burst of speed, the smaller blue wagon pulsed around the black SUV and exited the freeway. The Traveler momentarily lost sight of the rabbiting vehicle in the clutter and shadows before reacquiring it a few streets east of the freeway where it made a left turn. Midway down the block the speeding car slewed sideways, stopping abruptly. Then a large bearded man hopped out and hurriedly entered into one of the storefronts.

From the Traveler's vantage point, with the aid of the high powered binoculars, it seemed like he was witnessing a Los Angeles freeway chase on CNN. Although there weren't any police cars in hot pursuit, it appeared to the Traveler that the person behind the wheel of the black SUV didn't want to be left in the dust.

The Traveler watched with detached amusement as the SUV collided with a diminutive walker, sending the pasty body cartwheeling through space. *That had to hurt,* he thought, as the creature wound up with multiple piercings courtesy of an inconveniently placed wrought iron fence.

Continuing on the same trajectory, the black SUV struck a much larger male zombie head on. The result, however, was exactly the opposite; a viscous spray of fluids painted the hood and windshield as the giant walker disappeared under the front of the speeding SUV. Then, like a corpse in a wood chipper, shredded skin, flesh, and tattered scraps of clothing vomited out the other end. From the Traveler's skybox seat, even without the benefit of sound to accompany the gory visual, the steam venting from the truck's destroyed grill testified to the ferocity of the impact.

"They're effed," the Traveler said aloud as he continued to watch the spectacle unfold.

***

That was one big dude, Wilson thought as he turned on the wipers to clear the gore from the windshield. The flopping blades spread the greasy liquids over the entire glass, further obscuring his view.

"What's that sound?" Sasha asked.

Wilson slowed the truck and performed a U-turn. "I think the thing is stuck underneath," he said, stabbing a finger at the floorboard.

Sasha shook her head side to side. "No, not that sound... I hear something hissing. Like maybe a tire leaking air?"

"Shit."

"What is it?"

Wilson noticed the flashing idiot light on the instrument cluster. "The engine is overheating."

He nosed the stricken vehicle in towards the curb next to the Subaru. When the truck stopped moving, an explosion of superheated water and steam erupted under the hood. Wilson shook his head, fearing that the truck was done for. Then he grabbed the Louisville Slugger and looked down the street in both directions searching for any new threats before he exited the Suburban. "Wait here while I check things out," he said to Sasha, slamming the door shut without allowing her time to protest.

Part of Sasha wanted to curl up and melt into the seat but the thought quickly dissipated. Wilson's last foray from the safety of the truck was still etched in her memory: the unexpected thrashing he had given the zombie was brutal and totally out of character for him. The total feeling of helplessness that owned her as she lay paralyzed by fear on the verge of a nervous breakdown was something she never wanted to experience again. There was no way Wilson was leaving her and going in alone. "Dammit Wilson," she muttered as

100

she threw the door open in a fit of rage. The moment her bare foot touched the scorching pavement she realized that her shoes were still in the back seat, but before she could turn to retrieve them something ice cold clutched her ankle and yanked her out of the SUV. She twisted her body on the way down and landed on her right side, where she found herself staring directly into the hungry jaundiced eyes of her attacker. Sasha braced one foot on the running board and commenced the tug of war for her life.

***

The Traveler popped another Ritz cracker into his mouth and crunched hungrily. "What are you going to do now, carrot top?" he said aloud, the cracker crumbs spraying from his mouth and dusting the dark walnut floor. He watched as the redhead exited the steaming SUV, bat over his shoulder, and stormed into the drugstore. "No guts no glory." *Oh to be young again,* the Traveler thought.

Seconds after the driver disappeared the Traveler watched the passenger door open, revealing a scarlet-haired young lady.

"Nice... a lithe young redhead. Me like..." the Traveler said, continuing his running commentary. Then he noticed more walkers emerging from the darkened stores. "Better watch yer back lassie." As he spoke, her upper body disappeared behind the rig she had just stepped out of. "Can't hide from 'em there..." he warned the soon-to-be-surrounded cutie. He inhaled the rest of the crackers, chucked the wax wrapper on the pristine floor, and buried his face in the binoculars.

***

Wilson's eyes were slow to adjust to the shadowy interior, but his other senses picked up the slack. The darkened drugstore smelled like death and cheap cologne. *There are probably more than one of the creatures in here,* he silently warned himself as he choked up on the gore-stained baseball bat. He finally regained some eyesight and noticed a gray haze swirling in the air; just then a rattling sound, like someone shaking Yahtzee dice, came from behind the pharmacist's sliding window. By the time Wilson gathered up the resolve to see what or who was making the noise in the back of the store, Sasha's unmistakable shrill screams sounded outside.

***

Here I come to save the day, the Traveler thought, complete with the theme music playing in his head as he watched the guy carrying the bat burst from the drugstore. The Traveler loved Mighty Mouse cartoons as a kid and even idolized the tough little character. He was always the littlest guy in the room when he was growing up. To say he had a Napoleon complex would be an understatement. After high school, to prove a point, he tried to join the Marine Corps, but because of his size he was turned down. It proved to be a blessing in disguise, because if they had taken him he would have been sent to Vietnam in the waning years of the war. Instead he joined the Atlanta Police Department and rose through the ranks until retiring with a full pension in the year 2000 at the ripe old age of forty-four. He had every intention of working a cushy PI job and living the double dipper lifestyle until his life took a series of interesting turns. Now, more than ten years later, here he was trying to find a way to join up with the little group of survivors and get to Colorado Springs alive.

***

Sasha's screaming continued unabated. Wilson hit the door at full speed leading with his forearm, circled around the battered front end of the Suburban and tripped face first over Sasha's outstretched body. He looked like Pete Rose stealing second as his head and chest absorbed the brunt of the fall. He momentarily lost consciousness yet somehow kept hold of the Louisville Slugger. After a second or two, Wilson resurfaced from the dark. Still the screaming continued. He vigorously shook his head to get rid of the cobwebs; the tactic didn't work. He continued seeing double, although he desperately wanted his senses to return to normal... for Sasha's sake.

Sasha braced her foot against the running board and locked her knee. The searing pain from the monster's crushing grip raced up her leg as the thing started reeling her foot towards its mouth full of jagged teeth.

"Hold on, Sis," Wilson said as he commando crawled under the truck and jammed the bat, handle first, down the zombie's throat. Then he used both hands to pry the ghoul's fingers open. "Good thing it only got ahold of your leg with its *bare* hand. The big bastard was carrying a meat cleaver in the other," Wilson said, as he inspected

102

the abraded skin and hand-shaped bruise already blooming purple and fuchsia around her reed thin ankle.

"It still hurts like hell," Sasha said, while scooting backwards on her butt to get away from the groping hand.

From the other side of the Suburban, three shotgun blasts boomed in quick succession.

Wilson popped his head over the hood of the SUV to see who was doing the shooting. His stomach clenched when he realized he was staring down the barrel of Ted's shotgun, and from his vantage point the smoking muzzle looked as big as a manhole cover. It was the first and hopefully the last time he had ever had a gun pointed at him. Wilson had never felt so vulnerable. At that moment he wished he was a turtle and could pull everything inside of a shell, *especially* his head.

"I almost shortened you by a foot," Ted stated as he stalked around the SUV. "Where is your sister?"

Wilson, still recovering from his near death experience, couldn't find the words to reply.

Ted looked at the wrecked front end of the Suburban. "Will it start?"

"I think it'll start... but it won't take us very far with an empty radiator," Wilson said glumly, pointing at the yellow-green fluid lapping at Ted's shoes. Then he appraised the situation he had gotten him and his sister into. The creature under the truck was still rooting around, waiting for anyone to get within the grabbing zone. The sight reminded Wilson to light a fire under his sister to get her moving. "Sasha, get your stuff and this time don't forget your shoes."

He looked across the street; Tube Top still writhed on the fence. On the far side of the SUV, three corpses with fresh head wounds were splayed out in awkward positions scattered at five foot intervals. In the other direction, there were more walkers than Wilson could count streaming from the side streets and open storefronts, slowly lurching towards his position.

"Take this." Ted thrust the shotgun to Wilson. "I think there are only three shots left," he said as he emptied his pockets of shells and hurriedly dumped them in Wilson's free hand.

"I don't know how to use this," Wilson said, his brow wrinkling. He tried to hand the gun back.

Ted brushed past him, ignoring the gesture. "I have to drive... get in," he ordered rather convincingly.

Sasha retrieved her shoes and bags while being very careful to stay out of the butcher's reach. She inched around the Subaru and squeezed into the back seat behind William. The man didn't have a "human" color about him, he was unmoving and appeared unconscious. Sasha thought that he wasn't breathing until a dry rattle escaped from his thin bloodless lips. The way he looked just a foot in front of her face reminded Sasha of one of those wax figures in Madame whatever-her-name's museum.

Ted and Wilson jumped into the car at the same time, the stench of the dead entering with them, a choking eye watering odor that made breathing nearly impossible. For good measure, Wilson had repossessed his Louisville Slugger from the butcher's throat. He had a feeling he would need it again before the day was over.

The zombies were closing and now within twenty feet of the Subaru. A handful approached from the north but most of their numbers were trudging from the south, which Sasha was already well aware of.

Ted started the car and rapidly backed away from the curb, running over two walkers in the process. Suddenly the back end of the Subaru rose up off of the street, pitching the backseat passengers forward. Without traction the rear wheels spun freely and the rpms instantly increased, making the engine sound like it was in danger of blowing.

"Shift it into four wheel drive," Wilson said as he fumbled to reload the shotgun.

"How is that going to help? It's all wheel drive anyways," Ted said heatedly as he pounded a fist on the steering wheel. He was clearly not a fan of backseat drivers.

The gearbox balked with a clunk as Ted gave in and shifted the car into four wheel drive low; next, he shifted the transmission out of reverse and into drive. Although Ted wasn't about to admit it, the kid did have a point--the low gearing would transfer the engine power to the wheels that needed it most. "Betsy, don't fail me now," he thought as he mashed the accelerator. The engine emitted a low growl as the front tires gained purchase and began to pull the car forward off of the undead pair.

Sasha pointed a trembling finger towards the rear window. "Wilson..." was the only word she could squeak out.

A gnarled hand slapped the hatchback.

Wilson recoiled, whipped his head around, and poked the shotgun through the partially cracked window looking to acquire a target. From his cramped spot in the rear seat there was no way for him to engage the creature without getting out of the car... *that* was not happening, he said silently to himself.

Ted checked both side mirrors. The mangled zombies that had been stuck under the car were now slowly crawling along the passenger side and a third creature wavered nearby. Ted made it a point to check the rearview mirror before backing up. After determining that the coast was clear, he pulled away from the curb and consciously left haste behind; the last thing he wanted to do was get the car high centered again.

The zombie that had been pawing at the rear window stabbed its pustule-riddled arm into the slow moving car and grabbed a substantial handful of Wilson's hair.

Wilson instinctively yanked his head back while bringing the shotgun to bear. He knew the gun was loaded but he had never shot one before. With the gun barrel resting on the zombie's chest, and acting on faith alone, he pulled the trigger. The report wasn't so bad, but the recoil nearly broke his wrist. The resulting blast peeled the pectoral and shoulder muscles away from the zombie's breastbone nearly severing its left arm. The residual kinetic energy spun the monster to the ground, tearing the last strands of flesh and tendon free leaving the arm dangling against the passenger door with the fingers fully intertwined in Wilson's red hair.

The blast caught Ted by surprise. The proximity of the barrel to his head when it went off caused him to forget about the whole "take it slow" mantra that was running through his head. He stabbed the accelerator, peeling out in reverse, wrenched the wheel to the left and skidded to a halt facing the two dozen walkers standing between them and the road leading back to the freeway onramp.

"I think I sharted," Ted said quietly, sounding embarrassed.

"I don't care about your underwear. Someone help and get this thing off of me," Wilson begged as he wrestled with the clammy arm.

"I can't stop now... look behind us."

"Easy for you to say, you don't have an extra twenty pounds of dead meat hanging from your head," Wilson shot back.

Ted stole a furtive look in the rearview mirror as the large group of walking dead were about to overtake them. He put the car in drive and drove away, being careful to keep his speed under twenty miles per hour. He didn't want to risk a collision and have the Subaru suffer the same fate as the much bigger Suburban. Outside, the pale arm swung back and forth, occasionally banging against the door.

Wilson rolled his window all the way down and reeled the arm into the car--placing it between his knees while he worked to get the stiff fingers to relax.

Sasha moved as far away from the rotten appendage as she could.

Wilson was getting more pissed off by the second because the dead hand wouldn't let go. "Ted, I *need* you to pull over pretty soon, this thing is bleeding all over my shoes."

"Eww," Sasha exclaimed as she pulled her feet from the floorboard and closely inspected them for wayward bodily fluids.

Wilson noticed her bare feet first and then the welt on her ankle--which was turning a shade of purple Prince would probably admire. "Sasha... put your damn shoes on," he said gruffly, sounding too much like their mom. And then he asked in a more calm, caring voice. "How is your ankle?"

"I'll live..." Sasha's face sprouted a big grin as she tried to suppress a laugh. "Forget about my ankle. You should see yourself with that arm growing out of your head. That would be a great picture to post on Face..."

Wilson watched his sister's face go slack and then the tears started. He was already fully aware of how much the world had changed in the week since the outbreaks, at least in Colorado, the place that he called home, and he had a feeling Sasha had just come to the same realization.

Wilson wanted to console Sasha but he was in no position to give her a hug (dead man's arm and all), so he renewed his efforts to free himself from its grasp. "Ted, do you have a Leatherman or some kind of multi-tool... maybe a pocket knife?

"You're just going to have to wait a sec," Ted stated.

Sasha wiped her tears and watched William's head loll back and forth on the headrest. His seat was reclined nearly horizontally, so far back that Sasha was forced to stare at his sweaty face. She noted his eyeballs fluttering intermittently behind darkened eyelids. Her only option was to stay vigilant and hope that he didn't turn into a zombie and bite her face off.

Ted put his palm on his partner's forehead. "Hang on Will... I'm getting us out of here," he said, choking up a little. Then he wiped the sweat from his face with the back of his arm and focused on slaloming the little car in between the random clusters of walkers.

***

The small tire shop was two blocks from Interstate 25. Ted pulled into the parking lot out of necessity--he was fed up with Wilson's incessant whining and close to being sick from the decomposing flesh in the back seat.

Ted removed the first aid kit from the glove box and tossed the red and white nylon pouch in Wilson's general direction. "There's got to be something sharp in there," he said as he started rummaging around in the large plastic sack sitting on his lap.

Wilson opened the kit hoping to find a pair of scissors or a pocket knife, anything with an edge. At this point he would resort to shaving his head to be rid of the severed arm. Tucked deep in the recesses of the tri-fold kit, Wilson found a pair of red-handled scissors.

"Be brave Sasha... you've got to do this. You won't even have to touch it. I'll hold the arm up to give you some slack and then hack off as much hair as you need to."

With her hands trembling Sasha began cutting on her brother's locks--being sure to keep one eye on William.

As Sasha worked away, Wilson heard the same rattling sound present in the drugstore earlier. "Whatcha got there Ted?" he asked.

The question went unanswered. Ted was counting under his breath, zoned out, concentrating intently on the task at hand.

"William... can you hear me?" Ted lightly slapped the other man's sunken cheek.

He got no response.

Ted looked back and said, "Can one of you hand me a bottled water from my pack?"

Much to Wilson's chagrin Sasha stopped "Operation Arm Removal" to fulfill Ted's request.

Thinking the worst, Wilson inquired, "What kind of drugs were you looking for back there?"

Ted cracked the seal on the bottle and held it between his legs. With some difficulty he pried open his partner's mouth with one hand and funneled a palm full of pills in with the other. Then he washed them down with a small amount of water and held William's mouth shut. The unresponsive man heaved a couple of times, but the pills stayed down. "He hasn't had his drug cocktail for more than a week," Ted finally replied.

"What made him sick?" Sasha innocently asked as she finished her gruesome task. After a couple more snips the arm fell free complete with the clump of Wilson's bright red hair still clutched firmly in its grasp.

"They're to keep his immune system up. William is HIV positive, but when he takes his drugs you would never know it. All of these..." Ted shook the bag of pills. "They keep the symptoms at bay. No pills... and he crashes pretty quickly."

"I feel foolish," Sasha confessed. "I thought he was infected." Immediately she regretted her choice of words.

***

The Traveler slowed the Ford as the front entrance to the Heights gated community came into view. Apparently the last person to leave didn't have time to close up shop. The ten foot tall gate on wheels was in the fully open position. He drove through the stucco and iron entry, passed the vacant guard shack and negotiated the big Ford around a mound of putrefying flesh and bones, disturbing a number of feeding ravens in the process. The murder exploded into the air at once, cawing angrily at the interruption.

The Traveler ignored the pissed off birds and trained his binoculars on the blue car. The occupants were still sitting in the vehicle, which hadn't moved since he left the house on the ridge five minutes ago. He had been watching and waiting for the right time to make contact. The trick would be in timing his move right. Trail them too close and they would make him. On the other hand if he let them get too far ahead he would be forced to take chances to catch up, possibly getting himself into trouble.

The sun slowly slipped behind the Rockies; the Traveler estimated it would be fully dark in less than two hours. He had a hunch that these people, now down to the one car, were trying to make up their minds: hole up somewhere for the night or continue on and risk getting stranded in the dark, vulnerable and out in the open.

Suddenly the blue car started to roll, moving in the direction of the tollway. The Traveler watched the driver take the onramp, weave the car between stalls and walkers and continue south on I-25 in the mostly unoccupied northbound lanes.

"Fools," the Traveler muttered under his breath. "You're gonna make this difficult for me aren't you?" He tossed the binoculars on the seat next to him and made certain the .45 caliber Kimber was close at hand. To lessen the chance of being seen, he nosed the stolen truck into the clogged southbound lanes of Interstate 25 and began to shadow his quarry from a distance.

Chapter 17
Outbreak - Day 8
Over the Gros Ventre Wilderness Area,
Southern Wyoming

"Wake up Daymon," Duncan drawled over the comms.

The voice sounded vaguely familiar, and once again it was tearing him from the peaceful realm buried under layers of horror deep in his subconscious. The fair maiden would have to wait. Daymon snapped to, surly and disoriented. "How long did you let me sleep old man?"

"Obviously not long enough Mister Cranky. Shit, if I woulda known this was all the thanks I was gonna get... I wouldn't have even bothered."

"Sorry," Daymon said sheepishly. "I was having another *good* dream."

"Well lucky you... I don't have a *good* anything unless I'm awake and the Cialis has kicked in."

It was way too much information and Daymon didn't even want to go there so he changed the subject. "Have you made up your mind yet... are you taking me to Driggs... or have you already shanghaied me all the way to Eden?" he asked.

"That's why I woke you. We're edging south of Jackson Hole. Cade advised me to steer clear of the city. Something about surface-to-air missiles... I think I *will* take his advice to heart. That's the reason I'm skimming the tree tops... trying my best to stay under the radar."

Daymon peered down at the numerous mountain lakes encircled by lush green forest. They sparkled like so many diamonds, producing a hypnotic effect, flashing beneath the helicopter.

Duncan's voice interrupted Daymon's National Geographic moment. "We're seventy-miles from Driggs... if that's your destination I'm taking us through a slot in the Tetons. If Eden's your choice then we have to go south around the end of the Tetons. My brother's compound is well planned out and secure. You've seen the countryside from the air... the best aspect is how remote Eden is. And most importantly Oops will welcome you... no doubt about it. Keep in mind that the Eden compound is a collective of sorts and we are going to have to pull our own weight... Driggs or Eden--which is it?"

Daymon sat with his thoughts for a couple of minutes. "I'm more comfortable alone and I *need* to go home... to see my house with my own eyes... get some closure at least."

"Are you serious son?" Duncan drawled. "I actually kind of like you... matter of fact you remind me of myself when I was young. I'm still a loner, but these days being a loner ain't conducive to being alive." After a few moments of silence, Duncan finally gave up. The kid's mind was set and Duncan wasn't going to argue the point. Daymon was a big boy.

Duncan gently nudged the Black Hawk on a course that would take them through a slot in the mountain range, keeping them away from the armed stronghold of Jackson Hole. Duncan kept the helo close to the earth to minimize the chance of them being detected. Flying the big helicopter semi nap-of-the-earth required constant attention to the ground, the tree tops and the flight controls. It was a very dangerous stress inducing stretch of flying. Duncan couldn't wait to get to Eden so he could relax and stop running for a spell.

Forty minutes later the southeastern section of the small town of Driggs came into view. There were a number of walkers ambling about the deserted trash-strewn streets. A small group of zombies, on hands and knees, were intently feeding on some unlucky soul. Blood-streaked faces looked skyward as the DHS Black Hawk thundered over.

"Not an encouraging sign my man..."

"Let's see how bad it is over there," Daymon said pointing to the north. "My house is in a little subdivision about a mile and a half from here."

Duncan slowed to twenty knots to allow Daymon the time to get his bearings and guide him in.

"See that green water tower... look due north... there is a school with the baseball diamond and backstop. Drop me off there," Daymon said.

"Out in the open... are you crazy?"

"I'll know once we get closer. If you drop me at my house it'll attract too much attention. I work best out in the open... schoolyard please."

Duncan shook his head. "Let's recon your house with a flyby first... OK?"

Before Daymon had a chance to answer, Duncan banked the Black Hawk and overflew the faded yellow single-story school. Daymon used the opportunity to scrutinize the grounds from two hundred feet. The tall fencing was keeping the zombies out of the baseball diamond and outfield, but a few of the creatures were stumbling around the playground structures and there were three more in front of the middle school. *It should be doable,* Daymon thought, *as long as they don't follow me home everything will be OK.*

Daymon pointed out the port side glass. "There it is... the tan single-story ranch... there is a white house on the north side and a blue house to the south."

"Copy that... I see it," Duncan said.

"Whatever you do...please *do not* fly too close. I'm afraid the noise will attract too many of those fuckers to my block."

Duncan orbited the Black Hawk around the cluster of small ranch style homes, but stayed clear of the airspace directly over the tan house. "I only count three walkers... and it looks like there's no damage to your casa, mi amigo."

"The front door and garage appear to be intact," Daymon said, craning his neck to get a better look.

Duncan relayed his observations out loud. "Coming around back... fence looks good... and there's the door... it's closed. Good to go." He looked long and hard at Daymon. "Back to the school or onward to Eden?" Duncan asked. "*Last chance.*"

Without hesitation Daymon said, "It's been good knowing you Duncan. You had better take me down right now... before I puss out." Then he unbuckled the seatbelt and removed the bulky flight helmet. Lastly, while trying to keep his balance, he retrieved the Kelty pack and his weapons from the passenger area. Daymon felt his stomach churn. He didn't know whether it was caused by the helicopter's rapid descent or a healthy dose of fear. Whatever the cause it was too late to turn back now.

Duncan held the chopper in a hover five feet above second base and shouted to be heard over the blasting rotor wash, "*Take the shotgun!*" Daymon appeared not to hear him. "*Take my shotgun... that's an order!*" Duncan bellowed again at the top of his lungs.

Daymon reluctantly grabbed the stubby 12 gauge and opened the sliding door. His eyes met Duncan's one last time, then he nodded. The way he was crouched low, like a coiled spring, made it obvious that he was prepared to hit the ground running.

Duncan felt a slight bump as the wheels kissed the dry brown grass of the outfield and he watched the young man leap to the ground, duck his head and bound away from the helicopter at a full sprint. Daymon never looked back and the last thing Duncan noticed as the ground fell away under the Black Hawk were the man's bouncing dreadlocks as he effortlessly vaulted the cyclone fence.

***

Daymon landed softly and scampered across the street, his head constantly moving, on the lookout for the walking dead. The chain link fence rattling behind him resonated with metallic discord. The initial sprint from the chopper and his poorly thought out vault over the fence left him a bit winded and reopened his freshly scabbed over wounds. A spike of pain in his side urged him to slow down while the moaning coming from nearby zombies spurred him on.

Daymon noticed that several blocks to the west, the blue and gold helicopter hovered noisily. *What a brilliant move.* Duncan was drawing the walkers to him by creating a diversion that they couldn't resist. *Cagey bastard,* Daymon thought appreciatively.

After running three city blocks at full speed with the Kelty pack weighing him down and the crossbow bludgeoning his lower back with each footfall, he slowed to a trot to formulate a plan. His little house was on the left three blocks up ahead. *Front door or back?* he asked himself. Since he had already determined from the air that there weren't any threats behind the house, the decision was easy. He was going to go through the neighbor's yard that butted up against his and jump the fence, hopefully ending up behind his house without being seen.

Daymon caught sight of the three walkers the moment he rounded the corner. The trio staggered in the middle of 4th Avenue, rubbernecking at the hovering Black Hawk. Without thinking he went to a knee, readied the crossbow, and aimed for the nearest walker. He watched with satisfaction as the rotter crumpled sideways, then hit the asphalt face first, with the arrow protruding from the base of its neck. Oblivious to their brother's demise, the other zombies continued gawking at the helicopter.

***

Thirty foot aspen trees lined both sides of the street; Duncan held the bird in a near perfect hover a few feet above their whipping branches and watched Daymon's escape. He didn't feel at all comfortable with the situation, but it wasn't his decision to make, so just seeing Daymon make it to safety would have to be good enough.

Duncan cheered aloud when the first walker dropped. After dispatching the second zombie with a swipe of his machete, Daymon was up and running directly towards the remaining monster. Duncan chuckled as the ghoul's head went airborne and then bounced twice before finally coming to rest next to the storm drain. *Just a little off the top please.* Duncan's chuckle evolved into a belly laugh and then his trademark cackle as he rooted for his friend on the ground.

***

Daymon was almost home now, literally. He needed to navigate two yards and one more fence and he would be safely in his unkempt backyard. God how he hoped his home was secure.

The Robertson's Ford Taurus was parked in the driveway leading Daymon to assume the elderly folks were in the home. He stepped onto their porch with every intention of asking their permission to cut through the yard. *What the hell am I doing,* he thought, a millisecond before he rang the doorbell. For a moment he had allowed the familiarity of his surroundings to lull him into a false sense of security, and before he could regret his action a pair of bodies slammed into the ornate oak door. Daymon raised the crossbow, training it on the door as he backed off of the porch. Since he didn't want to further rile his undead neighbors, he stayed close to the house, ducking when he passed by the windows.

Once he entered their nicely maintained backyard, he couldn't help but stop and stare. The mere sight of his house brought goose bumps to his arms. After all that he had seen and been through during the last hellish week, it was a strange, yet comforting feeling to be back in his hometown, about to break into his own home.

***

Good going lad. Duncan breathed a sigh of relief as the cocksure fool cleared the fence, traversed the knee high grass, and bounded up the back steps. Then Duncan slowly rotated the noisy chopper towards the southwest and stole one last lingering look as Daymon disappeared into his house.

***

Daymon jiggled the doorknob. *Locked.* He remembered that he had left his keys *and* his Honda Accord at the fire station in Jackson before taking the trip to see his mom one week ago. He cursed himself for not hiding a spare key outside. Every time he had lost or misplaced his keys in the past, which was often, he swore he would follow through. Maybe it could be attributed to forgetfulness or maybe his penchant for smoking Mary Jane in his downtime-- whatever the case, the door was locked and he had no key, so he bit the bullet and shattered the glass pane adjacent to the lock with one soft tap from the shotgun barrel.

Once he was inside with the door locked, he relaxed a little. The house smelled just like he remembered: days old pizza and the overlying scent of jasmine incense. The latter was necessary to cover up the pungent smell of marijuana and it started him thinking--he hadn't given weed a second thought since the ordeal in Hanna a few days ago and he could take it or leave it now.

Scattered on the floor inside the front door, like poorly dealt playing cards, was the mail that had accumulated the week before the outbreak. When he was on fire duty, and not out in the field actively fighting a fire, he called the firehouse close to downtown Jackson home. The three-story brick building was built like a bunker and had the ubiquitous pole running down from the bunk area to the garage. Best of all, it was nearby all of the watering holes frequented by the out-of-townies and just two blocks from his favorite BBQ joint. The thought of a slow cooked slab of brisket set off a Pavlovian reaction, making him drool just a little.

After taking a quick check of the house with the crossbow cocked and loaded he returned to the kitchen and opened the refrigerator, more out of habit than the need for sustenance. *Good Lord.* The noxious smell of rotted meat and spoiled milk blasted him in the face. The nauseating odors, though not quite as bad, took him back to the farmhouse in Hanna. Since he was in there already he figured a warm beer wouldn't hurt. After cracking the seal and taking a small pull, the bitter taste and skunk nose instantly changed his mind. He poured the Bud down the drain and went to check on Lu Lu.

Chapter 18
Outbreak - Day 8
I-25
Castle Rock, Colorado

"I think we can make it to Colorado Springs before dark," Ted stated with a newfound optimism.

"If the road stays this clear... I think you're right. I can't believe those *dumbasses* didn't cross over and drive on this side," Wilson added incredulously.

"Humans are very unpredictable when under great duress. Especially when it involves large numbers of them forced to cope with unexpected calamity. You and I... we all possess a fight or flight instinct hardwired into our brain and act on it differently... that's why we're surviving--so far. Take the Titanic for instance: a majority of her passengers waited patiently on the listing deck for a rescue that wasn't going to happen while their fellows were already drowning in the icy water, many of them oblivious to their own fate--the others accepting it as fact and giving up. Hell, some of them busted out the bubbly while an impromptu band struck up music on the deck as the supposedly unsinkable cruise liner foundered. Those people that got trapped in traffic and died over there... they took the sheep route," Ted said, addressing Wilson's observation.

Suddenly William coughed repeatedly, a seismic event that caused his frail body to buck.

Sasha flinched from the outburst and held her Louis Vuitton handbag in front of her face, determined to block any potential showers of spittle.

Until now William's breathing had been punctuated with a wet rattle that resounded deep in his chest. It was apparent after the coughing fit that the drugs were helping his immune system fight what Ted had suspected was the onset of pneumonia. A dam seemed to have burst inside of the sick man and his breathing ceased sounding like a punctured bellows.

Sasha looked out the window, fighting the urge to hurl.

Ted offered words of encouragement. "That's it, Will. Keep fighting, the drugs will take effect soon." Ted was a trained psychologist, not a pharmacist; still, he was confident that the medicine liberated from the Rexall Drug would bring William back to him.

"Take a look at that," Wilson yelped from the back seat, pointing out the rising column of black smoke dead ahead. "It looks like a plane wreck or something."

Ted's attention was divided between William, dodging obstacles in the road and the mysterious wreckage ahead. While his eyes were fixated on the smoking blackened hulk, a lone walker materialized from behind a stalled SUV. Slow reflexes, dulled from lack of sleep and the monotony of the road, left Ted unable to avoid hitting the limping zombie. The Subaru's bumper sheared the creature's bad leg off at the knee. With an explosion of U.S. currency, the one-legged monster sailed over the hood and speared the windshield head first.

Glass peppered Ted and Sasha around the face and neck. Wilson, fully eclipsed by the much larger man in the driver's seat, emerged relatively unscathed.

Sasha, mouth fully open, cued the scream soundtrack and let one loose.

Adrenaline blasted Ted's brain but still he reacted a second too late. The Subaru fishtailed and completed a full, hair raising spin before he could stab the brakes and stop the car.

"*Shoot it!*" the stress-laced scream escaped Ted's mouth along with fragments of safety glass.

Luckily, William had been fully reclined before the impact; still, the zombie's gnashing teeth were dangerously close to making a meal of his entrails. The creature snapped and hissed, trying to wriggle through the windshield. Every twitch spilled more cash from the pack strapped to its back, making it rain dead Presidents onto William's lap. All of the creature's extra effort to get at the meat only lodged its stinking corpse more firmly into the spider webbed windshield.

Wilson retrieved the shotgun from the floorboard and leveled it at the zombie's face. He narrowed his eyes, braced for the explosion, and pulled the trigger. *Click.* Nothing but silence.

The zombie struggled to get its arms through the hole, spilling more money from the backpack in the process.

"Pull the slide, kid," Ted bellowed.

Wilson had seen enough shoot 'em ups on TV to know what that meant, so he followed directions and racked a shell into the chamber.

Sasha acted while her brother was fiddling with the gun-- jamming her precious leather handbag between the creature's salivating maw and William's motionless body.

Boom!

The deafening shotgun blast vaporized the zombie's head and deposited the remains of the windshield onto the car's hood.

Sasha, hands numb from shock, dropped the gore-slickened Louis Vuitton handbag atop the brain-splattered Benjamins and Grants heaped in William's lap.

***

Keeping up with the survivors was easier than the Traveler had anticipated. Someone had partially cleared the southbound side of the freeway, leaving a navigable lane between the silent procession of cars pointing towards Colorado Springs.

For some reason the blue car he was shadowing swerved unexpectedly, spinning a full three-hundred and sixty degrees before coming to an abrupt stop in the middle of the multilane tollway.

The Traveler pulled over to a clear spot on the shoulder, brought his binoculars to bear, and glassed the motionless vehicle. The cause of the accident was immediately apparent. A bruised and battered leg and a mangled bloody stump protruded from the battered windshield. He could see the pale foot working to get traction on the hood of the station wagon. Suddenly a torrent of sparkling glass and pink-gray mist erupted from the front of the car. The flailing body went still and the remains of the splintered windshield fell out of the car and slithered over the hood onto the asphalt.

A few hundred yards ahead a wispy column of gray smoke trickled heavenward. From the Traveler's vantage point the source of the smoke was obscured; however, the multitudes of walkers heading from the smoke towards his quarry were not.

"Shit." The Traveler's plan was quickly unraveling right before his eyes. *Fuck it,* he thought, *no better time than the present to introduce myself.* He tossed the binoculars onto the seat and put the 4x4 into drive.

He sped ahead and crossed the median at a spot where the barrier cables had been snapped. It looked like the smoking hulk had once been a helicopter of some sort. A soot-covered red and white cross and some partially obscured lettering was evident on the side facing him. Other markings on the crumpled tail indicated it had been U.S. military. A deep channel scarred the red earth, starting at the broken cable and ending where the thing came to rest. *Hard to walk away from a crash landing like that,* he thought, as he wheeled the truck across the median and drove back up onto the deserted side of the Interstate.

***

William had momentarily snapped out of his stupor. Whether it was from the shotgun blast or the brain-soaked loot in his lap could be debated later.

"Welcome back among the living," Ted quipped.

Wilson racked a new round in the shotgun and exited the car. Crinkling his nose at the smell coming from the dead corpse, he cautiously made his way around the front of the car. The extent of the damage was clear. Both of the Subaru's headlights were destroyed, the grill had caved in and, adding insult to injury, the left front tire was completely flat. Somehow the creature's severed leg had become lodged in the wheel well, probably causing the blowout.

"Ted, help me get this stiff off of your car," Wilson implored, while he tugged on its remaining leg. "Fucker's heavy, and this big ass backpack isn't helping any."

Ted exited the car shaking small shards of glass from his hair and beard. "With America falling apart *and* dead people walking around, where did this *imbecile* think he was going to spend all of this money?" he wondered aloud.

"Who did he rob? That's what's bugging me," Wilson said, grunting from the exertion of trying to move the dead weight all by himself.

Ted grabbed ahold of the corpse's gun belt and tugged. With their combined efforts they managed to extricate the walker from the car. Both men stood back and watched the headless corpse slide down the hood and impact the ground with a jarring wet slap.

"Well look at *this*. Stealing from your *employer* were you?" Ted mocked the dead Wells Fargo guard as he fingered the security badge he had found in its pocket.

This perked Wilson up. "Does he have a pistol? Because I'm afraid that shotgun of yours is way out of my league."

Ted gave the body a thorough shakedown. "*Dumbass...* the headless wonder here somehow lost his piece. There's an empty holster and a couple of full clips--little good that's gonna do you. Why don't you look around for the gun?"

"What are the odds..." Wilson stopped mid-sentence. A vehicle was approaching from the direction of the ruined aircraft.

The low growl of the engine was enough to lure Sasha out of the car with her three bags in tow.

Wilson handed the shotgun and remaining shells off to Ted and ordered Sasha to stay quiet and keep out of sight. Then he went back to the car to get his bat. When he returned he was more than a little dismayed at what he saw. Instead of heeding his instructions Sasha was busy consolidating her clothes from the brain-splattered bag into the others. "Forget about that stuff and stay down," he said, his voice conveying his frustration. Wilson had no idea if the person or people in the vehicle were friendly so he acted on the assumption that they were bad guys.

"This is *all* I have left in the world," she whimpered.

"*Drop the bags and get over here!*" The engine sounds drew nearer, prompting Wilson to climb up on the back bumper of the Subaru wagon and sneak a covert peek. Apparently situational awareness wasn't the group's strong suit. There had to be at least fifteen zombies that none of them had been aware of approaching from the same direction as the noisy vehicle and there appeared to be no way to avoid them.

"*We've got walkers!*" Wilson shouted. "And there's a big truck heading this way." He didn't know if his message was received over the moaning flesh eaters.

Two of the zombies were closing in on the passenger side of the stricken car. Ted stood guard over William, who was still riding a fine line between semi-coherent and passed out. Since the car was going nowhere, Ted chose to make this his last stand. He felt a cold ball forming in the pit of his stomach as soon as the undead pair saw him and started moaning. The female walker was getting dangerously close and had to be dealt with first. Ted noticed she had suffered a host of defensive wounds; scratches and purple bite marks peppered her hands and arms. The zombie's swollen black tongue lolled about in her mouth. Ted fought off the overwhelming urge to puke when he realized the black flies darting in and out of her yawning mouth were ravenously feeding on the succulent morsel. He leveled the shotgun at Slug Tongue but forced himself to wait and allow the creature to lurch and stagger closer. "Come to Papa," Ted said, trying to keep the thing focused solely on him.

Boom!

The deadly spray of lead buckshot struck the creature from point blank range, transforming the top of her head into a corona of vaporized bone and brains. The zombie was picked up and dropped flat on its back five feet away. Surprisingly, the black tongue stuck out fully intact, flies and all. Ted wasn't overly superstitious; still, the thought that he was being taunted from the afterlife did cross his mind.

Totally ignoring the mayhem, its eyes never wavering from the meat, the second zombie continued advancing as if on autopilot. He looked to have been about seven or eight when his first life ended. The undead boy's tank top was spattered with crimson.

IN HARM'S WAY: SURVIVING THE ZOMBIE APOCALYPSE

(Where was Dexter when you needed him?) If Ted hadn't known any better he would have just assumed the little guy had had a Cherry snow cone mishap, tousled his blonde hair, and sent him on his way. Instead, he racked the slide praying that the gun wasn't out of shells.

Boom!

The swarm of buckshot hit the child zombie with a glancing blow, spinning all seventy pounds of him around and into the front fender of the Subaru. The kid's left arm, which took the brunt of the blast, hung uselessly at his side like a wet sleeve.

Someone upstairs must have answered the foxhole prayer line, Ted thought. He really didn't believe in prayer because he was agnostic at best, and found that science and evolution made more sense to him. Besides, organized religion hadn't been very tolerant of folks like him and William.

Ted was reciting another prayer to the false God of shotgun ammo when Wilson entered the picture, swinging his Louisville Slugger like a steroid juiced clean-up batter. On his first cut the bat's sweet spot met the young walker's temple, doing little damage, but still knocking him to the ground. Three more rapid downward chops stilled the monster leaving viscous gray matter sprayed across two lanes of I-25.

Ted was about to thank his bat-wielding friend when the sound of gunfire took precedence. He snapped his head towards the loud booming. A jacked up 4x4 was stopped in the middle of I-25 no more than fifty yards to the south. The sunglass-clad driver fired a dozen rounds at the walkers, quickly reloaded, and resumed the offensive. Although Ted had no idea where the man with the handgun had come from, the simple fact that he was wielding the pistol with deadly precision against the zombies rendered it a moot point. An old Arabic proverb popped into his psychologist brain, *the enemy of my enemy is my friend.* He just hoped it held some truth to it. Ted used the momentary diversion to load the last two shells into the shotgun. "Come on kids, let's go," he shouted to the siblings as he knelt down next to the passenger door and hefted William's limp body over his shoulder into a fireman's carry. *Good thing I prefer my men small,* Ted thought as he maneuvered around the fallen walkers and trudged towards the waiting truck.

Wilson had Sasha by the arm and was half dragging her along as he followed in Ted's footsteps. Except for the clothes on his back, all he had was his prized autographed Louisville Slugger clutched in his blood-covered hand and the picture of their mom in his shirt pocket. During a brief lull in the shooting Wilson heard the man's voice calling for them to get inside the truck.

Boom!

Ted had aimed at the zombie's head, but considering that he was loping along and carrying someone he was happy that he hit the walker at all. The point blank blast produced a cavity the size of a cantaloupe through its chest, sending it flying. Ted held the smoking gun in one hand and had William's legs wrapped up with his other arm. Chambering another round one handed just wasn't going to happen. Sure, Schwarzenegger did it in Terminator 2 but Ted had already come to the conclusion that he was *not* Arnold. As he reached deep inside for the strength to reach the idling pickup without getting bit, the see-through walker struggled to its knees and swiped at him as he brushed by.

Wilson stepped to the plate and prodded the zombie with the barrel of his bat, knocking the off-balance flesh eater onto its back. He locked eyes with the soulless thing before finishing it off. "Stay down you bastard," he repeated after each vicious swing. Then Wilson started to cry. He didn't like who he was becoming but he couldn't seem to do anything about it.

"Come on Wilson," Sasha implored. She was literally tiptoeing her way through a maze of dead bodies and gore, keeping her precious bags above the mess and out of harm's way.

Unfortunately the honking horn brought Wilson back to reality. He looked down at what he had done to the former human, and it made his stomach turn.

Looking up at the immense truck, Ted wished he had a trampoline or maybe a pair of stilts--anything to make the task of getting his partner into the lofty crew cab a little less daunting. After a few moments divided between watching his back and manhandling William's buck-thirty into the truck, he looked for a hand hold and entered the crew cab as well. "Like they say, timing is everything. We were about to be overwhelmed out there... we owe you big time," Ted said between labored breaths.

I couldn't have said it better, the Traveler thought. "Is that thing out of ammo?" he asked, alluding to the shotgun in Ted's lap.

"No. There are at least two shells left," Ted responded.

"Then get your *ass* out there and help those two," the Traveler stated emphatically.

Somewhat taken aback, Ted jumped out of the truck and reentered the fray.

Walkers streamed in droves across the grassy median from the opposite side of the freeway, enticed by the raised voices and gunfire.

Sasha sprinted past Ted to the safety of the truck while Wilson backed away, swinging his bat at the zombies.

"Let's go kid!" Ted bellowed as he squeezed off a shot at the closest walker, stopping it in its tracks. He backpedaled next to Wilson and emptied the shotgun into the advancing crowd.

Sasha was in the front seat by the time Ted and Wilson reached the truck. Both men leapt in simultaneously: Ted in back and Wilson up front beside his sister.

The driver's pistol continued to buck, sending spent shell casings bouncing around the interior of the truck. He kept firing until the magazine was empty and the slide locked open. "Is everyone in your group accounted for?" the Traveler asked. He knew there weren't any others, he was just playing dumb.

"Yes... it's just the four of us. My name's Wilson and Sasha here's my sister."

Introductions were voiced from the backseat. "I'm Ted and his name is William."

The Traveler reversed the truck a good distance from the carnage before he slowed and turned around. "Hey Taliban... what's wrong with your *friend*... did he get bit? Did any of you get bit?" he asked suspiciously as he inserted a fresh magazine in the .45 and chambered a round.

Ted let the beard comment slide and answered for everyone. "I gave my *partner* one too many Vicodin. He's not infected... he's just comfortable," he lied. "As for the rest of us... sure we're splattered with blood and guts, but none of us have been bitten."

"Good enough for me. My name's Francis, but nearly everyone calls me Pug." He flashed a mouthful of crooked teeth in Sasha's direction. Trying to be discreet, Sasha looked out of the corner of her eye at the man's nearly vertical profile, marveling at how fitting the nickname was. Either the man had once been a pugilist--a very poor one at that--or someone had been *really creative* and nicknamed him after the breed of dog he most resembled.

"Where are you guys headed?" Pug asked.

"We *were* trying to make it to Colorado Springs *before* nightfall," Ted replied.

"Cutting it pretty close don't you think? If you all got caught out in the dark... it woulda been bad news for you. I've seen whole families dead in their car: men, women, and babies. You get yourself surrounded by enough of those things and you're effed. They will wait you out... 'til you die from exposure or go plain crazy and think you can run right through them. Either way you're effed," Pug said, laying it on thick.

"Where were you going?" Sasha asked.

"Thought you'd never ask, *sweetie*," he said, patting her on the top of her left thigh. "I heard that Colorado Springs is about the safest place to be in these United States. I guess it was fate that our paths crossed," Pug said, playing up his role in the rescue.

"Where are you coming from... Pug?" Ted probed. For some reason calling a grown man Pug made him uncomfortable.

"I was setting up Breck for the winter. Getting the lifts squared away... all that jazz," Pug lied. He had never been to Breckenridge--or on a pair of skis for that matter.

"Breckenridge is overrun?" Wilson said sadly. "That *was* my favorite ski hill," he muttered under his breath. He stared through the windshield wishing all of this were just a bad dream. Far ahead, on the horizon, he glimpsed two moving beams of light stabbing towards the heavens. It looked like a couple of white light sabers cutting the rapidly darkening sky. "Mister Pug. Did you see that... the lights up ahead?"

The driver tore his eyes from Sasha's bare legs and stared straight ahead. "No son, I missed it. If you spot it again let me know," he answered sheepishly. "And son... you can call me Pug. Mister just makes me feel old."

If the shoe fits, Wilson thought. He didn't know what it was but he was beginning to get a strange feeling about this guy.

Chapter 19
Outbreak - Day 8
National Elk Refuge
Jackson Hole, Wyoming

"They're aware of us now. I recommend we wrap this up," said Ian Bishop, former Navy SEAL, and current head of Spartan International, which was the private army funded and now deployed by the Guild.

"Please wait... I would like to finish my brunch first," Christian said as he plunged a dainty sterling silver spoon into his three minute egg, scooped out a dollop of nearly firmed yolk and moaned in delight. "Bring me more champagne," he ordered, waving the crystal flute in Ian's personal space, his little finger at attention in a display of aristocratic savior-faire as he danced the glass back and forth in the air.

The wind shifted, bringing with it the foul odor of rotten flesh.

The muscular warrior pressed the binoculars to his face and slowly panned the entire length of the perimeter fence to be sure none of the creatures were close enough to pose a threat. Then he pulled the Dom from the ice bucket and, in a ritual he had seen Christian's now dead assistant perform countless times, he dried the water rivulets from the bottle before refreshing the champagne. To Ian it was becoming clear that his boss was totally and irrevocably drunk with power. The Dom Perignon only made his actions harder to predict. Ian couldn't fathom why the man wanted to take his meal at the edge of the largest elk refuge in North America in the midst of the majestic Grand Tetons while fully surrounded by zombies, but he was used to following the man's sometimes eccentric orders and he did so without hesitation.

"Take all of this and leave us," Christian barked at his personal chef while making a sweeping gesture with his hands. Ian noted the sudden mood swings had become more frequent and intense. In the years he had been involved with the Guild and worked for Mr. C he had also grown used to putting up with his boss' minor vacillations in temper. It could be stress from the myriad things Mr. C could no longer control, he thought, so he filed it away to be pondered at a later date.

Tran cleared the china and service with a quiet efficiency learned from years of working for the billionaire king maker. Then he carefully folded the starched linen tablecloth and stowed the folding teak table, along with the dirty dishes, in the back of the Dark Green Range Rover.

The head of the Guild called for his chef.

With his head hanging slightly, the tiny Asian man returned and stood silent before the taller silver-haired man. He was fighting a losing battle to remain standing. The looming anxiety attack pressed against his lungs. His racing heart pounded against his sternum, fighting to escape like a caged animal.

"Thanks to you Tran, the eggs were exquisite as always."

The chef regained his composure, stuck out his chin, and with great relief manufactured the biggest toothy smile he could muster, yet he still kept quiet. The help were never to speak to Mr. C unless they were ordered to do so. Tran let his gaze wander over his boss' shoulder and fall on what remained of Fredrick. The Scandinavian-born man was once a handsome thirty-year-old, with fair skin, blue eyes and dirty blond hair. The bloated zombie used to be first assistant to Mr. C... until he spoke without permission. Tran recognized Fredrick, but not any of the other monsters on the far side of the fence, but he did know how they ended up in there. Every single one of them had done something to cross Mr. C--who had seemingly become angrier by the day. Tran wondered if the old man was host to a brain tumor and secretly wished it were true.

There were over one hundred "examples" milling around, and as the days wore on and more people decided they didn't like being forced to stay in Jackson against their will, the number of zombies populating the elk refuge swelled. The main road passed close by so the living dead on the refuge grounds became a dire warning reminding everyone in Jackson to toe the line.

One day after the Guild's private jets landed and the Spartan army rolled into Jackson Hole, a handbill was posted at the town's square, a small park festooned with towering arches constructed entirely from the elk antlers that had been collected over the years from off of the ground inside the refuge. Spelled out on the official decree from the Guild were the rules which were many and unreasonable. The exodus began the next morning. The bodies of those bold enough to try to leave began piling up moments later. A bullet to the brain had been a proven deterrent against defectors until recently.

"Mr. Tran. For dinner I would like Beef Wellington. And please decant the best Bordeaux in the cellar. A brunette for after dinner would be appropriate, don't you think?"

Tran nodded.

Once again Christian waved the man away.

"Mister Bishop, I have a strong suspicion that you are curious why I chose this location to dine alfresco."

"I'd be lying to you if I said that it hadn't crossed my mind," Bishop divulged. He knew Christian's intuition was legendary and the main reason he had risen to power. Ian also had a niggling feeling his boss was a mind reader.

"I know you don't make it a habit to lie to me Ian... do you?" Christian said in an accusatory tone.

"No sir."

"Good to know. I'm going to get down to brass tacks here. Jarvis swept the house for bugs and he found one in nearly every room. There were two in the boardroom and whoever planted them has been privy to all of our business. I trust the other members of the Guild about as far as I could throw them. I know that's a broad brush stroke... I get that." Christian stopped to gather his thoughts and maybe reign in his words. *Screw it,* he thought. "Ian, I need a real assessment of our situation. This plan of ours was supposed to be enacted *after* the collapse of society. Our members each had their respective parts of the country conditioned and ready for complete takeover. I'm worried. Although we only have a few hundred survivors to keep tabs on here in Jackson... the mere fact that they are survivors make them nearly impossible to subjugate. The sheep that we were going to rely upon to do our bidding after the collapse are all dead and hungering to eat us. I don't mean here. You've done a stellar job of cleansing Jackson Hole of the infected... and so far your campaign against defectors has been effective. Still, we must presume that the other Guild members are not going to have as easy a go of it." His eyebrows inched up.

It was Ian's cue to speak. "You are dead on about the other Guild members. I had reservations and I did let you know early on that the ex-Presidents were going to be a problem. They are used to being coddled inside of their respective bubbles. I don't think any of them have the patience to ride this out without infighting or doing something really stupid." Before he continued Ian paused in case his boss had something new to add, then went on. "I feel strongly that we should exclude the rest of the Guild from our spoils of war, if you will. And under no circumstances should they reap any rewards from *our* Minot mission."

Mr. C cleared his throat and downed the last of the warm champagne in his glass. With no place to set the flute he instead angrily hurled it at the living dead. "I had that executive decision made *before* a single one of those trucks left this town," he said with a smug, know-it-all look on his face.

Bishop nodded but silently called *bullshit* on the lie.

Fredrick hissed as if he were part of the conversation and in total agreement. The pallid abomination's Polo shirt was hopelessly snagged on the rusty barbed wire fence.

The leader of the Guild entered into a staring contest with the putrefying corpse. Realizing he had no chance of winning this one, Christian extended his hand, palm up, in Ian's direction. "Give me your weapon."

Ian warily eyed the gathering zombies and reluctantly unclipped his carbine from its center point sling, then passed it to his silver-haired boss.

"Hand me your sidearm please," Mr. Christian ordered, sounding more than a little annoyed.

Slightly relieved that he didn't have to relinquish his M4, but without saying a word, Ian removed his semi-auto pistol and handed it over.

The Guild leader stepped over a volcano-sized mole hill, dodged a pile of droppings from some four legged animal, and approached the rubbernecking ghoul. "Fredrick... what is it going to take for you to learn to keep your mouth shut?"

The zombie lunged against the fence, arms outstretched, bony fingers kneading the air as an eerie mournful hiss escaped from its leathered mouth.

Christian wasted no time. He shot Fredrick in the forehead at point blank range, experiencing great satisfaction as his twice dead assistant fell stiffly to the grass. Gray matter oozed from the fist-sized exit wound while black congealed blood leaked out of the puckered divot up front. "That's more like it, my little chatterbox." Christian returned the borrowed pistol to his head of security. Temporarily distracted by a nagging fly, he moved his head side to side like a sparring boxer, trying to keep it from settling on him. "Where were we before I was so rudely interrupted?" Christian prompted Ian.

"You said that you wanted my opinion... but first I think we should get inside the vehicle," Ian gently urged as he stole another glance at the gathering zombies. The former SEAL was afraid of no man, but the walking dead on the other hand caused a certain amount of anxiety to well up in him. If it were his decision, instead of keeping corralled zombies to serve as an example to would be defectors, he would have had women and children nailed to crosses in the town square. *Yes,* he thought, *crucified innocents would keep them all in line.*

Black clouds of buzzing flies accompanied the living dead as more corpses began to push up against the rickety fence.

132

Fredrick, eyes wide and mouth open, continued his eternal staring contest as his comrades unwittingly trampled his supine form into the muddy field.

***

Tran sat motionless, relegated to a patch of damp grass, eyes closed, while his boss and the assassin lounged in total comfort inside the SUV. He said a Hmong prayer to ward off the monsters of his nightmares and waited patiently, with a calm sense of serenity, for this dangerous time to pass.

"There's no need to worry about listening devices in this vehicle. I just picked it out from the dealership this morning; there are only ten miles on the odometer. I must admit I do find it intoxicating being able to take anything I need, anytime I want to." Ian suddenly felt foolish for saying those words to a billionaire--especially to his boss--a man that was already used to having anything he wanted, anytime he wanted it. He collected his thoughts for a moment. "First things first: there can't be any of those things walking around... *ever*. Let me worry about keeping the citizenry in check."

"As you wish Ian. Do continue."

That was easy, Ian thought. "I propose we keep our cards close to our chest as far as the Minot missions are concerned," he said, wondering how long it was going to take his very astute boss to catch the cat that just jumped out of the bag.

His boss perked up. "*Missions?* You just said you didn't lie to me... but you were keeping this from me *Ian*." Christian steepled his fingers and parked them on his chin, all the while seeming to glare into Ian's soul. "And that's the same thing as lying. I'm disappointed in you..."

Ian interrupted his boss; he didn't want to give him enough time to nurture his budding resentment. "As soon as Jarvis told me about the first set of listening devices I decided to send a team of my most trusted operators to bring back a ghost shipment--just for insurance. I'm sorry Boss... I take full responsibility. It was all in the name of operational security that I withheld the backup mission from you. For what it's worth, at the time I didn't know how secure the compound was or *who* was listening." Ian's stomach clenched as he

133

mentally readied himself for a double barreled blast of fury from his boss.

"It does give me pause. Caesar had his detractors in the Senate and ultimately he was done in by those closest to him. I will not suffer the same fate. If it happens again you *will* be fed to them," Christian said, stabbing a finger at the zombies.

"You have my word Boss," Ian said as he felt his chest tighten and he tried to pull his eyes away from the creatures.

Robert Christian thought, for a brief second, that he detected fear in Ian Bishop's usually emotionless eyes. He had a knack for remembering people's weaknesses and archiving them for future use. If Mr. Bishop *ever* stepped out of line again he knew exactly how he was going to punish the man, and it was not going to be pretty.

"Mr. Christian, why don't you carry a pistol?" Ian asked.

"Ian my boy, *you* carry my pistol," Christian answered with a detached faraway look on his face.

Chapter 20
Outbreak - Day 8
Schriever AFB, Quarantine and Research
Tent, Colorado Springs, Colorado

The steady whirring from the centrifuge masked the ever-present background hiss of the large fans working to keep the environment clean and the tent under positive pressure. On the counter, a large glass beaker sat atop a Bunsen burner; the honey colored liquid inside roiled from the blue flame flickering underneath.

Fuentes had been explicit when requesting the specific equipment for his thrown together laboratory, and the soldiers from Fort Kit Carson, without regard for their own safety, ventured into the city to fill his shopping list. They had delivered in full. Even without the moving corpse the lab could be easily mistaken for something out of a horror movie. The only props needed to complete the picture were a tesla coil spitting electric sparks and an insane scientist running to and fro--the bespectacled, wiry Doctor Sylvester Fuentes nearly filled the latter part.

To make it easier for the doctor and his much taller and much more beautiful assistant, Jessica Hanson, to work on both specimens at the same time, Fuentes had arranged the bodies so that they were lying face up on stainless steel tables only a few feet apart. Although the infected were immobilized with the kind of thick leather straps originally designed to keep the insane and unruly inmates in control, only the Asian zombie writhed, snapping and hissing, whenever Fuentes or Hanson came anywhere near him. The second man, an agent for the Department of Homeland Security, didn't show the usual signs of reanimation. Although the color of his face was ashen and wax like, his chest still rose and fell with a slow steady tempo and a heart monitor beeped out a slow cadence.

A stark white sheet draped the man from the waist down while the fabric around his feet and ankles was dotted and streaked crimson where his blood had seeped through.

"The decomposition of the Alpha isn't accelerating as rapidly as we thought it would Doctor. It's been what?" Jessica ticked off the days since the outbreak with her fingers, stopping at the middle finger of her right hand. "It's been eight days and the muscle and tendons still look like they were excised from a nearly fresh corpse..." She wore a pained look, staring at Fuentes through her plastic face shield, waiting patiently for his input.

"That worries the hell out of me because it shoots holes in my nine month theory," Fuentes said. "And since every attempt at a proactive immunization has already failed, the antiserum has got to work. If it doesn't then we are at a dead end."

Jessica grimaced.

"That was a bad choice of words and I'm sorry," Fuentes said softly as he fished an Oreo from the pocket of his lab coat. "Did you determine if he really was bitten? We need to be certain because we can't rely on assumptions alone. The word of his fellow agents or the aircrew that brought him here doesn't mean a thing. We *cannot*, in good conscience, use that man as a guinea pig--*unless* we know beyond a shadow of a doubt that he is infected."

Jessica cleared her throat before answering. "I examined his legs and couldn't find a definitive point of entry. Mostly he's covered with deep scratches on his lower extremities. One wound on the top of his foot could have been from a bite, but I dismissed it because he had shoes on when he arrived."

"Check the shoe. If there is a puncture mark going all of the way through then I think we should take a chance and test the first sample on him," Fuentes reasoned.

"When did the people who brought him in say he was supposedly infected?" Jessica inquired.

"Hours ago, but he's a big boy... I'd venture a guess at two-fifty at least. Even for a slow burn--this one shows longevity," said Fuentes.

Jessica proceeded to go through the pile of clothes to get to the discarded shoes. She tossed his lightweight black windbreaker aside, the letters DHS stenciled in yellow across the back. A pair of Levis, the denim on both legs shredded and bloody, was tossed unceremoniously atop the windbreaker. She uncovered the shoes and inspected the left one. "Shoot! I should have checked closer. There's a perfect bite pattern and it's evident where the canines went through the nylon tongue. Poor guy should have been wearing boots. How did he arrive here?"

"He was brought in on a DHS Border Patrol helicopter. I talked to the pilot to try and get a feel for the conditions out there." Fuentes removed his glasses and wiped his eyes.

"How bad is it?" Jessica asked with a look of bereavement on her face.

Fuentes sat down heavily and watched his last ounce of hope go round and round in the centrifuge. "The pilot didn't know much, but one of the Homeland Security guys told me--off of the record--he even made me promise not to repeat this..." *Fuck him though,* Fuentes thought. "He said that there are pockets of survivors spread out all over the United States. He also said the East Coast is a fuckin' blood bath... his words, not mine. The most depressing news though... he said that conditions are really bad south of Springs. New Mexico, Arizona and on into California... the infected are overwhelming the last of the living."

Jessica took a deep breath and then checked her watch. "How did this one get infected?"

"The pilot said there were thousands of dead around Sunport International Airport. They got swarmed outside of Albuquerque when they set down to refuel. A group of walkers got the jump on them and before they could finish filling up the helicopter... half of the people that fled Arizona with him died... he said he was forced to take off and leave them on the apron surrounded by the Z's."

Jessica glanced at her watch once again and then interrupted the doctor. "A few more seconds." As if on cue the centrifuge slowed down and stopped completely.

"Doctor Hanson. I want you to record the subject's vital signs while I ready the injection," Fuentes ordered, truly hoping they could save the man's life.

"Yes sir... right away," she answered.

Fuentes loaded sixty mils of the antiserum.

On the table the final ounce of fight left the man's body. He convulsed once and went motionless.

"Doctor... he's turning. We've got a limited window. Hurry... please." Jessica knew that she shouldn't be telling Fuentes how to do his job but still she kept talking. "He *has* stopped breathing Doctor... and I'm losing his pulse."

The heart monitor emitted a high pitched squeal as Agent Stockton flat lined.

Jessica reached across and turned the volume down so that she could communicate with Fuentes.

"Doctor Hanson, stand back," Fuentes said as he quickly crossed the room in her direction, holding the syringe, needle pointing skyward. He clamped his hand on the dying man's cold forehead and without hesitating slid the six inch needle into the soft flesh under the agent's right eye. Fuentes was aware that injecting the antiserum directly into the man's thalamus was a long shot, but seeing as how the man's heart had just ceased beating he was confident he had made the correct decision.

Chapter 21
Outbreak - Day 8
Sentinel Butte, North Dakota

Cade had a clear view of the entire convoy from where he
had set up his hide. His job was to take out the Humvee gunners first
and then the drivers next.

Captain Gaines would target anyone that was armed first, and
then "squirters" or personnel trying to run away were his secondary
targets.

Cade patiently waited, running Desantos' instructions
through his head one more time.

*"We're going to wait, conserve our ammunition, and let our adversaries
handle the Z's. When we go hot, do not hit the trailers... I do not need to tell you
what could happen if you do. Lastly, don't kill them all, let's try to identify any
leadership or ranking personnel and capture them."*

The report of the hammering .50 caliber M2, or Ma Deuce as
it had been affectionately called by multiple generations of soldiers,
was loud enough to wake the dead... or at least loud enough to get
the attention of every single one of them for miles around. Walkers
poured from the truck stop. Cade guessed they had been either
employees or infected that were left behind by desperate people just
trying to survive. He had been there--the will to survive saw him
through--just barely. Portland to Springs had been no cake walk. He
hadn't even had the time to process that cross-country ramble
through hell let alone spend a little time with his family before
jumping back in the saddle again.

The .50 chewed up the dead but the gunners were leaving too many crawlers for Cade's liking. They dropped in large numbers but didn't die, and he could tell by the way the gunners raked the M2s back and forth haphazardly that they were not trained professionals. The shooting lasted less than a minute before the big guns went silent. Then the Humvees disgorged armed men; from their helmets to their boots they were clad all in black. The sporadic cracks from their carbines echoed off of the buildings as they walked among the fallen zombies, methodically putting down any of them that still moved.

One of the black clad storm troopers entered the UPS truck Cade had left blocking the four lane highway.

Good luck with that, Cade thought. Not only had he cut the wiring harness out from under the dash, but he had also yanked the ignition from the steering column and discarded it into the scrub brush beside the road.

The trooper emerged, shaking his head and motioning for the driver in the lead semi to join him. The driver warily climbed from his safe cocoon, negotiated the corpse-strewn road, and exchanged words with the man in black. After conferring for a moment the driver climbed up and disappeared between the cab and the trailer of the Kenworth.

They're going to try and unhook the trailer, Cade thought. It didn't matter, because he knew the truck was wedged so tightly that they were going to need one of the big semi wreckers to clear the road. *Besides,* Cade thought, *they weren't going to be alive long enough to wait for Triple A anyways.* To his horror Cade realized that Duncan's gallows humor was starting to rub off on him.

Click. Click. Click.

Cade recognized the go sign. His first shot hit the gunner in the throat. The energy the .338 Lapua delivered shredded the man's carotid ending his life. *Effective, but a little low,* he thought.

"Good hit," Maddox said calmly.

After acquiring the second gunner Cade changed his elevation and windage incrementally and readied his shot. *Breathe in. Exhale. Gently squeeze.* The suppressed Remington spit lethal lead down range. The second gunner didn't know where his death came from. The

140

bullet hit him in the nose, caving in his face; the energy spun his body around sending it corkscrewing down into the Humvee.

"Good hit," Maddox announced.

Ronnie Gaines put his Remington MSR to good work as he systematically culled the dismounts, rapidly dropping and acquiring new targets.

The Humvees were not up-armored models; this allowed Cade to get easy clean kills on the drivers.

While Gaines finished off the remaining troopers taking cover behind the uphill Humvee, Cade took out the dismounts crouched on his side. In seconds the armed men were down and the helos were inbound. The way the security personnel froze up, virtually cowering, gave Cade pause. He made a mental note to take his observation up with Desantos.

At gunpoint, the truck drivers wisely exited their rigs with their hands held high. The driver from the lead vehicle, a reed thin man with bushy black hair exploding from under his ball cap, performed a slow motion pirouette in the center of the road, scanning the hills for the death dealers.

Desantos had been watching the fight unfolding via the monitor in the Ghost Hawk. An unarmed UAV orbited high over the ambush site, continually beaming live video to the helo. "Let's go and get 'em Night Stalker," Desantos ordered his pilot.

"Copy that," Ari answered. He instantly nosed into a steep dive, taking the helo from 1000 feet AGL to nearly nap of the earth flight in seconds.

"Not wasting any time huh Ari?" the General quipped.

"Waste not want not..."

"When can we go back and retrieve my stomach?" Desantos asked.

"Cowboys are supposed to have cast iron stomachs; therefore, yours should still be banging around here somewhere."

"Smartass," Desantos muttered.

The crew chief and the spook exchanged glances and for the first time in days they both found a reason to crack a smile.

***

After picking up the two sniper teams the Ghost Hawks took up positions for over watch, one on each side of the kill zone, hovering silently at three hundred feet.

The two CH-47s thundered over the hillock and flared before setting down near the gas station. Eight soldiers clad in full woodland camo MOPP chemical/biological protective gear and carrying M4 carbines stormed from the rear ramp of each dual rotor chopper. Two men from each squad fanned out, providing security while the rest of the soldiers loped towards the truck drivers. After the drivers were zip tied, sitting with their backs to the guard rail, the MOPP suited soldiers turned their attention to the three trailers.

Cade sat, eyes glued to the flat panel, and watched the teams go to work. One soldier wielded heavy duty bolt cutters and had the locks off and the doors open in short order. The men scurried in and out of each truck sweeping high tech Geiger counters checking for dangerous rad levels.

"This is Watchdog, how copy?" The voice that everyone on the hovering Ghost Hawks was listening to over the net belonged to the leader of the cobbled together NEST (Nuclear Emergency Search Team) team.

"Archer Actual, good copy, proceed," Desantos answered.

"All levels are acceptable. I repeat all levels are acceptable. Watchdog out."

"Archer Actual, thank you Watchdog, we will be wheels down in two mikes."

"Copy that," the Sergeant in command of the NEST team replied.

"The landing zone is secure Ari," Desantos said. Then he hefted his SCAR carbine and held it barrel down between his legs waiting for the Ghost Hawk to touch down on the highway.

The men on the ground, including the drivers, covered their faces to guard against flying debris, and two of the truck drivers sacrificed their ball caps to the rotor wash while protecting their eyesight.

As soon as Cade, Desantos, and the rest of the operators boots hit the ground, both Ghost Hawks bolted back into the cloudless blue sky to resume an orbiting over watch.

Desantos beckoned Tice over and said, "You have been endorsed by Major Nash--my words not hers. Her praise was more eloquent. You're the expert... so I'll stay out of your hair. Just let me know if there is anything you need."

"I need to see what we have in those trucks first. All of the different weapons in Uncle Sam's arsenal were kept at Minot, so there's no telling what's inside. Once I know a little more I'll brief you and we can go from there... but I'm definitely going to leave the heavy lifting to the NEST guys," the spook said before he turned and began to jog towards the first trailer.

"One more thing," Desantos said, raising his voice, "don't get bit on my watch."

The lanky spook turned, gave the baby Desert Eagle strapped to his thigh an affectionate pat and said, "My days of kicking doors may be over... but I still know how to use this."

***

"Wyatt my boy... good shooting. I must say, you still know how to reach out and touch someone. How many is that now?" Desantos regretted the words as soon as they left his lips. *Hell, we're all wearing big boy pants here,* he thought.

"Counting the living dead?" Cade asked.

The General watched the NEST guys poring over the trailers and took a moment before answering. "No, the zombies don't count. They all died the moment the fucking virus jumped out of the Petri dish. I'm afraid you've caught me in a "*glass is half empty*" kind of mood. Let me ask you something... forget about your body count. Did the sight of all of the infected coming out of Denver hit you in the gut like it did me?"

"If we're counting only breathers--the count is more than fifty--but less than one hundred. If we are talking about how many walkers I've waxed... one simple answer: not enough," Cade replied, hoping to dodge Desantos' last, but most important question.

Desantos pressed. He needed Cade's honest opinion. "What's your take on *Denver?*"

Boom! Boom! Boom!

143

The unmistakable report of the CIA man's .45 caliber pistol rolled over their heads. Tice stepped from behind the nearest trailer and mouthed the word *"crawler"* as he walked towards them.

Desantos gave the spook thumbs up. "Third time's the charm." Then he continued trying to pick the younger operator's brain. "Before I was so rudely interrupted I was asking you your take on the dead coming out of Denver?"

"My take? I truly hope that the first option has the desired effect," and after a long pause Cade finished his thought. "Because if we have to resort to the second option... then we might have to leave Springs anyway. Sure, the President can hole up in Cheyenne, but that doesn't help little Mike, Sierra or Serena. And I've got Raven and Brook to think about..."

Mike looked out on the Laramie mountain range. The granite peaks refracted the sinking sun, glowing like the last stubborn coals in a fire pit. He meditated for a second--desperately trying to quiet the little voice telling him to just say *fuck it* and take his family deep into the Rocky Mountains and ride this thing out.

"I have those same feelings towards the whole thing. Once we are wheels up I'm going to have Ari call Springs for a SITREP (Situation Report)."

Tice approached and said, "I've got bad news Mike..."

"Let me have it."

"It seems that at least a third of the devices are unaccounted for," Tice said, concern creeping into his voice. "Two of the trailers are filled with W-80 variable yield nuclear warheads... the kind meant to be delivered, air to ground, usually fixed on the nose of a cruise missile. The other truck is empty save for an Air Force officer, and she is badly beaten and in need of medical attention. NEST took some readings and found that the empty trailer is still hot. It had nuclear warheads in it recently, but apparently they were off loaded somewhere *or* they may have been transferred to one or more vehicles and delivered to multiple different locations. Long story short General... you don't have a single *broken arrow* situation on your hands... you, sir, have a whole quiver of broken arrows out there... *somewhere.*"

Desantos processed the information and considered the ramifications as he watched the NEST team working like a well-oiled machine, quickly loading and securing each of the three hundred pound warheads onboard the two Chinooks. "We're just going to have to put one foot in front of the other and deal with one threat at a time. Can you work with these W-80 warheads, and most importantly, can we safely use one or more of them for Option Two?" he asked.

"No problem General, these brigands stole everything they would need from Minot... enough fuses and all of the necessary hardware, tools and diagnostic equipment to arm *all* of the devices and burn several cities to the ground. If your D-Boys are planning on delivering the weapons personally... then I can make them operable ahead of time and adjust the yield to your liking... but we are going to have to set the timer manually. The W-80 has two blast settings-- either five kilotons, which is *my* recommendation, or a hundred fifty kilotons which is very effective but if you are less than twenty miles away you can kiss your ass goodbye, plus the fallout from the hundred fifty... *no bueno* for Springs and Schriever."

Wanting to explore all of the possibilities Desantos probed further. "What are the other methods of delivering the warheads?"

Cade followed the conversation, hanging on to their every word, his head panning back and forth like he was watching a Chinese ping pong match.

Tice adjusted his Detroit Tigers ball cap and said, "The only other way is a hell of a long shot. They could be deployed *as designed,* but I would have to remount them on a cruise missile... but that begs the questions... where are we going to get an AGM-129 *and* where are you going to get the B-52 to deliver the cruise missile?"

"Come again." For once in a long while Desantos was not following.

"I was being a smart ass, Mike," Tice said grimly. "The W-80s can *only* be hand delivered."

"All jokes aside... is the officer going to survive?"

"I think she will survive. She's got some broken ribs, but her career as a model is shot. Her captors smashed in her nose and knocked out a few teeth."

Questioning the spook, Cade asked, "Did you get any Intel out of her?"

"Affirmative," Tice answered, nodding his head. "She was conscious but she's suffered a helluva concussion. My team found her in the back of the sleeper cab; the fuckers had her blindfolded and gagged and trussed up with zip ties...so tight that she's probably going to lose some fingers."

A crackling fusillade of automatic rifle fire briefly interrupted their pow-wow.

Cade continued to mine the spook for details. "What did the officer say about the captors... did you get any of that out of her?"

"No... not before she lost consciousness," Tice said. "But the two guys who were driving the truck, they seem to know something but won't talk... they clammed up real tight when I tried to question them."

"Tice... once your team is finished loading the devices, bring the two drivers to my helo. Lopez... I want you to make sure their vehicles are disabled and remove all of the weapons and ammo," Desantos ordered.

Cade received a telling look from his good friend. He'd seen it a few times over the years, and what followed was never pretty. He knew without a doubt that *one* of those guys was going to talk and the one that failed to would not live long enough to regret it.

Speaking to Desantos, Lopez asked, "What should I do with the other drivers?"

"Cut them loose and leave them for the Z's."

Cold blooded... that's my Cowboy, Lopez thought.

Desantos waved his arm in a circle. "Load em up... we're Oscar Mike in five," he yelled to be heard over the Ghost Hawk's twin turbines.

Chapter 22
Outbreak - Day 8
Schriever Air Force Base

Slowly and deliberately the phosphorescent green dot silently cruised across the glass screen on the monitor only to magically reappear and trace the same path relentlessly. Department of Homeland Security Agent Archie Stockton had been infected with the Omega virus hours earlier; it had been five minutes since his heart had stopped beating and Doctor Hansen had declared him clinically dead.

Fuentes stood over the prostrate body stretched out on the stainless steel table, the beefy arms and legs restrained with thick leather straps. The big man's body was pasty to begin with, but under the white fluorescent lights bombarding the autopsy table his skin glowed like the face of the moon.

"Still no vitals, Doctor," Fuentes growled as he watched the thin green line motor along.

Jessica rotated her watch around her thin wrist and read its face. "He has been gone for nearly six minutes. If he comes back soon he might be recoverable but cerebral hypoxia is just around the corner."

Fuentes clucked his tongue and said, "If big guy here doesn't react to the anti-serum soon he's coming back as either an eggplant... or a zombie."

The Chinese Alpha battled its restraints and hissed and clacked its teeth at Doctor Fuentes' backside, which was frustratingly out of reach.

"That's six minutes... time of death..." Jessica was poised with pen to paper, about to record Agent Stockton's untimely demise and list Omega infection as the cause of death when the big man shuddered before her eyes and drew in a prolonged lungful of air.

The heart monitor came beeping to life and the green dot started bouncing haphazardly up and down across the glass display.

Jessica stepped back with a bewildered look plastered on her face when the soon-to-be-cadaver's eyelids snapped open. Jessica didn't know what to think. Although the man had drawn a breath, his eyes, the windows to the soul, looked like most of the newly turned: milky white.

Fuentes, fully cognizant of the Alpha eyeing his posterior, was not startled by the display of life the agent had just exhibited. Instead he sidestepped to the head of the table, perched his glasses on his nose, threw caution to the wind and peeled back Stockton's fluttering eyelids. The pupils dilated. *Good sign*, Fuentes thought, checking his enthusiasm. "Hanson... have we been documenting *everything?*" The doctor emphasized the word *everything* because he had a penchant for forgetting things in the short term. He was known for documenting everything on sticky notes, and since the apocalypse got under way those marvelous yellow pieces of paper seemed to be in short supply. When she nodded, he smiled in satisfaction. "Good job Hanson... because I haven't," Fuentes said.

Chapter 23
Outbreak - Day 8
Over Casper, Wyoming

Jedi One-Two, the second Ghost Hawk, flew in tight formation, shadowing the fully loaded Chinooks like a sheep hound watching over its flock. They were enroute to rendezvous with the Hercules for the first of their last two scheduled aerial refuelings.

Jedi One-One remained behind, lazily circling the ambush site, while Cade and Desantos acted out their version of good cop/bad cop.

"I have a feeling you two are just hired help... isn't that right?" Cade asked, playing the good cop. He noted the men's body language. The bigger man held his chin high and stared daggers at the spook and the operators. The smaller of the two squirmed a little, avoiding direct eye contact. He wore his blonde hair high and tight, military style. The multiple piercings in both ears contradicted the haircut. Full sleeve tattoos covered both arms: skulls, daggers, and flames were inked on every square inch. Apparently *"I think I'm a badass"* was the central theme but Badass wasn't fooling anybody.

The other man was just this side of giant; he had a ruddy complexion and a hawk-like nose that had already met its share of knuckles. The man's black ponytail was pulled back so tightly he was left with slits for eyes. The dead giveaway that he was going to be the more defiant of the two were the series of black tears tattooed underneath his right eye. They weren't just for show; they were for telling. Ponytail had either spent time in prison--killed a man--or a combination of both.

"So you're the snitch-bitch of the marriage. That's my guess," Desantos said through clenched teeth, his face inches from Ponytail's.

The man visibly bristled but remained seated.

Without warning Desantos punched Ponytail in the face, making sure to twist his hips to put all of his body weight behind the strike. Blood sluiced from yet another broken nose. "Talk now or your teeth are next. Keep in mind... talking without them is going to be a pain in the ass... and you *will* talk... or else." Desantos could tell by the man's eyes that he was curious about what was going to happen if he remained silent.

"What's the or else," the man croaked, spraying bloody spittle on the floor of the helo.

Cade silently eyed Badass, whose lower lip had begun to quiver.

Desantos' patience was shot. "Ari, find me some Z's!" he shouted over the faint engine noise, mainly for Ponytail's benefit.

Ari pointed the helicopter west following the refueling waypoint prominently displayed on his HUD display. *God I love this bird's glass cockpit,* he thought to himself. "Keep an eye out for walkers," Ari requested over the onboard comms.

Ponytail's face grew whiter by the second because he knew that he was about to find out exactly what the asshole soldier meant by *or else.*

The spook spotted them first. "Port side nine o'clock," Tice said into his mic. "Seven bodies moving south."

"Copy that," Ari said.

"Last chance," Desantos intoned, glaring into Ponytail's eyes.

Ari closed with the herd and held the bird in a steady hover fifteen feet over the hungry Z's. The creatures were "first turns" and looked pretty beat up. *The man might stand a chance,* Ari thought as he watched the zombies reaching and staggering, fighting to stay upright in the ship's rotor wash.

Ponytail's Adam's apple bobbed up and down. It looked like he wanted to speak but the words wouldn't come.

Cade helped Desantos get him to his feet. Clearly he didn't want to leave the helicopter; the doomed man fell back to his knees, nothing but dead weight.

Cade drew his Gerber and cut the zip ties from Ponytail's wrists while Desantos propelled him into thin air. Ponytail rolled the windows up, flailing his arms all the way to the ground. He hit hard, feet first, and rolled. By the time he found his balance the Z's were on top of him.

Tice mouthed the words, "Harsh way to go," under his breath and tore his eyes away from the carnage. Maddox could care less one way or the other; he was spent from the constant running and gunning and promptly closed his eyes, thankful for the few hours of shuteye he was going to get during the ride home.

Lopez, not sure where he stood, just looked away, content that God would sort it out.

Hicks, the crew chief, was lost in his own thoughts reliving his part in the mercy killings at the Long Acre Retirement Villa. One thing he was certain of, the man dying down below was involved with bad people and didn't deserve an ounce of his mercy.

Cade made sure Badass got a good look at his buddy's death throes. "Ready to talk?" he asked.

While the zombies tore at Ponytail's guts, Badass spilled his. The poser was a trove of information and he sang like a canary all the way to Colorado Springs.

Chapter 24
Outbreak - Day 8
I-25 Between Castle Rock and Colorado
Springs

"Holy shit!" Wilson exclaimed.

Sasha jumped in her seat, startled by sound of her brother's voice. "What is it Wilson?" she griped.

Wilson pointed in the direction they were headed and said, "Look at those black specks... right there on the horizon... they look like freakin' UFOs."

In a matter of seconds the moving specks grew larger and morphed into a number of matte black bat wing and dart-shaped jet aircraft. The ominous looking machines were nearly silent until they passed directly overhead. Then a low timbered howl washed over the valley as the fast movers disappeared over the northern horizon.

"What the heck were those?" Ted asked from the back seat.

"Batman's boomerang," William said in a foggy out-of-it sounding voice. "And he's bringing me my pills..."

"Why don't you give him another? There's still a stretch of driving and we might hit a whole mess of walkers when we get to Colorado Springs. Besides, he'd be better off sleeping the rest of the way," Pug proffered.

After rifling through the bag full of pills Ted found one of the night-night Vicodin pills. Without a fight William swallowed the *medicine*, and then asked for a nice Riesling to wash it down.

Ted propped William up in his seat and cinched the seatbelt a little tighter. "That ought to keep him happy for a while. *Everyone satisfied?*" Ted spat, feeling more than a little pissed off. More so at himself for not wanting to deal with a loopy William, than at the pushy driver who was a total stranger to everyone in the truck.

Pug finally answered Ted's earlier question about the over flight. "Those black airplanes... I remember seeing a documentary about them on cable. The bat wing jobs are B-2 Liberty stealth bombers and the others are B-1 something or others... I forget what they called 'em. At any rate, I've got a bad feeling that Denver is going to be glowing in a few minutes."

"No way," Wilson blurted.

"Where else are they going flying so low and fast?" Pug countered.

"I hate to admit it... but I think Pug's right," Ted opined from the backseat.

Wilson's conscience was nagging him, and he suddenly felt that he owed Pug full disclosure. "Do you want to tell him or should I?" Wilson asked Ted, referring to the disaster they'd left behind in Denver.

"*You go right ahead,*" Ted intoned. He'd clearly picked up on Wilson's meaning and wanted nothing to do with the conversation.

Wilson sighed. He didn't want to be even remotely linked to the surge of dead following them from Denver, but his mom raised him to be truthful. The monsters weren't going to stop at some roadside attraction and get sidetracked. They were going to be a problem for the entire South valley, a real big and very hungry problem. Wilson sat in silence and looked out the window for a couple of minutes before he said, "The walkers started doing some weird stuff... moving in a pack like wolves following the alpha male. When we escaped Denver there were eight of us."

"What happened to the others?" Pug asked, trying his best to sound concerned.

"Those *fucking* things overtook them... it was awful. Cheryl was torn in two." Wilson pinched the bridge of his nose and continued speaking, hiding behind the dark shroud of his eyelids. "We were being followed... it's like they're goddamn bloodhounds or something... and they are back there somewhere." Wilson opened his red rimmed eyes and stared straight ahead.

Sasha rubbed her brother's shoulder, searching her teenaged mind for some comforting words. "It was a good plan and we *did* escape Denver. Don't beat yourself up brother... *you are not to blame.*"

Ted finally piped up from the backseat. "They were hunting for *anything* living. For Christ's sake I saw a bunch of them corner a pack of stray dogs and devour them in seconds... fucking seconds. And sooner or later, after they consumed anything with a pulse-- including Fido--they *were* bound to leave the city... *it was inevitable.*"

"I'd tend to agree with ol' Ted here," Pug said. "Besides, it sounds like you're frettin' a lot over a few walkers. How many did you say there were?"

"I purposefully *did not,*" Wilson said, barely above a whisper. "And if all of the walkers that were behind us when we fled Denver *are* still following us... then you *do not* want to know how many of them there *are.*"

Pug was about to open his mouth and try to force a number out of Wilson when the female zombie lurched into the truck's path. He had already been aware of the creature in the distance, limping along the side of the road, but he hadn't anticipated her abrupt change in direction. A slight glancing blow from the left front fender spun the zombie around.

In that brief moment, Sasha realized that the walker had an infant strapped to its chest and that the small body was wildly flailing its chubby arms in the air. "Oh my God, did anyone else see the baby?"

"Get your eyes checked young lady. All I saw was that solo walker," Pug lied.

"Well I *did.* Stop this truck *right now.* We've got to check... just in case," Sasha said vehemently. She jammed her fist in her mouth and began to gnaw on her knuckles. It was her subconscious reaction to stress and a very hard habit to break.

"We don't have time to stop... it's gonna be dark in a couple of hours," Pug said. "Besides... you know the mom and the child are both in the same boat. They're *fuckin* dead."

"Are you sure? You were going pretty fast," Sasha said, her voice brimming with hope.

Wilson spoke after a few seconds of uneasy silence. "I'll go back and check... because if I don't, it's going to bother me forever." He wasn't doing it only for his sister's sake. It was also for him... the fact that he hadn't put the neighbor's toddler down after he bashed her parents' undead brains in still weighed heavy on his heart. He could still see little Sarah slamming against the baby gate, her beady dead eyes hungering for a hunk of his flesh.

Pug remained silent, weighing whether he should let the young man out and then drive away, leaving him for the dead. Then he remembered that the Ted fella in the backseat had a shotgun, but he couldn't for the life of him remember if it was loaded. *Curse you old age*, he thought. It was very tempting, but he took the high road and pulled over.

They all heard and felt the low rumble of the engines before the jet airplanes screamed back overhead. The stealth bombers were cruising at a much lower altitude than they had been on their northbound flyby.

Wilson gaped at the planes as they blotted out the sky over the truck; they passed so close that he could see the gray U.S. Air Force markings. He turned and peered out the rear window towards Denver, half-expecting to see mushroom clouds blooming on the horizon. *Nothing.*

As if he were reading Wilson's thoughts, Pug said, "We're OK. It looks like they didn't nuke Denver. Time's a wastin', you wanna take my pistol... so you can do them both?"

"No, but thanks," Wilson said icily as he exited the truck, bat in hand, and started his hundred yard trudge towards closure.

Sasha watched with rapt attention while she continued to chew on her fist.

Wilson moved closer to the walker. He had covered only half of the distance before his gut feeling was confirmed--he covered the remaining fifty yards thinking only about what he needed to do.

With only fifteen feet separating him and the hissing ghoul Wilson readied the Louisville Slugger. At five feet the undead baby in the carrier started to moan along with its mother. The chorus chilled his soul. It wasn't a fair fight--his rage versus the zombie's mindless drive.

Sasha watched the events unfold through her fingers. Wilson's bat lashed out. He didn't stop swinging until well after the zombies quit moving. She folded her small form on the seat and thought about her mom, trying to visualize her warm happy smile and the little tilt of her head when she was about to offer up an unwanted piece of wisdom. It was all gone now. Try as she might she couldn't even remember what her mom had smelled like--the reassuring scent that meant she was present and everything was going to be all right. And worst of all Sasha feared that she had lost her rock... the always steady and predictable Wilson seemed to be a different person... he now seemed cold and detached.

The door opened. Sasha cringed a little, knowing that she was stuck between Pug and the changed man that Wilson had become.

"Well. Was I right or was I right?" Pug asked smugly.

Wilson wanted to lash out, but he had left it all on I-25. Instead he softly said, "I knew you were right from the get go. The beauty of the whole thing is that now *I am alright.*"

Pug didn't know what the kid was getting at and he really didn't give a shit. He wanted to get to the U.S. Capital and he wanted to get there before dark. In the distance a group of white lights suddenly appeared on the far horizon and began sweeping the sky.

"Look, they're expecting us," Ted joked, trying to ease the tension in the truck.

"Then that's where we're going," Pug stated as he pulled back onto the road and accelerated quickly. Although he was anxious to get to his destination he watched his speed a little closer. He didn't want any more walker encounters now that he was so close to his objective.

***

The Stryker sat in the middle of the interstate, silhouetted against the backdrop of darkened high-rises in downtown Colorado Springs. From the roofs of the buildings, feelers of light probed the sky. Cheyenne Mountain, Pikes Peak and the rest of the Rockies circled the city like a fourteen thousand foot granite fence.

The survivors, being chauffeured by the strange man named Pug, were instantly blinded by the high intensity lights atop the armored vehicle's sloping nose.

"Turn off the motor and exit your vehicle," a disembodied voice ordered through a loudspeaker.

Since the Stryker's .50-cal was pointed directly at the Ford, Pug wisely did as he was told.

"What do you think they're going to do with us?" Sasha whispered.

Wilson stepped out first and said, "Whatever it is... it can't be any worse than the shit we've been through already."

"Wilson. Quit cussing, it's not like you."

"You're not my mom," he hissed back.

"Quit yer bickering and do as you're told," Pug implored. He wanted to blend in, not draw the ire of the U.S. military.

"What should I do about William?" Ted asked anyone that was willing to listen.

"Leave him for now. If you drag him out they might think he's infected and get a case of the itchy trigger fingers," Pug advised.

Once everyone, excluding William, was assembled, the voice told them to slowly turn all the way around.

Wilson got a good look at Ted's splotchy cut up cheeks and forehead and hoped that it didn't hurt half as bad as it looked.

Two armed soldiers emerged from the vehicle and approached to within ten feet of the survivors. "Are any of you armed?" the older of the two asked as his eyes passed from Pug to Wilson to Ted and then stopped on Sasha for a second.

Pug recognized the rank on the soldier's uniform and addressed him properly. "Yes Sergeant. I have a .45 and there's also a shotgun in the backseat, and Babe Ruth here..." Pug elbowed Wilson, "his baseball bat is in the front seat."

Ted spoke up. He had to warn the soldiers about William. "My partner is in the back seat... *I assure you, he is not infected*... but for his safety, I had to sedate him."

"Are you a doctor?" the sergeant asked.

"I'm a psychiatrist."

"A shrink," the other soldier, the younger of the two, studied Ted for a moment and clucked his tongue. "You're going to be real popular at Schriever."

The younger soldier was soon joined by another from the Stryker and together they went through the Ford, searching all of the compartments and under the seats. After the soldiers collected the weapons, Sasha's handbags and Pug's backpack, they politely ordered everyone back into the Ford. The three soldiers disappeared behind the Stryker and after a moment a tan Humvee emerged, driven by the older sergeant, who pulled alongside the Ford and instructed Pug to extinguish his headlights and follow closely.

During their meandering drive along the perimeter fencing, dusk slowly gave way to night. In the failing light, Pug took note of the various buildings and aircraft, cataloging everything in his mind for future reference. The Humvee paused outside of the southwestern gate; nearby, two mounds of rotting corpses served as an all-you-can-eat buffet for the crows and ravens.

The entrance was protected by a Bradley fighting vehicle. Two guard towers stood one hundred yards apart, manned by no fewer than ten heavily armed soldiers. After a two minute wait a solitary soldier emerged and waved them through both sets of gates.

When darkness finally prevailed the base virtually disappeared. To ensure that Schriever wouldn't become a beacon to the dead, all of the streetlights and porch lights had been unscrewed or removed altogether and every window had been blacked out.

"Extreme measures..." Ted said, alluding to the silent lifeless grounds. "I wonder how many people made it here alive."

"From the looks of all those planes we passed... quite a few. I just wonder where they're all staying," Pug stated.

"Those searchlights in the downtown district don't make sense to me," Wilson said, staring westward at the ambient light dancing off of the underside of the forming thunderclouds.

"Give it some thought Wilson... why do you think this base is blacked out?" Ted asked.

"So the dead heads don't get curious," Sasha said, smiling in the dark. "Those lights must be super intriguing to them. Kind of like Facebook used to be to me."

"*Used to*," Wilson muttered.

Pug continued following the Humvee to a desolate corner of the air base. Soon, out of nowhere, a giant hangar materialized from the darkness and the doors began to part, revealing the muted night lighting inside. The Humvee didn't slow, it just rolled right through with the Ford still on its bumper.

As soon as the immense doors rolled closed, the red lighting switched off and was replaced by the sterile light cast from long rows of ceiling-mounted white fluorescent bulbs.

"Wow... you could park an ocean liner in here," Wilson noted.

"Or a couple of jetliners," Sasha said smugly.

Wilson was relieved to see that the old Sasha was still in there somewhere. He was amazed at the sense of security that a couple of fences and a few armed U.S. soldiers fostered in her... and in him.

The Humvee rolled to a stop and the sergeant exited, clutching the three bags belonging to the survivors. Without saying a word he unzipped the two expensive leather bags and rudely turned them upside down. In an avalanche of bright colors, Sasha's clothes, tubes, and vials of perfume and makeup as well as her long dead iPhone clattered to the concrete. "A young lady of means I see." The grim faced sergeant then gave the bags a violent shaking. Once he deemed the status symbols empty he motioned for Sasha to reclaim her belongings.

"My *single, airline attendant* mom bought those for me at the Duty Free store," Sasha retorted in a huff. "And it is *all* that I have to remember her by."

"Understood," replied the soldier without a hint of compassion.

Pug's black REI backpack got the treatment next. His clothes, although not as frilly, were dumped on the hangar floor along with several packages of Mountain House freeze-dried food, a pocketknife and a folded map of the Western United States. The sergeant upended the empty bag but didn't stop there.

Pug felt his stomach tighten as the soldier rooted around inside of the empty pack.

After the prolonged sound of ripping Velcro, the sergeant removed a distended Camelback hydration system from inside the pack and tossed the full bladder onto the floor, where it hit with a wet smack, jiggling for a few seconds.

"Whose is this?" the sergeant inquired, holding the pack at arm's length.

"It's mine sir," Pug answered hesitantly.

"Sorry I tore it apart. You can take your belongings in with you during your quarantine..."

"Quarantine?" Ted said incredulously.

Fully expecting someone to object, the sergeant rolled out his standard spiel: "None of you are being singled out. Every person coming in from the outside has been subjected to the same twelve hour quarantine. You will be provided with clean clothes and bedding and our well stocked library is at your disposal. Are there any questions?"

Of course Ted raised his hand. "William is not well. Um... his medicine is in the truck and without it he'll be miserable... and eventually he will die."

As if on cue a woman soldier in desert ACUs, her face hidden behind a surgical mask and clear eye protection, appeared, pushing a wheelchair obviously intended for the incapacitated man.

The sergeant lowered his voice and said, "Listen... they will keep him quarantined for a few hours... if he is going to turn it will happen soon--if he doesn't--someone will take him to the infirmary where he will get the appropriate medical treatment."

"How do I know that you're not blowing smoke?" Ted shouted.

The sergeant put his hands up in a gesture of surrender meant to put Ted at ease and said, "Don't worry; the man will be in good hands." Clearly the discussion was at an end.

Little did they know that each one of them was going to be ordered to strip, while a person of the same gender gave them the incoming prisoner once-over: lift, cough, and spread. This was necessary to ensure the medical staff could check *everywhere* for bites.

After they were forced to shower for fifteen minutes in near scalding water, the medical staff checked them with a bulky thermal scanner. Lastly Sasha and Ted were taken to another room to have their injuries attended to.

Sasha had a few superficial scratches on her face that only required Neosporin and bandages. She was given a meal and then placed in a locked cubicle with a Twilight novel and twelve hours to kill. She settled in happily enough, engrossed in Edward and Bella's romance as only a teenager could be.

Ted's face received the same treatment, and after it was cleaned and bandaged he was taken to another cubicle. He declined the book and the meal; he wanted to get the clock started and the quarantine over with. If his math was right he should be free before noon.

Since both Pug and Wilson weren't injured, they were fed and offered their choice of reading material and mercifully started their time in the cubicles a little sooner.

Pug grabbed a thick hardcover copy of War and Peace.

Wilson opted for a Stephen King novel. He figured if he did finally fall asleep he'd rather have nightmares starring Captain Trips than the rotting creatures outside of the fence.

William, still unconscious, was whisked away in a wheelchair by one of the soldiers in full level 4 biohazard garb.

Chapter 25
Outbreak - Day 8
Eden, Utah
Eight hours earlier

Logan adjusted his body armor ever so slightly and moved his legs to get the blood flowing in his lower extremities. The binoculars went back to his eyes and his free hand went back to worrying his long handlebar mustache. He had been lying on the pine needle-covered forest floor with a rifle and a pair of binoculars watching the two-story cabin for the last three hours. Up to now, most of his experience with waiting had been done in the DMV or behind some math-challenged prick in the express checkout at the Safeway. Before they moved on the building he wanted to have a better idea of how many additional personnel and weapons they were up against.

Since Logan hadn't served in the military, he usually relied on Lev's or Gus's opinion on security matters, but if either one of them weren't available he reluctantly consulted his U.S. Army survival manual for a solution.

The library shelves in the compound were filled with every book that Logan could get his hands on that had to do with prepping or surviving off of the grid. Logan was a pretty good shot. He was also well read and had been preparing for the *shit to hit the fan* since the day he first learned about the Y2K bug. The event was supposed to kill a good portion of the world's computers, turn out the lights, and in a lot of people's worried minds, generally stop the earth from spinning. Logan was in his compound with a few trusted friends and fellow preppers in 1999 when the New Year rolled around and nothing happened. Undaunted, Logan continued prepping for any other eventuality, a financial crash, errant asteroid--*anything* but the zombie apocalypse which had been near and dear to his heart, but only in movies and books and the occasional zombie walk--*until now*.

For the past two nights in a row they had detected someone probing the compound's defenses.

Lev proposed that they have a QRF (Quick Reaction Force) ready the next time someone came too close for comfort.

Chris Levdahl and Logan had been friends since high school. After the two men graduated from Highland High, Lev went into the Army and was later deployed to Iraq where he served two tours, coming back tanned, fit and restless.

Logan stayed in Salt Lake and split his free time between service for the LDS church and preparing for the unrest that he knew was inevitable. Before the outbreak Logan and Lev devoted countless hours stocking the compound with food, weapons, and ammunition. The property was tucked away, hidden and secure, surrounded by dense woods nearly fifty miles from Salt Lake City. At least that's what they thought.

This latest incursion, number three, had happened earlier during the day. Luckily the game camera that the trespassers tripped captured grainy images of both men and instantly relayed the footage, via radio frequency, back to the security center inside the compound. The men in the picture wore woodland camouflage and were armed with AR style rifles--not deer guns. After calling a quick meeting and weighing everyone's opinion, the consensus in the compound was that the two interlopers were not locals out hunting game (or zombies for that matter) they were more likely bad guys with equally bad intentions. The group also made a bold decision to turn the tables on the men and make them become the hunted.

A six-person team was quickly assembled, kitted out, and set out after their quarry.

***

Hunting cabin three miles from the Eden Compound

Logan keyed the mic on the two-way Motorola. "*Levdahl... any movement in the cabin on your side?*"

"*Negative... all quiet over here,*" Lev replied. He was hunkered down with a Les Baer Tactical Recon bolt action sniper rifle chambered in .300 Win Mag. The scope on the rifle allowed him to cover the west side of the building from three hundred fifty yards, seeing everything clearly through the high powered optics down to the gauge stamped on the nail heads holding the plank siding on.

Logan looked to his right where Chief was positioned with his M4 trained on the cabin. Chief, sensing the scrutiny flashed thumbs up. For some reason, yet to be divulged by the Native American, he insisted his fellow survivors call him Chief. He was the most level headed person among the twenty-two people that called the compound home and by far the oldest among them.

Peering over his shoulder to his left he could barely see Jamie. She wore a ghillie suit which was made up of various pieces of fabric and organic matter affixed to her clothing; it served to break up her slender profile and helped her blend in perfectly with the surrounding foliage. The barrel of her Winchester Model 70 was also wrapped like her suit and pointed towards the rustic cabin. Jamie had been reluctant at first to get on board with her friend Logan's prepping lifestyle but as soon as TSHTF she was all in.

Lev looked at his watch and keyed the radio. "Logan... Lev here. I suggest we give them fifteen more minutes and then I want to make a little commotion and try to draw them out. They're definitely novices based on the trail they left for us to follow... not to mention the lack of noise discipline. Maybe they're getting it on in there. You and I know how the man/woman ratio is skewed these days. It seems like I'm in Alaska or some shit."

"Copy that... and thanks for the visual, buddy," Logan said as he checked his Timex. Then he stared at the Chief until he got his attention. He opened and closed his hand three times and then tapped his watch. The Chief nodded. Next, he got Jamie's attention and repeated the same silent message. Because the Motorola two-way radios were in short supply and weren't as user friendly as he would have liked, Logan made a note to self to try and acquire real communications gear, especially since they were now utilizing them in a tactical capacity.

***

Ten minutes had passed and the hunting cabin was still quiet as a mortuary. Lev motioned at Gus, a thirty-eight-year-old Salt Lake City Sheriff, flashing him an open hand. Gus nodded, shouldering his Mossberg.

Sampson, a forty-year-old ski instructor from Park City, Utah, received the same silent update from the team leader. He grinned, flashing his newly whitened teeth at Lev and then shouldered his AR-15, aiming it at the front door.

Logan first introduced Lev and Sampson during a ski trip to Park City before the outbreak. When Logan informed Lev that the ski instructor was one of the few that would be welcome at the compound in Eden, Lev immediately balked, calling bullshit on Logan's judgment and before they were finished skiing that day, Lev and Logan decided it would be best if they just agreed to disagree. There was even a small wager placed on whether Sampson would be a no show in the event of a catastrophe.

The always meticulously groomed Sampson was the compound's post-apocalyptic metrosexual. It pained him to do so, but Lev had to admit he was wrong when the guy turned up at the compound two days after the outbreak, alive and without a scratch on him. Over the following days he had proven himself a productive member of the group and had also taught Lev a valuable lesson: never judge a book by its cover.

Logan set the binoculars aside and spoke into the radio. *"Two minutes."*

Lev responded with two silent clicks of his radio, put his rifle down, and drew the Beretta from its shoulder holster. Then, pulling himself off of the ground, he silently worked his way towards the cabin while remaining inside the tree line.

Lev was about to sprint the last thirty feet from cover to the cabin door when the sound of a laboring engine reached his ears. He pancaked to the ground and quickly low crawled to cover behind a clump of fiddler ferns growing from the center of an old deadfall.

"Change of plans. What do you propose we do now?" Logan asked, sounding concerned.

"*Observe,*" Lev succinctly replied over the two-way radio.

The growling of the engine grew louder.

Looking at Logan, Gus stabbed two fingers towards his eyes and then pointed at the gravel road indicating he was aware of the approaching vehicle.

Logan tightened his grip on the M4 and made sure the selector was on fire. His attention was divided between the front of the cabin and the washed-out goat trail masquerading as a road where he knew the vehicle would eventually emerge. He was certain that the two men they had tracked to the cabin could be dealt with fairly easily, but the approaching vehicle changed the odds instantly.

"Watch the road... I'll cover the door," Lev said as the door began to open.

Logan watched the woods disgorge a dirty white Toyota Land Cruiser followed closely by a silver 4Runner. Both vehicles were loaded to the headliner with supplies and sat very low on their springs. Even though the dealer plates were still attached to the front and back of the two new Toyotas, they appeared anything but--their body panels were dented and dinged, and it looked like a thousand demons had sharpened their claws on the trucks' paint. Congealed blood and other fluids painted the front and sides of both vehicles adding to their beat up appearance. Two men occupied each truck. Logan couldn't be sure if they were armed or not from his vantage point, but he had to assume that they were.

Making eye contact with Chief, Gus displayed four fingers, relaying how many newcomers they would be dealing with.

Coinciding with the SUVs' noisy entrance into the clearing, the door of the cabin creaked open, and one of the camo-clad trespassers emerged carrying a black shotgun. He was of medium build and had a long billy goat beard and a gray ponytail snaking out from under his woodland camo boonie hat. He walked the length of the porch exhibiting a slight limp; Lev guessed that the man couldn't have been a day under fifty. With agility that belied his decrepit looks, the man jumped down off of the low porch and, with a huge grin spreading across his face, greeted the arriving men with backslaps and handshakes; judging by the spirited conversation that ensued the apocalypse must have been treating them kindly.

"We went from two tangos to six just like that... what do you think?" Lev whispered.

"That's a game changer," Logan said into the Motorola. "Both of the passengers have a sidearm and I can see at least one carbine propped up inside the 4Runner... on the passenger's side. I think we should lay low and then bug out when they aren't looking."

Lev thought it over for a second. "I like our odds... but given the unknown variables... I'd have to agree with you." *What would Gus do?* Lev thought. The sheriff was too far away to consult so Lev decided to trust his gut. *We need better communications gear,* his inner voice chided.

The cabin door creaked again as the second trespasser emerged and joined his buddies near the 4Runner. The kid's boonie hat was pulled down low over a snarled mop of blonde hair; he wore the same woodland camo as the other man and an AK-47 dangled freely from his shoulder. He looked like a baby-faced teen and the youngest of the group by far.

Lev had the best position and took it all in. He still struggled whether they should be taken out now or if live and let live was the best policy. He knew that sooner or later these guys were going to come snooping around the compound again and then they would have to be dealt with. If it were his decision he would take them out here and now, but it wasn't his to make alone. Logan had stressed from day one that all of the decisions that were made concerning the wellbeing or day-to-day workings of the compound would be handled democratically. So Lev waited.

The 4Runner driver poked his head into the Land Cruiser and pushed a button somewhere. The rear hatch opened automatically revealing two bound and hooded women. Baby Face grabbed the nearest woman and violently yanked her out of the cargo area, throwing her to the ground head first. Before he could grab ahold of the second prisoner she shimmied out of the truck under her own power and stood unsteadily, using the rear bumper for support. The men backed away silently and formed a loose circle around the prisoners. The upright woman's head swiveled back and forth inside the burlap sack. She took a few tentative steps and stumbled around blindly before the bearded man knocked her to the ground with a vicious hockey check.

Logan didn't like where this was heading. "We have to hit them while the women are down."

Lev whispered, "I was thinking the same thing. I left my rifle behind. I only have my pistol... so you're going to have to initiate."

The driver of the 4Runner was an extremely skinny twenty-something with an upturned nose and closely set eyes. A soiled wife-beater that swished when he walked hung loosely over his ratty cutoff blue jeans; the man looked like one of the "presumed innocent until guilty" stars on the reality TV show *Cops*. He crouched between the two women with his face hovering, menacingly, inches from their hooded heads. "You two ain't going nowhere... we're your new *friends*..." He paused to let the words sink in before continuing, "And you both better get used to it. We're going to be *friends* for life."

"Where did you find them?" Baby Face asked the man in the wife-beater.

"They were looting *our* Costco when we rolled up."

"Well let's see what we have. Please tell me you brought us some Ginger and a little Mary Ann," the gimpy man said as he pulled off both of their hoods.

"Holy hell," Wife-Beater blurted. "One of 'em must have been bit and turned on the way here."

The zombie lunged. Only the thin strip of silver duct tape covering its mouth saved Baby Face from being bitten.

Frantically the other woman rolled away from the writhing creature.

"Did the other one get bit too?" the driver of the Land Cruiser, a terribly overweight middle aged man, inquired.

Baby Face looked up dumbly and said, "I don't know."

"Well gawdammit... check the bitch for bites," the fat man barked. "And then check and see if the other one is still warm..."

"Eww Chuckie... you ain't goin' there again are you?" Baby Face said, revulsion showing on his face.

Chuckie smiled, displaying his lack of front teeth. "We'll see," he said with a wink. "If I get in the mood who knows what might happen."

Lev wished he hadn't been close enough to hear the last exchange. Bile rose in his throat and the urge to shoot them all tugged at his trigger finger. *Come on Logan,* he thought, *let's do this.*

Logan looked over at Gus and nodded, then whispered a quick reminder to Jamie and the Chief. "Head shots are *good,* but not vital, so remember to aim for center mass... they are *not* walkers." He aimed at the man standing closest to the bound women and squeezed off two shots. Crimson flowers bloomed on the scrawny man's wife-beater as he dropped in a heap.

At the same time Jamie struck Gimpy, who was standing next to the 4Runner, with a perfect head shot, dropping him like a rag doll. Chief wielded the M4 with deadly accuracy, pumping four rounds into Baby Face. The successive impacts walked from the young man's navel to his sternum, lifting him off of his feet. His body hit the SUV with a hollow thump and bounced off, ending up in the dirt where he died silently curled up in a fetal position. Chuckie turned, much faster than a man his size should have been capable of, and waddled away, only to come head on into the storm of buckshot from the sheriff's shotgun. Mister Rapist's face dissolved in a halo of gore, eliciting a satisfied grin from Gus.

Logan keyed the mic. *"Four tangos down on our side."*

Lev didn't have time to answer; he took the initiative and rushed the last two men from behind. One of them, a dead ringer for Howard Stern with long black greasy hair and a thin rat face adorned with oval wire framed glasses, was crouched near the rig's rear bumper with a chrome .45 clutched in his hand. He was intermittently stealing glances through the side glass trying to figure out who was shooting at them. The other man had just retrieved an assault rifle from inside the Land Cruiser and was in the process of charging the weapon. Both of them were using the vehicle for cover, totally unaware that they had already been flanked.

Howard Stern never knew what hit him; he took two 9 mm slugs behind the ear leaving some blood and brains of his own on the 4Runner before slumping to the ground.

Time slowed to a crawl for Lev as he swept his pistol to his left, bracketing the man with the assault rifle in his sights. "Drop it now," he said forcefully.

The man either didn't hear Lev or didn't want to hear him; he turned his head first, and then his body and the assault rifle followed in a slow deliberate arc.

Without a thought Lev shot the man in the neck, covered the distance in two quick strides, and then kicked the rifle away from the dying man. Lev watched as the lifeblood steadily pulsed between the dirtbag's kneading fingers, stared into the man's dimming eyes and said, "Good choice, asshole."

Logan's voice came over the two-way and spoiled the moment. "Come in Lev."

"Clear... two Tangos down," replied Lev. The entire encounter lasted less than ten seconds.

Sheriff Gus bolted into the clearing and pulled the woman out of the zombie's reach. The look in her eyes didn't say *thank you*, it screamed, *out of the fat and into the fire*, as she realized that a new group of armed men now owned her.

A single shot rang out as Chief took the initiative and put down the zombie.

"Sampson. You and Gus clear the house. Chief, keep an eye on the road, and Jamie, you need to take care of this one," Logan whispered to the camouflaged woman as she materialized from the foliage.

The prisoner's eyes widened and she recoiled and began scooting away on her rear after her first glimpse of the gun-wielding bush.

"Don't worry... we're not going to hurt you," Jamie said softly as she laid down her rifle and peeled off her hood and face mask.

A look of relief washed over the young woman; her shoulders and head slumped as her entire body seemed to uncoil.

Jamie flipped her blade open and held the woman's cold white hands as she cautiously sawed through the zip ties, and then with kid gloves she slowly peeled the duct tape covering her swollen mouth. "What's your name?"

The woman looked Jamie deep in the eyes and broke down. Between sobs she said, "Jordan."

Jamie held her and tried to think of some comforting words. "That's cool... we both have unisex names," was the best she could conjure up.

The creaky cabin door opened, snaring everyone's attention. Gus jumped off the porch and approached Logan. "The cabin is clear... really clear... it's spartan inside. There are only a couple of sleeping bags and a little bit of food. But I found these." Like he was displaying a trophy big mouthed bass, Gus held aloft two assault rifles and a sawed off shotgun.

"Good find Sheriff. Toss those in the 4Runner. Weapons and ammo are as good as gold now. Especially the ammo... I don't know about you, Gus, but I am not a big fan of reloading."

"I never had to," Gus replied. "The county provided as much ammo as we needed. Hell of a perk... while it lasted."

Chief gestured to the cargo laden SUVs and said, "Looks like these desperados were just moving in. What should we do with the gear and the trucks?"

"I say we take the stuff as the spoils of war," Lev said with a lopsided grin from the passenger seat of the 4Runner where he was sitting and reloading his pistol. "Besides, this thing still has that new car smell."

"Maybe on the inside... but it's *definitely* not smelling like lilacs on the outside. That thing looks like it crashed into a rendering plant," Sampson said, crinkling his nose while he munched on a liberated power bar.

Logan stared off into the forest seemingly frozen in a kind of trance and said, "I'm siding with Lev... but we need to get out of here twenty minutes ago. For one thing these guys might have more friends on the way and second, the gunfire might have gotten the attention of any walkers in the area... not to mention it's going to be dark in an hour or two." Logan sighed. He was trying to find the strength to dispose of the body at his feet. Most of all he was having a hard time getting used to the killing part of *surviving by any means necessary*. Logan had no problem dealing with walkers. In fact they were rather easy to kill without striking a chord. The living though...

not so much. The kid laying face up with his dead eyes wide open and the shock of dying prematurely frozen on his face was only number three for Logan.

He had killed his first two men during his flight from Salt Lake City over a week ago. It had been necessary to prevent them from stealing his truck. They were manning their twisted version of a civilian roadblock outside of Ogden and had demanded that Logan and Jamie exit their truck unarmed. Logan played the tape through and didn't like the ending... more so for Jamie than himself. As soon as he put two bullets into each of the menacing men he was a changed man forever. The look of surprise on their faces when things went sideways was going to the grave with Logan. And now he had added another death mask to the collection.

Lev stripped his kills of weapons and anything else useful before dragging the stiffening bodies behind the same fern-covered log he had used for cover. He retrieved his rifle and then sauntered to his friend's side. "What's the matter Logan... are you feeling sorry for the soon-to-be rapist piece of shit? It *had* to be done."

Logan shooed the ebbing thoughts of remorse from his head and softly said, "I know." Then he grabbed the skinny kid by one thin wrist and dragged the leaking body into the underbrush.

"Cover up the blood trails," Chief said loudly enough to be heard by the entire group.

"Everyone be sure to police up your brass," Sheriff Gus added.

Lev took the wheel of the 4Runner with Sampson riding shotgun. Logan had Jamie drive the Land Cruiser while he rode in the passenger seat with the carbine between his knees. Chief hurled some of the redundant supplies into the woods and then crammed his large frame into the rear cargo area along with Gus. Initially Jordan did not want to get back into the truck where she had already spent untold terrifying hours trussed and hooded, but after some coaxing she eventually yielded and crawled into the Land Cruiser with the others.

***

After one-and-a-half grueling miles bouncing along the rutted single track road, Lev turned left onto the smooth blacktop and stomped on the brakes. The truck's knobby tires chirped as the 4Runner came to a complete stop.

Jamie, who had been following closely, almost drove the Land Cruiser up the 4Runner's tailpipe.

"Sorry for the abrupt stop but we've got a few walkers on the road. They're about a hundred yards up ahead," Lev said over the two-way radio. "Their backs are to us... scratch that, they made us and they're coming this way. We are going to have company very soon."

"Can't we just go around them?" Logan inquired as he shifted in his seat to get a look at the zombies.

"I say we do 'em now so we don't have to worry about them later. Takes the same amount of ammo either way," Lev said matter-of-factly.

"Copy that, Lev." Logan said as he exited the Land Cruiser with rifle in hand.

Lev, who was already out of the 4Runner and standing in the road, removed his camo blouse, rolled it up and placed it on the hood of the truck to use as a makeshift barrel rest.

Slowly picking up speed, the quartet of moaning zombies lurched and staggered down the center of the double-lane highway.

Sampson, who was also now out of the 4Runner, said to Lev, "The rotters *were* moving north, they must have been coming from Ogden or Huntsville."

Logan, who had just walked up, joined in on their conversation. "I hope they came from Huntsville... because we don't want to tangle with the living dead from Ogden. I think there were like... *eighty thousand* people in Ogden."

"Look alive," Lev said as he shouldered his Les Baer and chambered a round. He sighted on the nearest walker. The female zombie looked like any soccer mom except she was definitely a "first turn;" her pallid skin hung slack from her ninety pound frame. She had probably been in her thirties, Lev guessed.

The .300 Winchester round struck the walker on the right side of the forehead with a glancing blow. The energy was still great enough to cleave a vee-shaped wedge in her skull, causing a gray geyser of brain matter to erupt from the wound. Before he could chamber another round, Logan had already dropped the freshly turned walker on the left with two well-placed rounds from his M4.

Two staccato volleys from Sampson's AR downed the remaining two creatures.

"Hey Logan... get the eff in here. There are more walkers coming up behind us and some more of them over there," Jamie said, pointing out the open passenger door of the Land Cruiser.

Logan looked across the field where, silhouetted in the low hanging sun, more zombies lurched towards them. "Let's go... we need to get back to the compound before dark," he said. Then, heeding Jamie's words, he hopped into the passenger seat.

Jamie followed Lev single file past the sprawled corpses, being careful not to run them over. She winced and looked at Logan after something popped under the SUV's big tires.

Logan grimaced and said, "Better them than us."

***

State Route 39 ran perpendicular to the compound's two mile long, gravel covered front entry road. The swinging gate which was set back from the road and camouflaged with native foliage was concealed so well that if a person didn't know where to look they would be hard pressed to locate it.

Logan jumped out of the Land Cruiser and manipulated the manual release he had hidden near the base of a red volcanic rock. Suddenly he froze and looked skyward.

Lev also heard the thundering thwap-thwap of rotor blades cutting the air immediately overhead. The aircraft flew close enough to the ground to make the 4Runner vibrate. *"Come on Logan, hurry up,"* Lev barked. They had to assume that the helicopter wasn't friendly and that meant that they needed to get to the airstrip in a hurry.

Chapter 26
Outbreak - Day 8
Over Eden, Utah

Duncan checked the coordinates a second time, decreasing altitude and slowing the Black Hawk at the same time. The dirt strip looked the same but the colorful airplanes were gone. Either he was overflying the wrong clearing or his old eyes were failing him. The next thought that crossed his mind was that maybe he had keyed in the GPS coordinates wrong. Duncan brought the helo to fifty feet AGL. "Good work," he said aloud when he spotted the mottled brown and green shapes. Since he was here last all of the aircraft had been expertly camouflaged and wheeled into the tree line on the periphery of the unimproved airstrip.

He settled the bird in the knee high grass as close to the edge of the clearing as possible without endangering the rotors. He cut power and waited for the rotors to slow considerably before exiting the DHS Black Hawk with his hands reaching for the sky.

Six armed men approached with their black guns trained on him. Duncan smiled; each of the men wore a different style of camouflage making them look like armed calico cats.

"*Keep your hands up!*" the man in the lead yelled convincingly.

Duncan complied.

"What's your business here," the same man stated in a more even keeled tone.

"I'm Duncan Winters... Logan Winters is my baby brother. I was here a couple of days ago... in a medevac Black Hawk."

"What is your brother's nickname?" the man asked.

"My mom and dad, may they rest in peace, gave him the nickname Oops. Safe to say at their advanced age he wasn't planned," Duncan said, a shit-eating grin spread across his face. He loved to divulge Logan's secret to his peers and did so every chance he got. He noticed that some of the armed men were finding it hard to keep from smiling as well.

The man who had been doing all of the talking extended his hand. "That is correct. Good to meet you Duncan, my name is Seth. We'll take you to the compound where you can get a bite to eat and put your feet up if you want to. Logan and a few others are out on a patrol and should be back before nightfall. Did you have a long flight?"

Duncan made a mental calculation and said, "About six hundred miles, give or take... my butt is sore. Cold beer and a stump is all I need."

"You got it," Seth said.

"Thanks for your hospitality," Duncan drawled. Leaving the flight helmet in the helo, Duncan perched his Stetson on his head and followed the patchwork army to the compound.

"What's it like out there?" came a voice from behind him.

Duncan answered without looking back. "It's bad out there. From a few hundred feet in the air, not so much, but on the ground--near the cities--better watch your six. I have seen a lot of good folks die this last week." He walked a few steps in silence and then continued, "Make that a six pack and a stump... I've got a little forgettin' to do."

Seth stopped abruptly in front of a thick patch of undergrowth and saplings and said, "Here we are."

The wall in front of them swung inward, foliage and all.

"Impressive," Duncan said under his breath.

Chapter 27
Outbreak - Day 8
Ten miles east of Schriever Air Force Base
Colorado Springs, Colorado

Five minutes had passed since the Ghost Hawk descended to just above the treetops and the flight got bouncy. Badass had been giving Cade the stink eye ever since.

"Ari... how close are we to Schriever?" Cade asked.

"Ten mikes out Wyatt... why, you got a date?" Ari pulled the stick back and violently popped the chopper over a taller pine tree and then just as sharply dove back to the treetops. The maneuver sent every testicle onboard into hiding. "Because if you do... I can push it a bit. Might have to leave the 47s behind to fend for themselves though..."

Cade held his SCAR carbine barrel down between his knees. He tightened his right hand around the fore grip and lashed out at Badass. The synthetic buttstock was a black blur as it struck the small man on the chin. Like he had just been on the receiving end of a Taser gun, Badass slumped in his seat unconscious and badly in need of some new dental work. "No need Ari... problem solved. But I do have one question for you, sir."

Ari jinked the helo around another stand of trees and said, "Shoot... I'm all ears."

"Why are we flying NOE (nap of the earth)?" Cade asked holding down the rising bile.

"Just for the practice, gotta stay sharp... just in case the dead evolve and figure out how to arm themselves," Ari joked.

Bad fucking joke, Cade thought.

Tice looked on, wondering what the prisoner did to deserve the sleeping pill, then mentally shrugged, owing it to general principles.

The helicopter abruptly slowed and gained some altitude. The boxy silhouettes of the buildings and hangars spread out across the AFB stood out in sharp contrast against the serrated Rockies in the background. Desantos and the other operators stiffened up, preparing for the imminent landing.

"We're going in quiet and low just in case," Ari said, his voice suddenly taking on a serious tone. "Durant, stay frosty on the countermeasures... we are at war."

"Repeat what you just said, Night Stalker," Desantos demanded.

"We're at war, sir. I was scanning frequencies and listening in on a side channel and caught some chatter over the net. Apparently a 4th ID patrol out of Carson was attacked with antitank munitions and decimated... happened somewhere in Wyoming," Ari said.

The General had suddenly developed a tic in one eyelid. "*I want to know who in the hell was talking about matters of national security on an open freq!*" he yelled.

Ari struggled mightily with the other piece of information he was sitting on. Ten minutes ago he started hearing snippets of a conversation that was improbable at best and quickly wrote it off as someone's fucking dismal idea of a practical joke, but he continued hearing the same mind-blowing words from the mouths of dozens of other excited soldiers and airmen on multiple frequencies. Even if it meant he became the laughing stock of Colorado Springs he felt compelled to repeat them to his good friend and superior General Desantos. "Looks like our jaunt to the CDC was worthwhile. Apparently the good doctor really is *good*. He either kept a man from turning... or he brought an infected man back from the dead. I've heard people talking about both of those scenarios." Ari shrugged. He wasn't getting his hopes up, and until he heard it from Shrill or Nash it was not a fact. "General, nothing that I overheard came from a *need to know* so I have a good reason to believe that they probably don't have their facts straight."

"Well I'll be damned," Lopez said, his face beaming. "I guess humpin' all those stairs at the CDC with Satan over my shoulder paid off." He looked up, closed his eyes, and made the sign of the cross.

"Change of plans, Ari. Drop us off first and then take the spook to Carson. Get me as close to the doctor's tent as you can," Desantos ordered.

"Copy that sir."

Desantos put his gloved hand on the CIA man's shoulder and peered into his eyes. "How long is it going to take to assemble and arm the devices?"

Tice briefly closed his eyes and performed a mental calculation. "Sir, two hours apiece to assemble them. That is assuming all of the parts I need are available. How many devices do you want operable?"

"Three."

"That *is* a lot of destructive power," Tice said wide eyed.

"The threat warrants it. Two of the devices are for the op and one is a backup... just in case plan A and B fail."

The spook's eyebrows scrunched together. "What is plan B?"

Every soul on the chopper was hanging on a thread, waiting for Desantos' answer.

Desantos watched the shadowy outlines of the other three black helicopters peel away and vector towards Fort Carson and then cleared his throat. Except for Badass, everyone in the cabin leaned towards him. "Plan B is pray that plan A works... because if it doesn't... the measures we will be forced to take pale in comparison to plan A."

Classic Desantos, Cade thought. He always played his cards close to his vest. If you need to know... then you will. Apparently the rest of the passengers didn't need to know.

By the time Jedi One-One crossed over the eastern wire, both Chinooks and the other Ghost Hawk were well on their way to Fort Kit Carson with the load of nuclear warheads and the accompanying equipment.

Chapter 28
Outbreak - Day 8
Eden Compound

Logan worried his handlebar mustache, twisting the ends into sharp points while he rode in silence. *It could have been Duncan buzzing the treetops,* he thought, *but then again it could just as easily have been the black clad storm troopers we saw from a distance on our last outing.*

Confident that there wouldn't be oncoming traffic, Lev drove the new 4Runner hard, drifting it on corners, kicking up rocks and an epic swirl of dust that coated the trailing Land Cruiser.

The DHS Black Hawk was already sitting on the edge of the grass and the rotor blades were tied down when the dusty SUVs rocketed from the tree line and sped across the clearing.

Logan hailed Lev on the two-way radio. "Do you see any personnel?"

After a few seconds Lev responded. "Negative, but be ready for anything when you get out."

Logan hated being told what to do but humility quickly kicked him in the ass. He was fully aware that real combat experience trumped his book knowledge and Lev was almost always correct when it came to anything security related. "Copy that," he said.

As soon as both SUVs skidded to a stop everyone piled out, charged their weapons, and trained them on the forest trail that led to the compound.

With a flick of his wrist Lev silently ordered the others to follow him. They drilled on silently movement with emphasis on proper spacing on a daily basis. Keeping separation between each person was important as it ensured that the group couldn't be taken out all at once if they were attacked.

Logan found it strange that there wasn't anyone posted in the clearing when they arrived.

As if he were a mind reader Lev whispered. "Where's the sentry?"

Before anyone could answer, the man responsible for watching the perimeter walked out of the shadows, gun held at a low ready position.

"Seth... why did you leave your watch?" Logan demanded.

"Sorry... I won't let it happen again. I was only escorting your brother to the entrance... he is one funny guy."

"Be alert. There are walkers on the road... so I think it wouldn't hurt us to double up the guard. I'll send another body out, but in the meantime *use* the radio... call if you see anything, and remember to keep quiet... the helicopter got them interested... the dead will start gathering if they find out we are here," Logan said.

"Will do," Seth acknowledged.

"I'll stay out here with him," Lev offered. "Maybe I can bag a couple more rotters."

Logan shook his head. "Let's hope not Lev. You and I both know what a couple of those things can lead to..."

"A very bad day," Lev concluded, "*a very fucking bad day indeed.*"

***

After a short hike through the trees they stood in front of the camouflaged steel entry to the compound. Even though the door was half-inch-thick plate Logan could hear Duncan holding court on the other side.

All conversation ceased and the cavernous room suddenly got quiet when Logan, Lev and the rest of the patrol filed through the door. Jamie peeled away from the group in order to escort Jordan to get some medical attention. Although the Flex Cuffs the kidnappers had used to restrain the young woman's hands had cut off the circulation for hours, she was going to keep her fingers but without a proper cleaning Jamie feared that the vicious red abrasions encircling her wrists would become infected. Logan made a bee line for Duncan and wrapped him in a bear hug. Then they held each other while exchanging back slaps and private conversation.

Duncan finally managed to free himself from Logan's python-like grip and put his hands on his shoulders, then looked the younger man in the eyes and said softly, "Baby bro... I thought I was never going to see you again."

Logan smeared a stream of hot tears with his forearm and said, "Welcome home old man."

Chapter 29
Outbreak - Day 8
Schriever AFB, Research Tent

Desantos didn't know which he should do first: cover his nose to fight off the stench of the Alpha or beg one of the doctors to loan him a pair of sunglasses to counter the miniature sun illuminating the creature. Furthermore, the steady hissing noise inside the windowless pressurized tent made him feel like Jonah in the belly of the whale.

Desantos quickly came to the realization that he was in dire need of sleep and food. Back-to-back-to-back ops with a newborn thrown into the mix was kicking his ass. His body was trying to tell him he was at the end of his rope and if he didn't acknowledge that fact soon someone was going to get hurt. He held one hand up to shield his eyes and thrust the other toward the much smaller scientist. "Doctor..." he said curtly, pumping his latex gloved hand.

Fuentes snapped off the glove and said, "Better wash that hand."

Ignoring the doctor's advice Desantos moved closer to the Alpha carrier. "Based on what I heard through the grapevine... I came in here expecting to see this one walking and talking," he said, poking the zombie in the chest. The dead Chinese national didn't feel the small brush of warm flesh, but the proximity of fresh meat sent tremors through the Alpha's body. Teeth grated as it bucked and strained, futilely rubbing ulna and tendon against the leather bonds.

The doctor fingered the Oreos in his pocket, longing to pop one in his mouth. "I'm sorry you had to hear about Archie from anyone but me."

Desantos exploded. "*Archie!*" He said the name as if it belonged to his mortal enemy. "*You named this thing... like a fucking pet. I don't know whether to puke or put a bullet in you!*"

Fuentes recoiled and said, "No. No... *This* isn't Archie." The scientist filled Desantos in on the DHS agent. He went over how he became infected and the events leading up to the awakening and finished with, "Archie is recovering in the other part of the tent."

"I owe you an apology for the outburst, Doctor... I'm still pissed off about the leak. How did the news get out?" Desantos asked, resisting the urge to rub his face with his unwashed hand.

Fuentes looked away. He didn't want to admit that it wasn't the first time Hanson had let information get away from her. "Doctor Hanson couldn't keep it to herself. She's full of hope... so much so that she let it slip to one of the soldiers in the dining hall a few hours ago. How much harm could it have caused?"

"Good grief... the chow hall is the *one place* on a military installation... any branch for that matter... where innuendo, rumor and plain ol' bullshit gets passed along as *fact*. Hell... word of this probably spread faster than a Bangkok whore's legs and probably more efficiently than *Omega* itself," Desantos railed.

"I'm sorry. It was never our intention to leak this because there is no way of knowing if the antiserum is going to be effective long term. I fully intended on waiting until we observed him for at least twelve more hours before bringing it to your attention. In a perfect world we would study Mister Luckiest Man on the Planet for weeks or months before getting our hopes up. For all I know Mister Stockton could still be carrying the virus... he may even succumb later and die... *again*."

Desantos finally relented and rubbed his rheumy eyes. "My hopes were riding high, Doctor. I was looking forward to interrogating this *Alpha fucker*. Pardon the language unbecoming of a General... but I'm damn tired."

Suddenly the air pressure changed inside the room and Doctor Hanson backed her way through the hanging slats of the inner air seal, a cup of steaming coffee in each small fist. Upon seeing the General chatting with her mentor, the demure civilian scientist suffered a sudden bout of Tourettes. "Oh fuck me... shit. Forgive me for the potty mouth General... curse words usually *are not* in my vernacular. Take this Doctor... but be *very* careful it's *hot*. I just got some on my hand," she lied.

Five-foot-two-inch Jessica Hanson squirmed as the intimidating soldier glared in her direction.

"Ms. Hanson," Desantos growled.

"Yes sir?" She stood rooted and wrung her hands, waiting for the boom to drop.

Desantos bowed his head, letting his chin rest on his sternum, and began to work the back of his neck. "Every person on this base... all the way down to the door kickers and the sharpshooters culling the dead downtown... are abuzz about your *cure*, Ms. Hanson. Will you kindly bring *me* up to speed about your *cure*, Ms. Hanson?"

"I'm sorry," she stammered. "I was so tired... the highs and the lows. I just blurted it out." She shook her head slowly side to side. "Believe me, I tried to reel the words back in but I couldn't spin it any other way."

Fuentes sipped his coffee and watched the woman wilt under the General's line of questioning. *Maybe she's finally going to learn from this,* he thought.

Desantos raised his head and looked the lady in the eye. "The genie's out of the bottle now... so we're going to have to keep up this charade no matter what happens to Mr. Stockton. The morale of the soldiers, marines, airmen and even the civilians in Springs depends on it."

Thinking the civilian scientist had learned her lesson, Fuentes intervened. "Doctor Hanson, go and check Stockton's vitals and let me know immediately if there are any changes... for the better or the worse."

Hanson, feeling like she was being sent on a time out, cast her eyes down and said, "Right away sir." Then she addressed the General directly. "Once again... I am embarrassed and very sorry for my actions... if I could turn back time I certainly would."

"You and me both, now carry on ma'am," Desantos said dismissively.

Once Hanson was out of ear shot Fuentes continued. "Are you saying we are to *lie* to them? Because this *charade* will require quite a bit of *lying*... and not just the *little white lie* type either," he said, clearly taken aback.

"You used that man like a lab animal and you already lied by omission... in a roundabout way, and for both of your sakes you better pray the agent pulls through," Desantos warned.

"Doctor... General..." Hanson blurted as she frantically burst through the inner air seal. "Mr. Stockton's condition has changed."

Fuentes sensed the first ice pick stab of the migraine probing his brain. *Maybe it's payback for putting six inches of hypodermic in Stockton's brain and prolonging his agony,* he thought as he dug his thumbs into his temples. The doctor flattened his lab coat with both palms and composed himself, fully ready to perform last rites and fire up the cranial bone saw and see what went wrong under Agent Stockton's dome. Fuentes, not awed by rank, went through the air seal ahead of the General.

Hanson leaned over the gurney, eclipsing the patient's upper body and head. After Fuentes angled around Hanson he noticed that the man was still tethered to the bed, but oddly he wasn't fighting his restraints. *That is odd,* he thought, *maybe he is finally dead and didn't really turn after all.* Stranger shit had happened in the world of science. At any rate, Fuentes was going to pick the man's brain, *literally,* and see how Omega had reacted to the antiserum.

"Hanson, check his liver temperature so we'll have a better idea of time of death."

"No need Doctor," Hanson said without looking up from whatever she was doing.

Desantos, clearly agitated, said, "Now is not the time to start doing things your way, *Doctor* Hanson... you are already skating on thin ice."

Hanson backed away from the bed, a wan smile crossing her face. "He's pulled through. I was leaning in so I could hear what he had to say. He wants to know if Gill or Jessie made it out of the airport alive... it seems they were onboard another helicopter. I told

186

him I didn't know." She looked at the General and continued. "And that's the truth... I'm not in the business of lying."

Desantos shot her a chilly look and took Fuentes by the elbow to confer in private. "What's the best prognosis?" he inquired.

"If he's asking questions... with specificity... pretty *damn* good I think. He was gone. *Dead*. No pulse or respiration for six minutes with no oxygen getting to his brain. I am amazed he's even able to talk, let alone hold a conversation or ask questions. It's either a miracle from on high or Omega can be beaten. You can go ahead and speak with him General. It's not going to kill him..." Fuentes offered.

Desantos had to see it with his own eyes. He didn't believe anything could defeat the virus. It even looked like God had thrown in the towel and said, "*No mas mankind, you're on your own.*"

DHS Agent Archie Stockton was hooked to a heart monitor. His heartbeat depicted by moving green pixels steadily and silently blipped along. Desantos marveled at the man's skin tone--it was about the same color as Mike Junior's. This man, he thought, looked healthier than most. Desantos wavered, wondering whether he should try to talk to the big man. *Fuck it*. "Agent Stockton, can you hear me? My name is Mike... I heard you had a hell of a flight from New Mexico. Hanson told me you had some friends and fellow agents that you were concerned about."

Standing on her tip toes, Hanson whispered a quick reminder in the General's ear, "Gill and Jessie are the names of his fellow agents."

Desantos leaned close to the agent and said, "Archie, I understand Gill and Jessie were on another helo."

The mere mention of the fellow agents caused the man to stir. He slowly opened his eyes a crack. "Can you kill the lights?" he said, his voice raspy and hoarse.

"Hanson, extinguish these," Desantos said, pointing at the bank of klieg lights hanging over his head. "How are you feeling Agent Stockton?"

After taking an inventory of his body, the agent said, "My whole body feels like I'm being jabbed with pins and needles... like when your foot falls asleep and then wakes up, only much worse and all over."

Fuentes moved to the foot of the bed and took over the questioning. "Do you remember being bitten?"

The agent shook his head vehemently, denying the doctor's allegation. "No. Not a chance. One got ahold of my shoe while another... a kid. A fuckin' dead kid tried to climb me like a ladder. I remember it clawing my leg and then falling away from the Black Hawk."

Desantos stood silently, hands on hips.

"What else?" Fuentes asked. He noticed the man's heart rate spike.

"Just waking up to the pretty lady's face... that's it."

Fuentes eyed the monitor and said, "Get some rest. I'm going to see that we have some food here for you in case you get hungry."

Holding his hand up, "Can you free me?" the agent asked.

Fuentes remained silent and let the General field the question.

"Unfortunately... not just yet, it's for your safety Agent Stockton. But soon..." Desantos said nodding his head. He hated playing the bad guy when he didn't want to.

"Fuentes, a moment in private please," Desantos said. Then he followed the wiry doctor into the autopsy room.

The rancid-smelling Alpha perked up; its cold emotionless eyes tracked the meat across the room.

Fuentes was growing tired of the operator's brash personality and in-your-face attitude. He stood his ground, looking up at the tall warrior. "*Yes General?*"

"Good work Doctor, but keep this under wraps until that man moonwalks from one end of this tent to the other. I want *you* to make the call. Anything you need to make more of the antidote or... "

"Antiserum," Fuentes said correcting the General.

"Anything at all... get a hold of me personally or Freda Nash if I'm not available. Please keep an eye on Hanson from here on out. No more solo safaris for her."

Desantos' sudden display of respect surprised Fuentes. He shook the General's hand and said, "We will get to work on the next batch right away and I'll be sure to keep Hanson in check. Also I wanted to thank you and your men for rescuing us from the CDC. I wasn't so gung ho about leaving at the time... but it was the right move."

"My pleasure Doctor," Desantos said as he parted the air lock.

"*Hanson!*" Fuentes yelled.

The Alpha cracked every vertebra in its neck whipping its head around to see where the noise originated from.

"Stand down *Archie*," Fuentes said with a small chuckle.

Hanson poked her head through the slats. "Is he gone?" she asked.

"Forget about the General. What you did was incomprehensible. If what the General told me is true... the whole base is riding high on a pink cloud."

With a pained look on her face Hanson silently held her arms to the front, palms up. It was an apologetic show of submission that she used when the words wouldn't come.

Fuentes knew that Hanson's transgression wasn't deliberate and it pained him to discipline her. He had always considered her the daughter he never had. Furthermore she was the hardest working and most detail oriented co-worker he had ever had the pleasure of working with in a lab setting. "Do not let it happen again," he whispered. "Let's get to work. We need to brainstorm and find a way to mass produce enough antiserum to keep the soldiers going so they can clean up the United States. If we are successful then mankind just might survive this little Omega beastie."

Chapter 30
Outbreak - Day 9
Mess Hall, Schriever AFB

It was well after midnight and without a doubt Brook, Raven and whoever else was bunking in the Grayson hut at the moment were fast asleep.

Cade firmly believed the mission wasn't over until his weapons were put to bed wet. He broke down the Remington, swabbed the barrel and cleaned and oiled all of the moving parts with his old friend Hoppe's No. 9. He took his time and meticulously reassembled the sniper rifle, double checking the bolt and the trigger pull. Lastly he inserted a magazine and cycled a few rounds through the high powered beast. His trusty Glock 17 received the same breakdown, cleaning, and scrutiny and then went back into the holster on his thigh. The SCAR didn't require his attention because the only action it saw was the buttstock-to-teeth variety.

Earlier Desantos indicated that he had something to take up with Fuentes and he had set off alone to the research tent. Lopez and Maddox stayed behind with Ari, Durant and Hicks helping them prep the helo for the next day's mission.

Cade decided to go get a bite or at the least some of Schriever's famous paint-removing coffee. Sleep when you die, *that* should be the motto of the Tier-One operator, Cade mused.

***

Cade passed on the eggs. He noticed they were runnier than usual. *Must be getting low on powder.* A handful of health missiles and a big cup of caffeine would have to pass for a meal. The little sausages (that were *not* on Brook's short list of approved foods) were the closest thing to real protein he had eaten in a couple of days. Even doused with a gallon of Tabasco, the bland packaged MREs that had sustained him for days just didn't taste like food.

Good thing Brook wasn't around to cluck her tongue and remind him what ingredients went into a sausage. Being married to a nurse sure had its advantages, and unfortunately its drawbacks. He was thankful the advantages far outweighed the latter. Cade smiled inwardly. He wished it wasn't so late. He badly wanted to see Brook and Raven before he was pulled away on the next op. Lord knows he could definitely use a little company to help take his mind off of the men he had just sent to hell.

The tired operator stopped in his tracks and panned his head, scanning the rows of tables and benches. He was amazed; there were more people in the mess than he had seen at one time since arriving at Schriever.

He resumed pacing through the maze of celery-green tables and chairs hoping to find a familiar face.

Cade noticed electricity in the air and the background noise seemed to have taken on a life of its own--rising and falling in crescendo--punctuated with bursts of laughter and guffaws. Gone was the usual demeanor-killing shroud brought on by mission creep. During the previous week the inhabitants of Schriever were stretched thinner than the only piece of Silly Putty in the *twenty*-kids-and-counting Duggar household. Everyone was running on fumes and so were the aircraft and vehicles.

Cade caught snippets of the different spirited conversations as he wound through the revelry trying to find a place to settle and decompress. It was obvious to him that the word was out, and the possibility that Doctor Fuentes had found a cure was on everyone's mind. To Cade it seemed like a switch had been thrown and everyone in the room had instantly cast off the day-to-day fear of dying and had fully embraced the idea of living--and not just surviving.

Although Cade had been listening in on the comms in the Ghost Hawk he didn't insert himself into the mix. If Mike wanted his opinion he would have asked. Up until now Cade had successfully

191

survived the tightrope walk of dealing with higher ups unscathed and he could see no good reason to jump off of the cable now.

Cade was just happy to see that the people he was fighting shoulder to shoulder with had been inoculated with a shot of hope, because in desperate times like these, with a few hundred thousand dead heading for Schriever, a little bit could go a long way.

"Soldier... Grayson. Over here, grab yourself a piece of pine." Dan waved a Schriever coffee mug to and fro trying to get the operator's attention.

The voice, rising above the others, snapped Cade from his moment of thought. He changed course and headed for the bearded Vietnam vet.

Dan pushed a chair in Cade's direction. It came at him with a nerve jangling squeal. Cade slapped his plate down, putting the sausages in danger of rolling off, and sat down heavily. "Thanks... I needed that."

"Good to see you my boy. Saw you swivel headin' around on auto pilot and thought I could use some company."

Cade tried to laugh but only found the energy for a grunt and said, "That makes two of us."

"Want some more coffee?" Dan reached out; his knuckles looked like they belonged on a street fighter's hand. Had it not been for the grease and grime Cade would have said something smartass and asked about the other guy's face.

"Sure." Cade downed the tepid liquid and handed over the empty mug. "Have them add the caffeine this time please."

"I think they're running low on beans and just burning the water," Dan added, cracking a half smile.

When Dan returned the first thing out of his mouth, even before he sat down, concerned the rumors of a cure. He looked over both shoulders before he said, "So I saw you carrying the top secret folder yesterday... what do you know about this purported cure? I know that you probably can't say anything because I'm not *need to know*, but theoretically if there were an antidote or something... *that would be the best news ever.*"

"Take a breath," Cade interrupted. "If I knew anything that was one hundred percent iron clad the honest-to-God truth... I would not hesitate to include you. *But I do not.*"

"What do you know?" Dan asked.

"I know I'm beat, bone tired and I can't go and sleep next to my wife because I'll wake up the whole family. I didn't have any contact with them for a week after Omega started burning and at times I feared the worst. What a fucking rollercoaster of emotions I stuffed while I was on the *outside*. And now... here I go leaving them on a daily basis with no guarantee I will return. How can I say that I am a good dad and husband when I'm subjecting my family to those same emotions? How can I expect to ever be forgiven for reupping?" Cade put his forehead in his hands for a few seconds and then fixed his eyes on Dan's. "Part of me wants to stay here... and then go to the briefing *without* seeing them. To be honest it will hurt me to see them... because I have to turn around and leave on another op in a few hours."

"You *have to* go and see them. If they can't go back to sleep... it's a few more precious minutes spent. Just chalk it up to what was supposed to be. You *know* you reupped for them. Whether you want to admit or not... *everything* you do... *every* decision you make is for them. Don't forget it. Every second we are on the right side of the dirt oughta be spent living."

Cade squeezed the grizzled vet's shoulder. "Thanks for letting me bend your ear," he said, stealing one of Dan's sayings. "Now I'm going to sneak in and get a couple of hours of rack time."

Chapter 31
Outbreak - Day 9
The House
Jackson Hole, Wyoming

The aroma of maple syrup and bacon filled the cavernous dining room; grand splays of wildflowers were scattered amongst the heaping plates of breakfast meats, scrambled eggs and waffles.

Robert Christian sat at the head of the wide mahogany table seemingly in a trance, staring out the picture window at *his* granite mountains, and with a grand sweep of his arm said, "Gentlemen, look out the window. That is *the* Grand Teton. John D. Rockefeller Jr., Teddy Roosevelt and Grover Cleveland were all great conservationists in their time; they had a vision for this beautiful place. They wanted to keep it pristine and wild. If they knew how many coffee shops were in this valley and that a million overweight and over-consuming tourists rubbed elbows in Yellowstone every year they would be spinning in their graves."

"What are we going to do to stop it from happening again?" Griffin Blackburn asked. He was the fifty-five-year-old heir to the Blackburn fortune, who until now had remained silent, finishing his brunch, wondering why only he, Cranston, Ross, and Buchannon had been asked to stay behind, while the other Guild members boarded their private planes in the early morning and presumably were safely home by now.

"I want us to be better stewards and further their work across New America; every city that we clean out will be preserved as a warning against unbridled procreation and the subsequent wants and needs associated with an out-of-control population. No more grid lock. No more pollution. If any of you doubt my resolve--have Tran take you on a drive down the Teton Pass Highway. There are about a hundred reasons for the population of Jackson to stay in line and give back for the cause. Soon the people will want to stay here... many more will want to come here. They will flock here... in moderation. Gentlemen, Mother Nature just gave mankind a piece of her mind and it was a long time coming. I *will* make sure that we never forget how bad we let things get here on Mother Earth."

Texas oilman Hank Ross drained his Bloody Mary and said in his thick syrupy drawl, "R.C. I gotta hand it to you... this place you picked for the Capital is magnificent. It's like Mother Nature made you a castle with granite ramparts all around. The entrances to the valley are easily defensible. And I see that the air defenses were delivered overnight."

"You don't miss much Hank. Have you seen the airport since you arrived?" Christian asked.

Dabbing at the corners of his mouth, Hank cleaned his white mustache and placed the napkin onto the half-finished plate of food. Tran instantly materialized from behind a hewn oak pillar and silently spirited it away. "Why... did some U.S. military hardware fall off of the truck?" Hank inquired.

"Bishop's boys are paying off in spades. They have liberated a number of fighter jets as well as a dozen attack helicopters," Christian said proudly. "But that's only a start... Bishop cleared the elk refuge of living dead and his men are quickly filling it up with National Guard armor and Humvees. We are very close to fielding a capable army of our very own," Christian said with a flourish.

You are covering your ass nicely, how do we cover ours? Mark Buchannon thought. "So when do we get *our* bombs?" the Dot Com billionaire from California asked. He was the youngest of the group and the most outspoken--always ready with a question even if he thought he knew the answer.

Christian had been waiting patiently for one of the men to bring this up. "That, young man, is a point of contention with me. Somebody bugged this very room... actually my personal assistant

Jarvis found that the whole mansion was full of listening devices and I know for a fact that they weren't here before the outbreak. Besides, who would want to spy on a blowhard, narcissist actor anyway?" Christian's cobalt eyes lingered on each man for a moment before he continued. "Until I know you can be trusted... the bombs will be tucked away for a rainy day--the gold, however, will be distributed as soon as it arrives." *Carrot and the stick*, Christian thought to himself.

Buchannon shook his head. He hadn't expected the offhanded accusation and furthermore it really pissed him off. "With all due respect *Mr. Christian*... how do we protect our sovereignty as part of New America if we don't have the capability to counter anything Valerie Clay can throw at us? I see how well you are protected here: anti-missile batteries, the Spartan army, jets, and helicopters not to mention Jackson's strategic location. I will be in Napa tomorrow nervously awaiting the black helicopters or better yet a hundred and fifty kiloton warhead to turn my valley to glass. What am I supposed to do, throw gold bars at them?"

"You must exercise patience, Mr. Buchannon," Christian countered.

The heavy chair screeched backwards as the brash young man rocketed from his seat and threw his hands in the air. "How would you feel if you were in my shoes?" he asked, his voice a mix of desperation and exasperation.

"*Insubordinate!*" Christian hissed, the veins in his neck bulging.

Strategically changing the subject, former President John Cranston said, "Fine way to send us off Robert, last night's entertainment was fabulous." With a mischievous grin, he hoisted his mimosa in the air and bowed his head. "I especially liked Heidi... blonde hair, splendid... "

"*Enough,*" Christian barked. "For my dystopian vision of New America to come to fruition we all must have patience. The people of Colorado Springs are about to receive a warning that they will not soon forget."

Chapter 32
Outbreak - Day 9
Driggs, Idaho

The fire glowed, a winking orange ribbon over the ridge line separating the gray horizon from the crackling treetops. Colorful exploding embers, like a fourth of July fireworks display, rocketed into the sky.

Daymon risked a glance uphill. The dead tumbled down the steep incline, cartwheeling and bouncing off of the snags and deadfalls, gravity helping them quickly close the distance to where he was kneeling. As the next shambling wave reached the crest of the hill the flames licking at their backs created the illusion that their heads were ablaze. The first waves of monsters were only yards away and they were bursting before his eyes like overcooked bratwurst, their outer dermis and the flesh underneath cooking from the extreme heat.

Still he kept hacking away. The bramble shafts were thick as a toddler's wrist. Every effective swipe of the machete was countered by two that bounced off of the thorny runners.

"Hurry... they're coming," the woman prodded. She was caught deep in the thicket, the shark tooth barbs piercing her alabaster flesh. She was the reason Daymon decided to return home and not go to Eden.

Daymon renewed his efforts. His wrist ached and his right shoulder burned from the constant exertion as he chopped away. He was making little progress--he might as well have been cutting down a sequoia with a butter knife.

Daymon sensed the zombie approaching from his blind side. In one motion he spun on his knee and snatched up the bow, and without sighting shot from the hip. The arrow stopped, buried to the feathers in the walker's cheek with the barbs and shaft protruding from the opposite side. It looked like an extreme piercing gone wrong. Undeterred, the blistered zombie trudged ahead, its taut burnt skin crackling with each step.

Lacking the time to reload, Daymon discarded the bow and fumbled for the machete. With a no look sweeping backhand he decapitated the crispy creature. The blackened body folded in on itself like a well-worn road map while the head, eyes darting, bounced out of sight down the hill.

"Be quiet," Daymon whispered, "or all of them will be on top of us." He reloaded the bow and continued slashing at the robust bonds, trying to free the one he loved.

"Leave me and save yourself," Heidi implored.

"I'm not leaving you again... I'll die first," Daymon promised. He raised the blade but froze on the downswing when a large man-shaped shadow darkened the ground in front of him. He turned his head slowly towards the looming threat.

Hosford Preston stood less than ten feet uphill, fully blocking out the ashy beige sky, naked save for a tattered pair of Fruit of the Looms which were no longer white. His body had suffered from hundreds of bites. Hunks of flesh had been ripped from the dead lawyer's three hundred pound frame, revealing glistening muscle and glimpses of bone.

Without thinking, Daymon dove for the crossbow in a desperate attempt to save them both. When he turned to train the weapon on Hoss it was too late. The polar bear-sized corpse was already on top of him.

Daymon jolted awake and shot up, wild eyed and disoriented. He rubbed the sleep from his eyes, trying to recall his nightmare. He remembered that Heidi was somehow involved, but the absence of morning wood told him that this dream couldn't have lived up to the earlier ones. Duncan had ruined those wonderful subconscious forays, on more than one occasion, by waking him up prematurely. *Asshole.* For some reason Daymon had a niggling feeling that he had been in the grip of a nightmare and Heidi had been in danger. The fact that he was still dreaming about her after not speaking with her in more than a week left him with a little bit of hope.

Daymon swung his legs over the edge of the bed and planted his bare feet on the carpeted floor. Using both hands, he placed the dangling strands of dreadlocks behind his ears and cocked his head. A summer shower hurled a steady patter of rain at the bathroom skylight and somewhere in the distance an engine rumbled.

He threw on his boots and gave them a quick lacing. Since the dead had started walking he had made it a point to sleep fully clothed with his weapons at arm's reach. The approaching vehicle meant that he might have to contend with men--possibly even marauders--so he opted to arm himself with the stubby combat shotgun.

Daymon padded into his living room, glancing forlornly at the flat screen that would surely never display another Utah Jazz basketball game. His stomach growled, reminding him to check his cupboards. He rifled through the dry food finding only graham crackers, Fig Newtons and a half eaten bag of pretzels. Finally he came across something he had been craving for a week. A family size can of cling peaches in syrup was tucked in behind an assortment of Top Ramen noodles. After hungrily wolfing down the fruit he stuffed the rest of the provisions into the Kelty.

The rain slowed to a trickle, little taps here and there, but the engine noise was ever-present. Daymon had a strong suspicion that the Black Hawk had caught the attention of more than just the dead, and he hoped those people weren't searching door to door.

Since the back of Lu Lu was fairly roomy he placed the Kelty backpack, his old beat up Bullard Wildland helmet, an axe, and his backup set of turnout gear behind the second row of seats. *Who knows,* he thought, *fire season isn't over yet and they may come in handy.* He propped the crossbow, stock up, in the passenger foot well and the shotgun, along with the two machetes, stayed within easy reach next to him on the passenger seat.

He listened while the vehicle continued what sounded like a grid search; on more than one occasion sporadic gunshots punctuated the still morning. Daymon couldn't discern if the gunfire was associated with the persistent patrol or just people like him trying to survive. Alone, and with no one to watch his back, he made a mental note to be very cautious; it was apparent that Driggs was no longer Mayberry.

***

The flat black Humvee crept down the street in front of his house. In the pre-dawn light Daymon could see a driver and a passenger. They wore black helmets and black uniforms; on the top of the gun truck a third person in the same attire manned the heavy machine gun. As the truck passed, Daymon noticed, stenciled on its door, a large red star encircled by a constellation of smaller red stars, all of them floating on a field of white. He never had been a very attentive student but he was pretty sure he had never seen that flag in any school books. The possibility that Idaho and Wyoming had been invaded by an army, foreign or domestic, sent a cold chill racing down his spine. Two things struck him as odd: one, they didn't seem very vigilant--like they were bored and only going through the motions. And two, they were riding in an armed vehicle usually only found in the U.S. inventory.

Very grateful that the occupants hadn't dismounted the Humvee and started a door-to-door search, he waited for the sun to rise over the western flank of the Teton Range, passing the time eating stale Fig Newtons and drinking semi-cool water ladled from the toilet tank.

***

Daymon hadn't heard the patrol for more than half an hour. He waited another full hour before deciding it was safe enough to leave his home.

Lu Lu was loaded and her gas tank was nearly half full. Jackson was a hair under thirty miles from his place in Driggs, and most of the driving was going to be through the countryside.

So far all of the walkers that he had seen in Driggs could be counted on two hands. The small city was home to more than a thousand people. During the winter and summer months most of the younger ones worked on the Wyoming side of the Tetons. The ski resorts in Jackson employed them in the winter and Yellowstone Park in the summer when it was jam-packed with tourists who flocked there for the mountain bike trails, camping, hunting, and fishing.

Daymon cracked the curtains and looked up and down his street. A partially eaten corpse was laying on the lawn two houses down. Daymon didn't know the man, but it appeared he had been in the middle of his honey-dos. An overturned lawnmower, its shiny blade glinting in the early morning sun, lay near the remains of his right arm. The dead man's attackers had picked his bones clean, leaving his ribcage resembling skeletal fingers reaching from the ground. Crows were doing their best to finish the job, burying their heads inside, mining the soft bits that had been missed. Other than the feeding birds, the only movement outside was one lone zombie ambling down the middle of the street.

Lu Lu had been garaged for two months but she still started right up. Daymon usually drove the Honda to and from work in the summer months, but in the winter he drove his trusty old 76 International Scout. The bright green and white truck was named after his great aunt Lu Lu. She loved their weekend drives through Yellowstone in the rattletrap. Her pet name for the Scout was Kermit. Daymon abhorred it, and he simply called her Lu Lu, mainly because every stitch of clothing his aunt owned was made of polyester colored much like his truck.

He let the Scout idle while he rolled up the garage door. Daymon surmised that the corpse down the street must have been sunning there for a while because the air rushing in was crisp and clean, not rife with the stench of carrion. He jumped in and slammed the door with a bang--instantly regretting it. Some habits were harder to break than others. Craning his head as he backed out, he noticed his transgression and the engine noise had summoned company. The single zombie was soon joined by two others and the moaning commenced. In seconds a much larger welcoming committee was lurching his way.

Chapter 33
Outbreak - Day 9
Schriever Air Force Base

Cade opened his eyes and took in the surroundings. The inside of the Quonset hut still harbored shadows while outside the sun was just starting its journey through the bluebird sky. He had succeeded at sneaking in at 0200 without waking his family. It was now 0700, and five hours of sleep would have to suffice. He found himself sardined on the bottom bunk bracketed by Brook on one side and Raven on the other; both were snoring. He didn't want to move and risk waking them so he remained still. His thoughts turned to the rumored cure. It was not just a rumor, that he knew--but he was very aware that medical breakthroughs never happened quickly. They most often happened on a glacial pace, after years of research and then after many more months or years of clinical trials. One alleged infected man and one dose of antiserum do not constitute a clinical trial. Unfortunately for Cade, at the moment he saw the glass as half empty.

After talking to Dan the night before, Cade had found that he couldn't quiet the machinery in his mind so he took a long walk around the base and thought about what a cure might mean for his family and the rest of the living population. For Brook, who was pregnant, a cure would mean a brighter future for their baby. Raven would also be able to lead a semi-normal life without having to remain secluded in a fortress behind fences topped with razor wire while constantly watching her back. The pace of life would slow down for him and that wasn't such a bad thing. Even though he lived for the adrenaline rush that walking the razor's edge in combat provided, he could just as soon flick the switch and assimilate back into the family life that he had enjoyed for some fifteen months before the outbreak. He locked that thought away for now. The upcoming mission, which he was due to undertake in just a few hours, had to take priority over everything.

"Daddy?" Raven's dainty voice interrupted his moment of contemplation.

"Yes sweetie," he whispered.

"I was thinking. Schriever is kind of like our own little island... isn't it?"

"Yeah... kind of," Cade said, wondering where his eleven-year-old's mind was steering this conversation. "Why do you think of it that way?"

"I have been reading Swiss Family Robinson," Raven said as she propped herself up on one elbow.

Cade stroked her hair and said, "I read that when I was a little older than you are now. So, who do you think you are more like: Fritz, Eric, or Knips?"

Raven screwed up her face. "Not the monkey... *Dad*." She said *Dad* like he had committed a mortal sin by comparing her to a monkey.

"OK then... how about Eric, he's about your age and by the end of the book he becomes a pretty good shot with the rifle."

Raven's eyes lit up. "I almost forgot to tell you."

"Tell me *what*... " Cade said.

Raven grabbed her dad's forearm to steady him lest the news cause him to roll out of the bunk. In her mind the revelation was going to be earth shattering. "*Mom let me shoot a rifle,*" she said rapid fire as a wide smile spread across her face.

"Did not," Brook said groggily.

"Yuh huh Mom," Raven countered.

Cade remained silent and let the facts present themselves.

"Alright... I confess. I did take her shooting, and I know you probably wanted to do it--you being the professional soldier and all,

SHAWN CHESSER

but you weren't around. In fact, Cade Grayson, you've been gone a lot lately. I'm starting to feel like an army wife all over again."

Cade looked at his arm. Raven still had it in her firm grip and was shaking it like a tree limb. "Raven, if you have something else to tell me please do so before the fillings fall out of my head."

Raven let go of her dad's arm and said, "I left out the best part of shooting the gun."

"I let her shoot some walkers," Brook said, stealing Raven's thunder.

Cade was shocked but didn't let it show. "Raven, this is real important. Look at me."

She tilted her head at Cade and they locked eyes.

After an uneasy silence that he used to process the new information he said, "How did it make you feel?"

Raven bit her lip, obviously racking her brain for the response that she thought her dad would want to hear. "It was bound to happen sooner or later," was her curt response.

That's my girl, Cade thought. "You are *eleven*, Raven; tell me how it really feels in here." He pressed one finger against her tee shirt, right over her heart.

"Kinda icky I guess," Raven said as she plopped her head dramatically on the pillow.

Cade looked at his daughter. She was eleven going on twenty and it was time to lay almost all of the cards on the table. "It's OK to feel that way sweetie, but remember they aren't like us anymore. They are *dead* and they don't feel. They don't know they're going to die. I really think that inside they're happy to be relieved of the burden of walking around bugging us."

"That makes me feel OK with it then, Dad," Raven said in a smart alecky tone.

Cade knew it was Raven's patented way of saying *we'll talk about it later*. He touched his mouth to Brook's ear and whispered, "Can we talk?"

Brook got out of bed, wrapped a sweatshirt around her waist, and followed her husband to a corner of the hut where Raven wouldn't be able to listen in. "I didn't think it would hurt her to

204

shoot one of those things... after all she has been through. You weren't there," she said defensively.

Noticing that his absences had suddenly become a recurring theme, Cade began to feel pangs of guilt. "Honey, I just wanted to say you did the right thing. It was bound to happen sooner or later," he said, parroting his little girl.

Smiling, Brook said, "Now where have I heard that one before?"

Cade winked at her and continued, "I'm sorry to leave you two again..."

Raven interrupted from the other end of the Quonset. "Mom, can we go see Mike Junior and the twins?"

"In a minute, sweetie," Brook said holding up a finger. "You were saying, Captain Grayson?"

"I have to leave in a minute... another pre-op briefing to attend. I'm sorry but I promise that I *will* be back."

"I know you will, I was just venting, and to be totally honest... I'm bored."

"If you need something to keep you busy while I'm gone, see to it that our daughter gets some practice with the Glock," Cade said with a sly grin.

Brook playfully punched her man on the shoulder and then embraced him, showering the big bad Delta boy with kisses. "I love you Cade Grayson."

Cade returned the kisses and said, "I love you too Brooklyn Grayson."

"Gross," Raven wailed and plowed her head under her pillow.

SHAWN CHESSER

Chapter 34
Outbreak - Day 9
Driggs, Idaho

The creatures grabbed at Lu Lu as Daymon slowly steered
her through their ranks. Greasy handprints and gray slime coated the
Scout's green sheet metal front to back. Daymon put the pedal to the
metal after parting the Dead Sea. Two left turns and he was travelling
south on Teton Pass Highway which ran parallel with the Teton
Range. He couldn't believe the damage in the center of the city.
Broulim's supermarket had burned to the ground; sagging metal
girders and the pristine sign standing guard over the parking lot were
all that remained. Across the street the Pines Motel had also been
torched. The main thoroughfare was an obstacle course of stalled
cars and dead bodies, the majority of them riddled with bullet holes.
The foreboding feeling that he was heading into the depths of hell
was getting stronger by the minute. He drove the next fourteen miles
without a zombie sighting and at Milepost 28 he discovered why.
Daymon saw the shimmering black mound from a mile away. He had
no idea what he was looking at until Lu Lu's exhaust note disrupted
the feeding frenzy. The coal black mound broke apart and took
flight. Thousands of crows, ravens, and starlings had blanketed the
missing residents of Driggs whose hundreds of bodies were giving
back to the food chain.
    "Holy shit!" Daymon exclaimed. He had a hard time
wrapping his mind around the sheer numbers of dead splayed out
before his eyes. It was like he was looking at an old photo of the

carnage wrought on the Jews and other "enemies" of the despicable Nazi SS during the holocaust. As he drove past he found it nearly impossible to tear his eyes off of the sight. In the back of his mind he wondered if maybe Heidi was somewhere in the tangle of rigor mortis-wracked bodies.

***

Maneuvering Lu Lu through the "s" turns was like driving a metal mattress. With every change of direction the truck listed considerably. *Must get new shocks*, Daymon told himself. *Or better yet, a new truck.* There had to be millions out there needing a new owner.

The last sweeping right hand turn allowed Daymon a clear view of the city of Jackson Hole, 8,431 feet below on the valley floor. Sparkling like an electric wire, the Snake River wound through the abundant foliage. Teton Pass was only a quarter mile ahead and Glory Bowl stretched up to the left. It used to be one of Daymon's favorite slopes to hike up and ski down. Locals called the post hole-punching slog uphill through knee deep snow "earning the run;" the last few winters he called it too hard on his old knees. Give him a gondola or tram any day.

The winking muzzle flashes shocked the daydreamer back from his youthful recollections and suddenly the Scout's sheet metal was vibrating from multiple impacts. It sounded like someone had thrown a handful of ball bearings at Lu Lu. Thankfully the gunner atop the Humvee had been leading the Scout, and only strafed the road with warning shots. Each .50 caliber round displaced a shovelful of blacktop, showering the Scout's hood and windshield with rocks.

Goddamn it, Daymon thought as he stood on the brakes, making the Scout slew sideways. After bringing the old rig to a complete stop, he thrust both hands out the open window.

Parked in the center of the road, two vehicles blocked his way: the black Humvee with the top-mounted fifty that fired the warning shots and Jackson Police Chief Charlie Jenkin's black and white Tahoe, which sat perpendicular to the Humvee. The Humvee looked identical to the one patrolling Driggs down to the red stars on the white background. Behind the roadblock loomed a wall of burned out vehicles blocking the roadway.

"Driver... throw the keys out the window. And keep your hands in sight," an amplified voice ordered.

"How the *fuck* can I do both at the same time?" Daymon muttered as he removed the keys and tossed them into the middle of the road, never once taking his eyes off of the unwavering machine gun.

He watched with growing apprehension as the Patrol Tahoe backed slightly and then rolled forward towards him. Daymon felt his chest tighten as his body received a blast of adrenaline. He recognized and embraced it for what it was--he was entering the fight or flight mode and he had only seconds to make his life-saving decision.

Daymon risked a one-eyed glance to locate the shotgun in case he had to shoot his way out. *I could blast the driver and back down the hill,* he thought to himself. The plan fell apart when he remembered that Lu Lu's sheet metal was no protection against the machine gun bullets and she sure enough couldn't outrun them... especially with her keys sitting on the ground ten feet away. He came to the maddening conclusion that he had fucked himself yet again.

The Tahoe rolled to a stop next to the Scout and with a soft whirr the driver's window motored down. Daymon couldn't believe his eyes. Chief Jenkins' familiar face stared at him from behind mirrored aviator sunglasses.

"Yo Daymon... what brings you back to Jackson?"

"I just came from Driggs. There's nobody left there, at least nobody living... "

"You saw the bodies then... on your way out of town." Charlie said as he removed his shades and rubbed the dark bags under his eyes. It was more of a statement than a question. Chief Jenkins knew the answer and the last thing he wanted to do was explain to Daymon what had happened to them. He hated the fact that he even harbored the knowledge.

"I saw hundreds of them... *fuck*, half of Driggs was rotting in the sun. Tell me they were all infected... *right?*" Daymon could feel some of the built-up tension leave his body as he waited for an answer. He and Jenkins had a pretty good relationship. They had worked together coordinating wilderness rescues and also on a couple of fires that had been close enough to Jackson to threaten the city. They weren't best friends but Daymon had no reason to distrust the man, but the black Hummer... that was a different story.

Jenkins shot a glance at the Hummer and donned his sunglasses. "*They*... happened to Driggs. Anyone that wouldn't comply and relocate to Jackson...executed on the spot. *Shot in cold blood*, even if they weren't infected."

"Why the black Mission Impossible get up? Dressed the same as those guys... sure looks to this country boy like you're playing for the *wrong* team."

Jenkins fiddled with something in the Tahoe. "*Listen*... I had no choice but to toe the line." Then he changed the subject and said, "You didn't tell me why you came back here."

"When I found out my Moms and Pops didn't make it... well I'm pretty sure they didn't anyhow, because I couldn't get close enough to check on 'em. I had to come here and check on someone," Daymon said, holding his emotions at bay.

Jenkins had an idea but asked anyway. "Who are you looking for?"

After an uneasy silence Daymon said angrily, "I came back here to see if my girl survived this *bullshit*."

"Weren't you seeing that Heidi gal...worked at the Silver Dollar?"

"Yeah, the pretty blonde bartender," Daymon conceded.

Jenkins glanced at the soldiers, and making a show of it, loudly asked Daymon if he had any weapons.

Schriever... here we go again. Daymon thought to himself. "A shotgun and a bow. Why... are you gonna confiscate them from me?"

"Everyone in Jackson has been disarmed. Second amendment... shredded. Constitution... shredded. I need to take the shotgun. You can keep the bow, it's one of the few concessions in New America. I guess they expect us to hunt and feed ourselves this coming winter," Jenkins wondered out loud.

The radio in the Tahoe crackled to life. "Are you going to need help?"

"Negative. I'll vouch for him, he's a Jackson native and he is on the *essentials* list," Jenkins said, trying to sound as if he were in charge even though he was pretty low on New America's totem pole.

"Is he infected?" the soldier on the other end asked.

Chief Jenkins head retreated into the SUV so he could speak discreetly into the microphone. "Negative. I'm disarming the citizen and I'll make sure he gets med-checked when I get to the station."

"Roger that," said the soldier.

Daymon looked uphill towards the Humvee. "Charlie, why don't we just take those guys out... take their Humvee and head west?"

"Don't look up... there are snipers in the rocks above Glory Bowl and they are deadly accurate shooters. It's too risky to run. Just give me the gun and follow me into town."

Daymon passed the shotgun through the window. "I need to get my keys."

"I'm going to turn this truck around and then you can get out and get your keys... *slowly*."

***

After the burnt out husk barely resembling a school bus had been rolled aside, Daymon followed the Tahoe through the roadblock. Cresting the Teton pass he spotted a lone bald eagle soaring the thermals, a normal sight in the valley. Trumpeter swans floated lazily in the lake and a flock of geese took flight as they crossed the two-lane bridge spanning the Snake River. Everything seemed normal in Jackson, and for a second Daymon forgot that America was overrun by the dead--until he saw row upon row of crucified men, women, and children, stretching as far as he could see down both sides of the blacktop. Some still squirmed, straining against the spikes as the crows and buzzards wantonly fed on their flesh. Whoever was responsible for this evil roadside attraction was making one hell of a statement by leaving them to die alone, slowly and painfully, facing one of the most beautiful mountain ranges in North America. Daymon seethed as he drove past no less than a hundred examples of someone's callous disregard for human life. Then he felt a dagger of guilt twist in his gut remembering the way he had allowed Hosford Preston to meet his maker. Finally he made a mental note to steer clear of whoever nailed these Americans to the cross. *I want no part of this New America*, he thought angrily.

Daymon clung to the notion that somehow his girlfriend was still alive, somewhere in Jackson Hole. Except for his folks (who he was sure had already joined the undead ranks), Heidi was the only person left in the world that he cared about. He put the mental blinders on and with that thought in mind, set out to find her...dead or alive.

Chapter 35
Outbreak - Day 9
Schriever AFB Quarantine Hangar

Pug glared at his watch, willing the little hand to move faster. He grew tired of War and Peace and cursed this Tolstoy fellow the second he realized the novel was about a bunch of stuffed-shirt aristocrats. Queens, princes and counts were too much like the governmental ruling class that he had recently grown to despise. How in the hell could the, now mostly dead, population of the United States keep electing and re-electing the same jokers from the same family lineages year after year baffled the fuck out of him. Pug pitched the thick book across the room only fifteen minutes into his mandated twelve hour stay. With a title like that it should have been about battles and shit, he thought.

Pug risked another glance at the watch. *Fifteen minutes.* He sighed and leaned back in the chair, resigned to getting some enforced shut eye.

***

Six hours into his quarantine Pug overheard snatches of conversation about a rumored cure for the Omega virus. Interest piqued, he pressed his ear to the wall in order to glean as much info about the breakthrough as possible.

***

Pug looked at his watch. *Ten minutes.* He quickly laced up his boots and donned his pack. After his incarceration he just wanted to get out of the cell and slink away without a lot of fanfare.

***

Five minutes. Heavy footfalls signaled someone's approach, and before long, the soldier that had spouted the canned spiel in front of him twelve hours earlier was standing by the zippered door about to free him. "Jesus... about time. I'm so hungry I could eat a horse," Pug said. "And Sarge, you better burn that freaking book. War and Peace my ass...what a bore."

The grim-faced soldier ushered him out of the cubicle and ordered him to stand still while he powered up a hand-held thermal scanner. After a few seconds the device beeped and the soldier swept it from the tip of Pug's boots to the top of his head, front, and back.

"Didn't you do this earlier?" Pug asked.

Without warning, the soldier jammed an old style thermometer into Pug's mouth. "Hold still."

After a long minute Pug cracked, "What, the tricorder didn't work?"

"Almost finished," the soldier said, sounding irritated. He checked the mercury and noted something on a chart. "You're good to go."

"Whew! Since I'm not going to turn into a zombie... where can a hungry American get a bite to eat?" Pug said with a grin.

"Not funny," said the soldier, shooting Pug a deadly look. "This is a map of the base. Clearly marked in red are the places civilians *cannot* go while visiting us."

Visiting, Pug thought. *Does he know something he's not letting on? What the hell...* "What's the talk I overheard about a cure?"

Recognition briefly flashed across the soldier's stoic features. "Just hope-filled rumors." Then he pointed to the map. "This is where you sleep. And this is the only mess hall. The base personnel are sharing it with you... be respectful."

"Thanks Sarge," Pug said as he folded the map and turned to leave.

"You're not waiting for your red-haired friend?" the soldier asked.

"Wilson? I'm done with him." Pug said as he shouldered his black bag and headed for the door.

Chapter 36
Outbreak - Day 9
Schriever AFB, 50th Space Wing Briefing

Freda Nash stood front and center looking over the men that held the fate of Colorado Springs in their hands. These last few days had definitely taken their toll on her and it was evidenced by the dark gray half-moons that had formed under her eyes. The petite Air Force officer looked like her head hadn't hit the pillow in weeks. Also the usual piss and vinegar that caused some people to fear interacting with her had all but disappeared. The last thing Major Nash wanted to do was send a single operator into harm's way without the information needed to run the op effectively. Solid intelligence, which was the foundation of any good operation, had been almost impossible to gather since the dead started to walk. Desantos and his men had broken into the White House to retrieve the nuclear football without knowing if the President was still alive, and then Nash had immediately sent them off on the CDC mission to bring back Fuentes and the Alpha carrier without so much as a floor plan or entry codes to the building. Now she was sending the team downrange once again, with nuclear weapons, and no idea where they needed to be deployed in order to destroy the approaching carrion juggernaut.

Time to put on the game face, Nash thought. She took a sip of water and cleared her throat. The mic was hot and the drawn out *harrumph* that reverberated about the Space Warfare room brought a smile from Desantos. "Good afternoon, gentlemen. I am going to keep this on point and move along quickly. After I finish, President Clay will address you all." Nash thumbed the remote and started the vivid picture on the large flat panel moving. An uncomfortable silence ensued--rustling papers and the droning thrum of computer fans the only noise in the room.

Cade recognized the scene for what it was. The panoramic view of the Denver skyline was taken from a fairly low altitude and a long standoff distance. The cityscape disappeared into the background as the optics zoomed out and the camera panned down revealing the full scale of the undead horde. Unlike the gray, grainy feed from the UAV footage taken over Denver the day before, this new color footage was sharp and crystal clear. The biomass of living dead appeared to almost slither down the freeway. The front of the herd, which wasn't as thick with lurching bodies, stretched nearly a quarter mile in front of the main body and appeared to change direction periodically, feinting left and then right and back again, apparently scouting the path ahead.

"This is real-time footage from an orbiting Global Hawk. As you all can see... the dead are still tracking straight for downtown Colorado Springs. I hate to admit that we do not have an accurate count... but our best guess is that we're looking at no less than twenty percent of the Denver/Aurora area population on the screen in front of us. Roughly four hundred thousand is the latest estimate, and though we're not in their direct line of travel, one incoming transport plane is all it would take to get their undivided attention and bring them here."

The picture on the flat screen disappeared. Nash allowed the numbers to sink in before she started the next bit of footage. "This sequence was taken yesterday, hours after the herd left Denver in pursuit of a group of fleeing survivors."

The image sprang to life. In one instant the herd was ambling along bracketed in the center of the UAV's optics. Abruptly the gimbal-mounted camera rotated away from the Denver skyline and zoomed in towards the south. The camera locked on to four fast moving stealth aircraft, tracking them as they passed thousands of feet below the Global Hawk's orbit.

"B-2 Spirit bombers and B-1 Lancers out of Ellsworth, South Dakota... watch closely," Nash said without emotion.

The black aircraft suddenly began spewing wobbly gravity bombs. After a brief free-fall the munitions began to strike earth. The fiery orange explosions walked down the center of the undead herd, destroying thousands of the shambling creatures. The concentric shockwaves and overpressure reduced even greater numbers of the zombies on the periphery of the procession to slower crawling versions of their former deadly selves. After the dust from the bomb runs had dissipated slightly, the UAV slowed and moved closer to the deck as the camera zoomed in for an intimate BDA or Bomb Damage Assessment of the target. Although massive amounts of ordinance had been dropped on the undead army, to the viewers' dismay the majority of the herd continued on its relentless death march towards Springs.

"As you can see, the hundreds of bombs dropped yesterday had very little effect on the dead." The Major looked at the operators silently, wondering how many of them weren't going to live to see another sunset, and then finished her speech. "There is nothing, short of abandoning Springs, that we can do to avoid contact with these unyielding monsters, and that, ladies and gentlemen is why, just like the anti Z operations that are currently being waged downtown, we are taking the fight to the enemy. Any questions?"

The room remained silent. Cade guessed that half of the people in the room were in a state of shock.

Major Freda Nash moved aside, making room for the President.

President Valerie Clay put her hand on the Major's shoulder as a sign of solidarity, then she adjusted the microphone and said, "First off I want to thank you all for putting your lives on the line each and every day. I know that every one of you has lost family members and for most of you... your entire families have vanished." President Clay scanned the room trying to project the empathy that she truly felt and then continued. "The virus that decimated our loved ones has been defeated..." Cheers went up around the room, momentarily drowning out the President's voice. She put her hands in the air, gesturing for quiet, and then continued where she left off.

"…thanks to Doctor Fuentes and Doctor Hanson, both formerly of the CDC in Atlanta. The man that was rumored to be cured is named Archie Stockton and yes, he has recovered surprisingly well. Just hours ago he died… and then started to turn." She paused to let the words sink in. "Thanks to Doctor Fuentes' breakthrough Mr. Stockton miraculously recovered. I want to assure all of you that more of the antiserum is being produced. But only in small quantities at first… so we are not out of the woods entirely. Our hope is… and Fuentes is very confident on this front… that eventually his work with the antiserum will pay off in the form of an antidote. One day we *all* will be inoculated against Omega. And lastly, General Desantos… the United States will forever be indebted to you for this mission that you and your men are about to undertake."

Putting some steel in his spine, Desantos thanked President Clay and humbly deflected the praise onto his men.

"God speed General," President Clay intoned, dabbing away tears. Then she motioned to her Secret Service detail and left the room in a hurry, flanked by the six serious looking armed men.

"Thank you Madam President," Nash offered as the door closed behind the trailing agent. "Desantos, you have already been briefed by Colonel Shrill… I will see you and your men for a debriefing *when* you return. And I want to personally say I am sorry that we don't have as much intelligence for you to go on as you are used to, but I know how good you and your men are at *improvisation*. Isn't that right Captain Grayson," she said with a wink directed at Cade who just nodded silently.

Chapter 37
Outbreak - Day 9
Downtown Jackson Hole

Chief Jenkins pulled into the police station which commanded prime real estate in the heart of downtown Jackson. Daymon nestled Lu Lu in beside the Tahoe.

"Am I under arrest?" Daymon joked, trying to break the tension after the somber drive.

Stone faced, Chief Jenkins stared him down and said, "I had nothing to do with those crucified people."

"Who did?" Daymon pressed.

Jenkins checked over each shoulder before answering. "Spartan mercenaries... they all answer to a man named Ian Bishop. Stay away from him. As a matter of fact... give his men and anyone driving one of those black vehicles a wide berth. If you want to stay alive in Jackson you *have to be useful* and most importantly you *have to fly under their radar.*"

"You never answered my question."

"About what?" Jenkins asked, playing dumb.

"*Heidi,*" Daymon said, pronouncing her name slowly. He sensed that Jenkins was trying to keep something from him.

Fumbling for words Jenkins said, "She got caught up with the wrong people."

"What the fuck do you mean the *wrong people?*" Daymon hissed.

"She was *invited* to a party hosted by Robert Christian at the *House*."

Daymon cracked his knuckles and asked, "*The House*... the big ass mansion on the hill that the asshole action hero actor used to own?"

"Yes, that's the one... but don't get worked up about it."

Shaking his head Daymon said, "It's too late... I'm well past worked up... I'm fucking livid."

"Listen to me," Chief Jenkins said urgently, adjusting his sunglasses. "Don't go near him or the house. Just stay the fuck away... or you will find yourself on one of those crosses feeding the birds."

"Who died and made this Christian guy king?"

"A lot of people died... then he waltzed right in and appointed himself king and *that* is why Jackson Hole is supposedly the Capital of what used to be the United States of America. Robert Christian is calling it New America and he claims to be the President... if that's the title that he's using. But I wouldn't know because I wasn't invited to the inaugural ball." Jenkins removed his hat revealing a deeply receding hairline. "They are fucking serious. Look over there... and there..." he said pointing at several olive drab missile launchers, each as big as an upended school bus and arranged in a ring around the valley. "Those are Patriot anti-missile launchers and they're protecting the entire city from any and all airborne threats."

"What threats?" Daymon groaned. "Only thing threatening me lately has been those stinking walking corpses."

"I shouldn't be telling you this but after what those animals did to the kids I don't effin care. The U.S. Government is setting up in Colorado Springs and Robert Christian has his little army canvassing the U.S. looking for arms and armament to use against them and anyone else dumb or courageous enough to stand up to him. So now you know why I'm walking on egg shells here... we are in the middle of a God damned arms race surrounded by flesh eating zombies," Jenkins said, shaking his head in disgust.

Daymon yawned. "I don't know anything about Colorado Springs," he lied. "Just point me to a place that I can call home and I promise I'll pull my weight... become a part of life here and make the most of the situation."

"Why don't you go back to the fire house? Your stuff is probably still there... and by default you're the new Chief."

"What happened to Chief Kyle and the others?"

"The entire fire crew was on duty during the Omega outbreak. Chief Monsour in Idaho Falls called for help. You know how strong the brotherhood bond is. Kyle and the guys answered the call. Hell... half of Idaho Falls was on fire after all of the looting. The entire crew went to pitch in and not one of them returned," Jenkins uttered solemnly.

"Shit... timing is everything. If I hadn't taken leave I would have been right there with them. As far as the *appointment*... I'll accept but I ain't fighting fires alone," Daymon said flatly.

"You'll get help. Just pray we don't have a summer lightning storm between now and then." Jenkins slipped the shotgun through the open window and placed it in Daymon's lap and said, "Don't get caught with this. Consider it a little insurance... *just in case*."

"Thanks Charlie. I owe you one... probably more. If you need anything... anything at all, just ask," Daymon said as he backed the neon green Scout onto Main Street. *And keep an eye out for Heidi*, he thought. He couldn't believe how peaceful Jackson Hole appeared from the outside. *Looks can be deceiving*, he told himself, as the gears in his head began to turn.

Chapter 38
Outbreak - Day 9
Mack, Colorado

The convoy, forty vehicles strong, ground to a halt near the
Utah/Colorado border. Stopping the metal beast was a long drawn
out endeavor. The resulting cacophony reminded Major Beeson of a
freight train coming into a station. The whine of downshifting
gearboxes along with the squeaking of brakes and the rattling clatter
of idling diesel engines sent Beeson on a mental journey--twenty
years back in time.

***

All of the time spent waiting and constantly drilling for
chemical attacks in the hundred and ten degree heat of the Saudi
Arabian desert had been maddeningly monotonous. Finally, Bush the
first made his pronouncement from on high. Mercifully the
Americans and the stalled ground war machine were allowed to cross
the border. The goal: liberate Kuwait. The convoy that rolled through
the berm that day, 23 February 1991, was no different in sound and
smell than the one Beeson now led. Saddam Hussein had no idea of
the ferocity of the hornets that were about to pour out of the nest
that he had just kicked. The coalition spilled into his country, nine
hundred thousand strong, ready and willing to kick some ass.

Sadly, Beeson, a young sniper, didn't get to fire a shot during
the one-sided, one hundred hour skirmish. After the war he rose
through the ranks, and after several years spent running ops with the
19th Special Forces group, he found himself leading them and

221

serving as base commander over Camp Williams where thirty-six hours ago he and his men were under siege by the undead flowing from Salt Lake.

***

Driven by primordial impulse, in search of food, the zombies began to amass around the base. Eventually, Major Beeson chose to conduct a strategic withdrawal. Under cover of darkness, the forty-five vehicle convoy carrying two hundred and thirty-seven soldiers escaped the base and the dead clamoring for their flesh.

Major Beeson and his men had only been able to traverse thirty miles over the course of the first twelve hours following their emergency egress from Camp Williams. The fighting had been so intense that all of the vehicles in the column looked like they had been painted in a two-tone color scheme: desert tan on the top and blood red on the bottom. After surviving the exodus from Draper and pushing south along the Wasatch front and away from Salt Lake City, the numbers of walking dead they encountered dropped off considerably.

***

After a day and a half spent fighting his way out of the Salt Lake valley and then traversing the backwaters of southeastern Utah, Major Beeson's Bradley sat idling atop a small rise in the middle of I-70 near the Utah/Colorado border. He stood in the cupola glassing the valley in the foreground. A menagerie of SUV's and pickup trucks sat, parked haphazardly, occupying the median and both shoulders of the road where I-70 slithered between two ochre sandstone nubs jutting from the red earth and creating a natural choke point. People moved about in the tree line and shadowy recesses on both sides of the highway. Two black Humvees with top mounted heavy machine guns, definitely not U.S. issue, sat parked side by side defiantly blocking the road.

What troubled Major Beeson most was the fact that so far this encounter on I-70 didn't have the same welcoming feel that they had received from the smattering of survivor communities encountered so far on their arduous cross-state journey. Looking through his high powered binoculars he could see that nearly every

person on the other side of the valley was armed with either a long
gun or some kind of assault rifle.

Beeson keyed his mic. "Samuels, get me a range to target."

Staff Sergeant Samuels pressed his face to the optics mast.
"Range... six hundred meters sir, be advised contact approaching
eleven o'clock. Looks like a ... *moped*," he replied over the comms.

The lone man maneuvered his scooter across the grass
median and motored up the hill straight at the lead Bradley.

Beeson lowered the binoculars and extended his arm palm
up, silently ordering the driver to halt.

Three SF soldiers from the 19th dismounted their Humvee
and with a flurry of movement detained the man, checking him for
weapons.

"Bring him forward," Beeson ordered.

One of the SF soldiers escorted the man to the front of the
Major's truck.

Beeson climbed down from his elevated position and seized
the initiative. "Sir, I need you to deliver a message to your friends
down there." The major, who possessed a full head height advantage,
approached the young man and stood near enough to invade his
personal space; Beeson's stony stare never wavered. "Tell them that
they must put down their weapons and pull the gun trucks aside so
we can pass without provocation. Any other actions will place each
and every one of you in harm's way. Consider this your *only warning*."

The slender young man looked like he could still be in high
school. The faux hawk hair-do running down the center of his head
the dead giveaway to his age. He was visibly trembling as the
enormity of the situation hit him in the chest with the force of a
falling anvil. The men in black had thrust him and the rest of the
survivors into the middle of this confrontation, and from the number
of men and machines that were gathered on the back side of the rise,
the townspeople from Mack and the seven New America soldiers
with their two measly Humvees were vastly outnumbered.

"Sir... I'll tell the NA soldiers exactly what you said," the kid
stammered.

Major Beeson arched his eyebrows. This was something
entirely new. First the dead walk and now some militia starts a land

grab. What's next, he thought, flying pigs? "NA soldiers?" he asked. "Now... why don't you take your time and fill me in, son."

"Can't I just go now?"

"What is your name, son?" Beeson said firmly.

"Dawson," the boy whispered.

The Major gripped Dawson's shoulder and said, "I will let you go *only* after you tell me *everything.*"

Dawson drew in a deep calming breath before he spoke. "These armed guys showed up here a couple of days ago. They told anyone that would listen that it was the politicians and the government who were responsible for releasing the virus on the population. Honestly sir... I was already fed up and that's all it took for me and the others to get on board with their New America concept."

Beeson glanced across the valley. The assembled survivors seemed content for the moment, apparently awaiting the return of their emissary. "What *is* their concept?" Beeson asked. He already knew how to win the hearts and minds of a populace and turn them to his side. Beeson learned the art years ago during the four-week-long Robin Sage exercise in North Carolina. It was the grueling fourth phase of the Q course that all SF recruits participated in. Beeson had put the learned skills to use on numerous occasions since and he had a feeling these NA guys were operating from the same playbook.

"They told us they were here to help us fight off the rotters and all they wanted in return was our consent to use the town as their garrison. It seemed like a pretty fair trade to all of us at the time. We had already taken care of most of the zombies by ourselves and were in the middle of setting up barriers on the roads leading in and out of Mack. The soldiers pitched in and helped... at least *they* were true to their word in that regard."

"Listen," Beeson said, "I know Mack is in the middle of nowhere but did it not occur to you that because your town sits on the Utah/Colorado state line it becomes that much more valuable from a strategic standpoint?"

The young man suddenly tensed and turned the tables on the Major, answering a question with another question. "Where was the

224

government when we were losing our people left and right? My *mom* and *dad* both got bit and turned into one of those fucking things. *Where were you and your Army then?"*

Beeson removed his helmet and plowed his gloved hand through his sweat-soaked, closely cropped gray hair. "Son... we were *all* up to our necks in this shit show now aptly named Omega. I am done pussy footin' around. You made your bed... now you are going to sleep in it. Get your ass down there and deliver my message."

Without speaking the kid turned and shakily mounted his underpowered plastic Honda and motored towards the blocking force.

Beeson yelled down to the Humvee, summoning one of the rough looking SF soldiers. "Sergeant Mackay, get on the horn and tell Springs about this New America militia and set up some security while I sort out this cluster."

"Yes sir," replied Mackay.

"Someone get Scully up here!" Major Beeson bellowed to no one in particular and watched through his binoculars as the retreating scooter wobbled and bucked across the packed earth separating the highway.

Staff Sergeant Scully skidded to a halt next to the Bradley and stated, "Sir. You called for me?"

"Scull, I need you to set up quickly. If my first message isn't well received... then I want you to deliver the follow up," Beeson said, still glassing the valley for hidden shooters.

"Copy that sir," Scully replied, while from a hard case he removed a wicked looking long gun with an enormous scope mounted to the top rail; then, as if the gun wasn't intimidating enough, he attached an eight inch suppressor to the business end. The gangly SF sniper worked silently and efficiently. He flicked down the bi-pod legs and removed the dust caps from the optics and began adjusting for elevation and windage. All of this took him less than a minute.

Dawson jumped off the scooter even before it had stopped moving, sending it skittering on its side producing a cloud of dust and debris, and sprinted between the assembled civilian vehicles at full speed arms and legs pumping.

"Scull, I want the person in charge to be target number one. Whoever the kid takes the message to--that's your man. Then take down the remaining soldiers first and any other combatants second." And after a brief moment of thought he added. "If the townies rabbit...hold fire and let them go. Poor bastards got themselves stuck between a rock and a hard place."

Already busy calculating ranges to individual targets, Scully calmly replied, "Copy that sir," and then trained the cross-hairs on the man he suspected as being the leader.

Even if these citizens had been coerced by the NA forces there was no way Beeson was going to order his column to turn around and try to find an alternate route. He had already determined that he was going to have to make a statement here... but he was troubled, struggling to determine the amount of force he should employ. *That's going to have to be decided by their actions,* he told himself. Looking to his gunner, he ordered, "Samuels, target the Humvee on the right and fire on my command. The Humvee on the left is your secondary target."

Samuels repeated the orders and said, "Copy that sir."

Across the valley a conversation ensued between the emissary and one of the black-clad soldiers. Beeson counted five NA troopers standing among the black Humvees and two more manning the vehicle-mounted guns. The one-sided shouting exhibition ended with the uniformed NA trooper punching Dawson, knocking him to the ground.

A sustained burst of crackling gunfire echoed from the rear of the armored column.

Beeson noticed the soldiers and citizens across the clearing visibly stiffen, surprised by the reports. *You're not under attack... yet,* he thought. Putting the binoculars down he keyed his mic and said, "This is Lobo Actual... I need a situation report, are there any casualties?" The last thing he needed was to lose any more of his men to the Z's. The slog south of Salt Lake had claimed dozens of his soldiers and at the time he feared that he and the men under his command weren't going to get out of the valley alive.

IN HARM'S WAY: SURVIVING THE ZOMBIE APOCALYPSE

"Lobo Three-Two, we had Z contact at seven o'clock. We have fifteen bodies down, repeat, one-five Tangos down. We have no friendly WIA or KIA. How copy?"

"Good copy, *that is music to my ears*, Three-Two. We should be Oscar Mike in five... Lobo Actual out." Beeson glassed the rear of the convoy and noticed several dismounted soldiers milling about, but thankfully the only zombies he could see were lined up next to the road unmoving. Satisfied everything was under control, he returned his attention to the front.

Beeson pressed the field glasses to his eyes and said, "Fire at will Scull."

The sound the bullet made as it left Scully's Remington at more than 2,600 feet per second was barely audible to those nearby. Consequently, the bullying NA trooper who was standing by the door of the Humvee didn't know what hit him. A fine spray of pink mist blossomed around his head as his body disappeared behind the black Humvee. Then three things happened simultaneously: the civilians, looking like teenagers running from a busted kegger party, bolted to their vehicles. Both machine guns atop the Humvees opened fire, spitting poorly aimed .50 caliber tracer rounds uphill, and Beeson gave Samuels the order to fire.

Scully targeted the gunner on the right first. The supersonic Lapua round killed the man and effectively silenced the booming .50 caliber. As he sighted on the next gunner the deafening cannon erupted atop the lead Bradley, sending a barrage of 25 mm shells downrange, and before the SF sniper could pull his trigger he watched the Humvee on the left disappear, engulfed in a maelstrom of orange flames and cooking-off ammunition. The NA soldier's corpse, still gripping the machine gun, jerked once and then began to melt before Scully's eyes.

Beeson ordered his men to cease fire and quickly assessed the situation. Frantically trying to get away from the burning hulks, the other vehicles below were turning around and speeding away out of sight over the crest of the hill. "Lobo Actual, message received... let's roll." The road weary officer didn't know if his response was the right one--and it was going to eat at him for a long time, but he had vowed to himself when they rolled through the horde of living dead at Camp Williams that he was going to see as many of his men to Colorado Springs safely as he could or die trying. It made him sick to his stomach that he had already let down a few of his men. They wouldn't be going home but he was still going to write the difficult letters that every commander despised. Almost more distressing than having to write the condolence letters was the sobering reality that more than likely there wasn't anyone left to receive the correspondence.

***

It took the forty vehicles from Camp Williams fifteen minutes to file by the still burning Humvees, the heat emanating from them causing the air to shimmer and dance. Both crispy NA gunners sat frozen, fully embraced by death, looking like they had tangled with a fire breathing dragon.

The Major decided to leave the wreckage and bodies in place as a reminder to everyone that the U.S. military was still a force to be respected.

***

Beeson's boys rolled through the town of Mack, Colorado. The business district consisted of an old fashioned drugstore/ice cream shop, a couple of uninhabited greasy spoon diners and a lonely rundown tavern--its darkened neon signs teasing the thirsty sleep-deprived soldiers with the empty promises of cold beer and fine spirits. In the blink of an eye the shadowy store fronts were behind them and the convoy was in the midst of the residential area on the east side of town.

Major Beeson couldn't believe the reception they were receiving from the few remaining townspeople. Thanks to the propaganda being spread by the NA soldiers, he and his men were greeted with animosity, angry sneers, and middle fingers. Thankfully the curse words and epithets hurled their way were drowned out by the noisy metal machines.

Beeson hailed Springs on the net to inform them of his contact with the New American troops and the town folks of Mack, Colorado. Colonel Shrill in turn warned the Major about the undead herd and gave him a rundown of the impending operation meant to destroy them.

IN HARM'S WAY: SURVIVING THE ZOMBIE APOCALYPSE

Bone tired, hungry and nearly Winchester on ammo, the 19th SF soldiers trudged on, their final destination: Colorado Springs.

Chapter 39
Outbreak - Day 9
Schriever Air Force Base
Colorado Springs, Colorado

Pug left the quarantine facility without so much as a
backward glance, walking briskly but not fast enough to garner any
undue attention from the many soldiers and airmen in uniform. His
first order of business was to distance himself from the misfits whose
lives he had saved--they had served their purpose--now he had to
discover his.

As Pug navigated the base, he periodically stopped to
surreptitiously recon his surroundings while pretending to consult the
simple map given to him after being released from the mind-
numbing quarantine. After spending ninety minutes snooping
around, he was fairly confident that he could move about the base on
the paths least likely to be patrolled by security personnel.

Pug found the food in the mess hall barely eatable and the
civilians' living accommodations, which were nothing but a hastily
erected tent city with portable Honey Buckets for shitters and no
running water, highly unacceptable. Schriever was no Embassy Suites,
but hopefully, if everything fell into place, he wouldn't have to
endure this Boy Scout's nirvana for very long.

Earlier he had discovered two things during his brief stop in
the shared mess hall: the rumor of a cure held more credence than
the grumpy Sergeant had led him to believe, and then there was the

minor inconvenience, coming in the form of a few hundred thousand walking dead on a collision course with Colorado Springs.

On his way out of the mess hall he passed a bank of silent pay phones. The light blue AT&T logo reminded him of his long dead Smartphone and just how far and fast society had fallen. No more Google searches to see who starred in what inconsequential movie. No more e-mail for the masses. No more apps. No more Facebook--he didn't even know what that was, but someone was surely going to miss it. *Shit,* he thought with a smirk, *people are going to have to start reading paper books again.*

Pug stopped at the last phone in the line and, feigning curiosity as an airman walked by, picked up the receiver. As he did so, he scratched a two inch vertical line into the soft brick wall next to the phone's privacy enclosure.

He took a covert look over his shoulder and slipped the steak knife that he had just stolen from the mess hall back into his pocket.

***

Pug chose an empty tent in a deserted corner of the base where hundreds of the canvas shelters had been set up in the days after Omega. By his estimation barely one-fourth of them were inhabited. To Pug it was obvious that the virus had been much more deadly and had spread throughout the population much faster than the government's predictions. He shuddered to think how bad it had been in New York, Chicago, and Los Angeles. *Who knows,* he thought smiling, *maybe I'll get to find out.* This was the man's big break; he was finally going to be *somebody* and he did not want to screw it up.

When Pug pulled back the canvas flap and stepped onto the plywood floor, memories from his youth came flooding back. The smell inside of the tent instantly reminded him of the dingy gray straight jacket with the sturdy metal buckles that he had been forced to wear whenever his foster parents wanted to *play* with him.

He tossed his hooded sweatshirt on one of the many cots, unzipped his bag and retrieved the Camelback bladder. After draining off the water he slit the bladder open with the purloined steak knife. It wasn't the sharpest tool on the base--*kind of like him*, he thought with a grin, but it did the trick.

The two pieces, still wrapped in plastic, slid out easily. He had taken the heavy duty freezer bags from the dead hoop star's house the day before and they had worked perfectly at keeping the water out.

Pug took the bigger piece out first, unwrapped the small pistol and placed it on the taut, cold-war-era canvas cot. The six inch silencer was in the second baggie. The can spun effortlessly onto the end of the compact pistol. After placing the gun into his waistband near the small of his back he was out the door.

***

Pug put one hand up to shield his eyes against the mid-afternoon sun as four noisy Chinooks followed by two smaller black helicopters thundered across the base before disappearing behind the tallest of the distant hangars.

He turned his attention to the courtyard. *The coast is clear,* he thought to himself, and then he strolled nonchalantly in front of the bank of worthless payphones. A shiver rocketed up his backbone; there was an identical horizontal scratch intersecting the vertical mark he had scribed thirty minutes ago. *The word was out,* he thought, *I have arrived.*

***

One hour later

Pug wandered around in the predetermined area before he spotted the telltale white rock at the base of a withered rose bush. He bent to one knee acting like he was examining the flora, while his free hand stealthily removed the hollow aluminum spike from the soil. *Right where it was supposed to be,* he thought. He had just executed a perfect dead drop exchange without anyone the wiser.

***

Pug took every precaution to ensure that he wasn't followed, doubling back, stopping abruptly and even going so far as sprinting back and forth through the tent city before slipping into his chosen abode.

You did it. The voice was back.

Pug sat on the rock-hard cot, still sweating from stress and exertion incurred avoiding the imaginary agents. Then, after a moment basking in the glow of his success, he opened the hollow spike, unrolled the piece of paper stashed inside and paused before reading the orders. He wanted to remember what it felt like to still have his anonymity. What it was like to be able to move about without everyone wanting to talk to him--pick his brain and ask about his exploits. The second he looked at the paper and read the words, his mission would be clear and his destiny revealed. Pug would be a rock star. *Here I come to save the day,* a child-like voice resounded from deep within his tortured mind.

Chapter 40
Outbreak - Day 9
Schriever Air Force Base
Colorado Springs, Colorado

Instead of accepting a ride on the Cushman with Desantos, Gaines and Lopez, Cade opted to walk from the briefing facility to the flight line. The thought of stopping by the infirmary and saying goodbye to his family one last time crossed his mind but he quickly dismissed the idea. Instead, he used the time to clear his head and start the difficult process of compartmentalization. Raven, Brook, and the peanut-sized fetus in her womb meant the world to him, but always before he went on a mission he said solitary silent goodbyes to his loved ones, tucking all of his thoughts and feelings for them deep into his subconscious. The ritual pushed all of the fears and what ifs into the background as well, leaving him free to act solely on instinct, training and a good amount of muscle memory.

***

By the time the flat black Ghost Hawks came into view he was locked down mentally and mission ready. Tice, the CIA spook, walked around the tail boom of the closer of the two SOAR choppers and greeted him with a nod and a wave. He had on his usual Detroit Tiger's ball cap but had changed out of the military ACUs. Instead, he had on a well-worn pair of blue jeans and his ballistic vest cinched tightly over a colorful Tommy Bahama's shirt. The man looked like he had just stepped out of a Hollywood casting

234

call for a Magnum P.I. remake. The only props missing were a big bushy mustache and a red Ferrari 308.

Returning the nod Cade asked, "What is it, casual Friday?"

"No, I figured I'd dress like a spook today," Tice said as he did a slow pirouette, showing off his getup.

Cade wasn't impressed. "So you're going to stand out like a bullfighter's cape... *and* you're tagging along again?"

Cracking a big grin and patting his pistol like he was on one big safari, Tice replied, "How in the hell could I miss out on an opportunity like this? Besides... I gotta have *something* interesting to tell the grandkids."

What bunker is your family safely tucked away in? Cade thought to himself. "So you're sold on the cure thing huh? Gonna have a big brood and live 'til the ripe old age of... pick a number, any number." Cade didn't allow him the time to answer. "That's a pretty cavalier attitude. I, for one, am not going to let the idea of a cure take the place of vigilance... and I suggest you do the same."

"I'm only trying to keep my mind off of the task at hand. Nash ordered me to come along and arm the devices when it's time. Shit... don't get me wrong, it's nothing but bravado and stupidity that's holding me together, and in case you are curious... I *am* wearing my *Depends.*"

That final crack broke the ice, causing Cade to smile. "Have you seen Desantos?"

"He was putting his kit in the helo the last time I saw him," Tice stated. "Hey man... I can't wait to get into one of those sand rail jobs. Are those things as fast as they look?"

"Faster," Cade replied, "and if Cowboy's driving... I hope you brought an *extra* pair of those Depends."

"Hell yeah..." the spook said enthusiastically as he walked away.

Making his way around the Ghost Hawk, Cade was forced to step over one of the ground crew, who was laying prone, readying the bird for flight.

"These helos need more upkeep than all of the Housewives of Beverly Hills combined," the man said as he sensed Cade nearby.

SHAWN CHESSER

Cade didn't get a chance to respond. Mike Desantos had called his name from somewhere out of sight, requesting his presence in the hangar adjacent to the tarmac.

When Cade located Desantos the man was in the middle of the monotonous task of reloading the magazines for his MP7.

"How many more do we need?"

"Only six, which means we will both have ten. Three hundred rounds apiece... that oughta do it... you think?" Desantos said tongue-in-cheek.

"If it doesn't, then we need to go back to Q and qualify all over again."

Both men laughed at the notion of a thirty-five year old and a dinosaur the General's age going through that grinder again.

"Cade... I've given this a lot of thought. This is my last rodeo. I am done. Finito. No mas."

"Sir, if anyone in the spec-ops community... or at least what's left of it, deserves to hang up his spurs, it's you."

"Thanks for your permission... I feel better already," Desantos said halfheartedly. He pinched the bridge of his nose and absentmindedly adjusted his tactical helmet. Somewhere outside the wire a murder of crows cawed angrily, no doubt fighting rapaciously over someone's carcass. After an uncomfortable silence the General continued, "I had a tough decision to make and if it were fifteen months ago it would have been a no brainer."

Cade knew exactly where this was going.

"I am going to recommend that Captain Gaines take over command of the Unit... he'd be a fine leader. Hell, he already is. That fucking mission to get the Alpha from Bethesda, *that* was a cluster fuck going in and he shoulda lost more than the seven operators. No slight on you, Wyatt, but you are still getting back up to speed." Desantos looked his good friend in the eyes and held the gaze.

Cade didn't feel the need to say anything but he opined anyway. "For what it's worth... Ronnie is the best choice for the command, Mike, no hard feelings here, friend."

"Well damn Wyatt, once again, I am glad that you approve," Desantos said with a wink and then collected the magazines and his

236

suppressed MP7 and strode purposefully towards Jedi One-One saying, "Let's get this goat rope into the air."

***

With a thunderous cacophony the Four Chinooks lifted into the air, the whomping of their twin rotors echoing off of the prefab buildings. Special Operations LSVs, or Light Strike Vehicles, were internally stowed inside three of the dual rotor helicopters. The fourth helicopter carried a chalk of Rangers and a trio of the three hundred pound nuclear devices, strapped down safely inside of the cargo hold. The Rangers of the 75th would be available as a quick reaction force if the mission was compromised or to help secure a landing zone if a medevac extraction became necessary.

As the Chinooks crossed the wire, the noise and rotor wash disturbed thousands of feeding blackbirds which took flight at once, momentarily blotting out the sun, wings flapping to escape the noisy metal monsters.

"This Alfred Hitchcock moment was brought to you by Night Stalker aviation," Ari Silver quipped as he waited a tick for the angry flock to dissipate so he could power the wasp-like Ghost Hawk into the air.

"Mike, did I already miss the Scrabble banter?" Cade asked Desantos as his stomach started to breakdance when the helo rocketed into the air.

"Yes... but I didn't... and Limo is still not a word according to Durant," Desantos answered, rolling his eyes.

Durant flashed an enthusiastic thumbs up as Ari banked the ship hard to starboard.

With a firm handhold on the bulkhead and looking more than a little bit green, Tice asked, "Do you guys ever get used to these G-forces?"

"Those are *not* G-forces, gentlemen," Ari said, talking over the inboard comms. "I got to ride a catapult launch off of the Reagan... in the back seat of an FA-18 Super Hornet... now *those* were G-forces. I quickly discovered that I was a *puker.*"

"*You... a puker?* I would have never guessed the way you bounce us over the tree tops trying to make *us* toss our cookies,"

Lopez intoned. "Now you know how sick I was carrying that dirty *demonio* up the stairs in the CDC. *Madre...*"

I wonder if Lopez is ever gonna get over that, Desantos thought to himself.

Tice hijacked the brief moment of silence. "While I have everyone's attention, let me talk about the devices. I wanted to rig them to detonate remotely but the fail safes are such that they have to be set up in place and *then* the codes can be inputted. These warheads were designed to be delivered on a cruise missile... so I did my best."

"What are the codes?" Desantos asked.

"I made it real easy to remember in case I go down... Independence Day..." Tice waited for one of the men to ask him when it was so he could good naturedly bust someone's balls.

"7-4-1-7-7-6," Maddox stated, "easy enough."

"No, it is not as easy as it sounds. You are not going to be able to roll the things off on the move and simply scram. The devices are in two pieces: the timers that I MacGyvered and the warhead itself. I know what I am doing... because I've worked around these things for a while, and even *I* couldn't mate the two pieces in less than three minutes."

Lopez couldn't keep quiet. "That's a lot of time to be in the middle of a Z swarm..."

"All the while trying to focus on the task at hand," Cade added.

"Best case scenario... how long will it take one of *us* to mate and arm the bombs?" Desantos asked.

Tice shifted in his seat to look directly at Desantos before answering the question. "That, General, depends upon how close to the herd you want the bombs."

"You are the expert. You tell me. How close do they *need* to be placed to decimate all of the Z's?" Desantos pressed.

"I would have to see them up close and personal... the herd that is," Tice stated.

Desantos mulled over his options. He didn't have the opportunity to gather all of the necessary info before the mission. The closer the herd got to Springs, the deadlier the fallout from any detonation would be... assuming the wind patterns worked in their favor. If the wind funneled down the valley, which was a rare occurrence, then it didn't matter if the detonations happened in Denver or ten miles outside of Springs... they would all be irradiated. The bottom line was, they really were flying by the seat of their pants, and that is exactly why he requested the silenced special ops sand rails be brought over from Fort Carson. The 10th SF boys had been using the stealthy, heavily armed dune buggies to a great advantage on their Z clearing ops north of Springs. Getting in close and quiet would be paramount if they were going to be able to take out the entire herd of dead with just the two five-kiloton devices. Desantos decided at that moment to do a real time aerial recon of the herd. "Ari, we need to buzz the walkers before you take us to the staging area."

"Copy that General. Durant, have you seen my nose plugs?"

Durant played along, "They're probably back in your billet next to the Costco-sized jar of Vicks Vapor Rub. You D-Boys are probably used to smelling the rotters by now. Night Stalkers... we pride ourselves in operating *above* the stench."

"You *prima donnas* better take us low," Desantos ordered.

Passing by on the starboard side of Jedi One-One, above eye level, rose the gigantic monolithic red rock formation known as Castle Rock.

"Walkers on the port side," Ari said.

Cade felt the Ghost Hawk slow as Ari took them alongside the herd at seventy-five feet above ground level. The smell was indeed intense.

In unison the walkers slowly panned their heads in order to see the semi-silent helicopter. White faces tracked the helo as the herd continued along I-25.

The scene reminded Ari of the old footage he had seen on the History channel where Russian soldiers filed lockstep past Khrushchev or some other long dead premier, marching stiffly, faces submissively turned towards their superiors in the stands.

"Why do you think they are following the Interstate?" Maddox asked Desantos.

Desantos obliged. "They're following the leader. We got to see the UAV footage of the start of this exodus yesterday. Some of it might be attributed to snippets of memory... we all spent a good chunk of our lives in a car, in a rocket seat as kids and then driving ourselves everywhere. Not to mention the fact that most people, even when they are still living and breathing, fall victim to the herd mentality."

Maddox bobbed his head up and down in agreement.

"I think the overpasses are the way to go. We place the bomb in the center... I will arm the device and then we'll call for egress," Tice stated. He focused on something outside and then asked, "These stone mounds on the right side... what are they called?"

"Castle Rock," Ari answered.

"That formation is in just the right spot to contain the blasts *and* provide a little bounce back. Call it a double whammy on the horde. The trick is going to be timing the movement of the Z's. If we don't pop them at *just* the right moment then we are going to have *glowing* walkers showing up at Schriever."

Ari waited until he was sure the spook was finished talking and then said, "I paced them at less than two knots. That means the main body is moving between one and two miles per hour... give or take."

"Put us down and we can hash it out," Cade said, obviously itching to get it done.

Ari's voice overrode the comms. "Gaines just called in, wondering where in the H- E- double-hockey sticks we are. His words, not mine. He's got the buggies offloaded and devices loaded and they're ready to go. Over the comms it sounded like Captain Gaines was eating potato chips... I was salivating at the thought and I had to ask him."

"*Well*, what was it Ari?" Lopez inquired.

"Popcorn... don't ask where he got it because he wouldn't tell me. He is saving some for us though," Ari stated.

"I'd love to see any one of you try and eat popcorn near those Chinooks," Sergeant Hicks, the door gunner/crew chief, quipped.

That last visual brought laughs from all of the men.

Desantos was glad to see that his operators were loose and ready to go.

240

Chapter 41
Outbreak - Day 9
Castle Rock, Colorado

Two minutes had elapsed between the Z over flight and CWO Ari Silver's God awful singing that was currently violating everyone's eardrums. "*Let's all go to the lobby. Let's all go to the lobby and get ourselves some treats...*"

"Make him stop," Lopez begged.

Ari brought the stealth chopper around the back of the well-worn five-story movie screen and settled her next to the cinderblock projection/lobby building.

Although Cade hadn't been to a drive-in theater in years, he still thought fondly of the Foster Drive-in back in Portland. It had closed and was out of business before Raven was born but the place had always been a favorite haunt of his and Brook's when they were younger.

Three of the Chinooks were already gone, headed back to Schriever; the fourth Ranger-laden helo was just spooling up, preparing to lift off and orbit at a discreet standoff range in case the third device was called for or the Rangers were needed to backstop the Delta team.

Cade exited the Ghost Hawk, instinctively ducking under the spinning rotors and formed up next to Captain Ronnie "Ghost" Gaines with the knowledge of the man's impending promotion safely under wraps inside of his head.

"Captain," Cade said in greeting.

"Captain," Gaines nodded.

Desantos, Lopez, Maddox and Tice--who was holding onto his Detroit Tigers ball cap to keep it from getting diced by the rotors--all sprinted from the Ghost Hawk towards the waiting LSVs.

Quietly, the Ghost Hawk leaped skyward, accidently sandblasting the operators assembled in the center of the immense parking lot. Ari was given the order to loiter and wait for Desantos to call the exfil request.

"We'd better hurry if we're going to get to the northernmost overpass before the lead element of the herd," Tice insisted.

"Do you have an idea of how far apart we should place the bombs?" Desantos asked the CIA nuke specialist.

"Those buggies I'm guessing are pretty much bare bone and don't come equipped with an odometer... if they did that would take the guesswork out of the equation."

"They don't," Gaines replied after double-checking the gauge cluster.

"We'll just have to count the blocks between overpasses then," Tice stated.

"There are roughly twelve blocks in a mile," Maddox offered up.

"Alright, lock and load... we already have visitors."

The walking dead, attracted by the raucous Chinooks, were amassing outside of the tall privacy fencing near the *Castle Rock* drive-in marquee.

"Comms check," Desantos said into his mic, and since this operation was hastily conceived, he told the men to use their names for the duration.

The other operators also checked in verbally.

"Since we have Tangos at the gate let's take the back route. These places used to funnel people around after the movie if I remember right," Desantos said, as he gunned the engine and spun the tires, spitting gravel on Maddox and Lopez in the second LSV. Cade rode above and behind his commander. The position allowed him to shoot the mounted M249 SAW, or Squad Automatic Weapon, a full three hundred and sixty degrees; strapped in next to Desantos was three hundred pounds of instant glass-producing nuclear death.

Maddox goosed his buggy, forming up behind, yet slightly out of range of Desantos' grit spewing tires.

The third LSV, driven by Gaines, had the second device strapped into the passenger seat and Tice riding high in the gunner's seat.

They came to the rear exit gate which was locked up with a tightly wound length of chain and a heavy duty Master Lock. Maddox jumped from the driver's seat, bolt cutters in hand. Even though he was the team's best lock pick, he was just going to brute force this lock. There was no need for finesse. Twenty seconds later the gate was open and the three LSVs blazed through.

Cade was amazed at how quiet the buggies were. He watched a cone to the front of the LSV, panning the machine gun left and right. He spied three walkers: one a *first turn* that he couldn't discern the sex of, and the other two newly-turned male zombies. They ambled onto the road one hundred yards ahead. Stealth wasn't necessary here, so he engaged them with two buzz-saw sounding bursts from the M249.

The ripest zombie of the three disintegrated from the breastbone up after the lethal lead encounter with ten buzzing 5.56 mm rounds. The other two Z's were punched to the ground, each taking their fair share of the second, twenty round burst.

Desantos wheeled around the downed creatures and steered the speeding vehicle towards the jagged Rocky Mountains dead ahead. On their right the afternoon sun caused the Castle Rock formation to glow orange, making it look like a miniature version of Australia's Ayers Rock.

The three vehicle convoy was forced to take a left at a zombie-choked intersection. They wound single file past a host of dead bodies, smelling sickly sweet after some time in the elements, and drove around a wrecked Suburban with a still-flailing zombie stuck underneath.

"Next right should take us over I-25," Desantos informed the others.

A series of clicks answered back.

"Desantos, this is Jedi One-One."

"Go ahead Ari," Desantos said.

"I have a feed from the Global Hawk and the freeway looks clear if you want to make a speed run for the far overpass. The herd is about a third of a mile north from there and closing," Ari stated.

"Copy that. Keep the info coming Night Stalker." Desantos' sudden burst of speed caught the others by surprise and they struggled to keep pace.

Good thing this rig isn't a Cushman, Cade thought, the memory of the ride with the maniac still fresh in his mind from the day before.

***

Schriever AFB Satellite Warfare Room

The creatures were still on relatively the same path as they had been since leaving Denver. The HD color feed from the Global Hawk allowed Major Nash to keep tabs on the mission taking place forty miles to the north; whether the drone was going to survive the twin nuclear blasts had been a matter of contention between her and Colonel Cornelius Shrill since they had hatched this hastily thrown together plan. The fighter-jet-sized, unarmed surveillance drone which had the capability to loiter over an area gathering real time data for hours on end was flying a circuitous racetrack pattern directly over Castle Rock. The high tech aircraft was supposedly shielded against EMP, or Electro Magnetic Pulse, the circuit-frying surge of electricity that was capable of shutting down most things electronic.

Colonel Shrill was still old school and didn't trust the modern battlefield gadgets that the military had become so dependent on in the last few years. He had a strong feeling the blasts were going to turn the drone into a hundred million dollar paper weight and he reminded Nash about their wager every chance he got.

The drone was going to survive according to Freda and she couldn't wait to see the cranky base commander eat crow. Whatever the case, she had her eyes glued to the flat panel monitor, anxious to see what hole cards fate was about to deal the human race.

244

Chapter 42
Outbreak - Day 9
Schriever Air Force Base
Colorado Springs, Colorado

Pug paused momentarily outside of the fifteen-story structure. He looked both ways along the white metal walls that seemed to go on forever. The base map in his hands indicated that this was one of the places that civilians were forbidden to go. The white tent pulsating directly in front of him was large, not circus tent large, but it was still dwarfed by the cavernous airplane hangar in which it had been erected, and strangely it seemed to be calling out his name.

The only security were two soldiers in white bunny suits lounging near the other end of the hangar. Pug remembered being processed the night before in the very same building.

Time to forge my destiny, he told himself. *Go big or go home,* the other voice told him. It had been talking to him more than ever since the outbreak and had really been driving him since he embarked on this journey. *I'm on a mission from God.* He didn't know whose voice it was but he remembered the line from a Blues Brothers movie and it made him laugh.

He ducked into the living, breathing tent before his laughter got him caught. Once inside, his nose was instantly assaulted by the unmistakable smell of death. Strapped to a gurney, less than ten feet away, the naked, decomposing zombie hungrily eyed him.

"You gotta be fucking kidding me," Pug said aloud. "Put something on would ya... a nice thick body bag would suffice."

***

I-25

Desantos deftly maneuvered the small LSV between the walkers and stalled vehicles. Some of the cars had grabbers inside so he was careful to keep the vehicle at least an arm's length away as he passed.

He nosed the buggy up the off-ramp and brought the vehicle to a sudden halt. Gaines pulled up next to him. Desantos put a pair of armored Bushnells to his eyes and said, "The north overpass is coming up. This one is too close so I think after we place the first device up ahead we need to go back and put the other device on the overpass behind us."

"I concur," Gaines said. "Tice was telling me the same thing as we were following you. He estimates the two overpasses are a little over a mile apart."

From the gun seat in the rear LSV Lopez let loose a burst from his silenced MP7, stitching a female zombie from the navel to the forehead. Her dome popped off, spewing sun-cooked brains on the ramp before she teetered and fell, rolling like a log down the embankment. The creature had been stalking them through the foliage beside the freeway and more were shambling their way.

The walkers were onto them. Even though the LSVs were very quiet, the total absence of any other noise made the engine and exhaust notes carry for blocks. There was no way they were going in stealthy so Desantos ordered his men to go all weapons hot.

***

Schriever Research Tent

Doctor Jessica Hanson entered the air lock door backwards, coffee in hand. *Success!* She was getting better, not one drop spilled. Jessica was suddenly startled and surprised to see a man standing near the autopsy table, his back facing her. He was shorter than she and when he turned to face her a tingle of warning scaled the base of her neck. His face was completely flat except for the lightning bolt of a nose, obviously broken multiple times.

"Can... can I help you?" Jessica stammered.

"I'm lost. I just got out of quarantine down the way and I'm clean... I swear," Pug said, putting his arms in the air in mock surrender. "I was hoping to find the civilian sleeping quarters and some food," he lied as he slowly lowered his arms and felt his pocket to make sure the map was hidden away.

Despite the man's ex-con looks, Jessica felt the urge to help him... and always a sucker for a stray, caved to the impulse. After a moment of thought she tilted her head and said, "I was going to wait for Doctor Fuentes to come back and help me wheel Archie over to the infirmary. Fuentes is the brains behind the cure... you *have* to meet him." Jessica mentally scolded herself for talking but she was still so excited about the prospects of the antiserum and Archie had been OK for quite some time now... *Too late Jessica... once again there's no way you can take back your words now*, she thought to herself.

Pug smiled, displaying his jumbled teeth and said, "I would *love* to."

"I have a proposition for you... a trade off of sorts," Jessica said.

"What is it?" Pug asked, sounding intrigued. The voices in his head screamed *yes, yes, yes!*

"Help me with Archie and I will show you around the base."

"Sounds like a fair deal... after all, I'm prone to getting lost. Why is this guy Archie here anyways?"

"Archie survived a bite," Jessica said dramatically, arching her eyebrows.

"A dog bite?" Pug asked, playing dumb.

"No," Jessica said conspiratorially. "He was bitten by an infected creature. He had the Omega virus in him and he started to turn. The doctor's antiserum brought him back."

"Really?" *Kill her now...* "Is there enough for everyone that gets bit?"

"Not yet... but we're working on it. Come on, I'll introduce you to Archie. He's a real nice man." Jessica turned and headed for the far inner air seal leading to the makeshift recovery area.

***

Eastern fence line
Schriever AFB

"The gun will rise slightly from the recoil so keep both hands on the grip... like this." Brook stood behind Raven, arms wrapped around her, showing her daughter how to correctly hold the compact Glock 19. "This long thing on top is called the slide. It comes back really fast so you have to keep your top hand out of the way or you'll get pinched. OK... the safety is on the trigger. I'm going to stand behind you. You put your finger on the trigger, aim and shoot when you are ready."

Brook backed away a few paces.

Raven's hands wavered slightly.

Bang.

The pistol jumped and Raven jumped, but the pop can didn't move. Brook was pleased to see that her petite eleven-year-old kept her grip firm and still had possession of the gun. "I only loaded six rounds but the gun can hold fifteen if you need it to. Take your time and shoot until the slide locks open."

Raven spaced out the shots. The third time was the charm, the Coke can which was sitting on the ground ten feet away suddenly flew backwards with a new hole in it.

"I got it!" Raven said excitedly with a big toothy grin.

"Good shooting sweetie... are you ready to try shooting at some Z's?"

"Not today," Raven answered anxiously. "Can we go see Carl and Mike Junior instead?"

"Annie, Mike Junior and the twins are back in their quarters now, but we can stop by and see Uncle Carl," Brook said, stroking her daughter's hair.

"OK. Let's go Mom."

***

I-25 Overpass

The three LSVs sped down the off-ramp and followed I-25 to the northernmost overpass.

"Multiple contacts," Desantos warned the others as he stopped the buggy at the west end of the four lane span, undid his harness and hauled his frame out of the low slung go kart on steroids. He raised his MP7 and dropped the nearest two zombies with precise headshots. Behind him, on the east side of the overpass, one of the M249's let loose with a long drawn out burst. Risking a glance backwards, Desantos noticed Tice and Gaines manhandling the first device out of their LSV while Lopez laid down heavy covering fire. Tice, in his unmistakable Hawaiian print shirt, quickly got to work mating the two bomb components.

Three minutes, Desantos told himself as he looked at his Luminox wristwatch. Then he turned his attention back to the encroaching Z's. "The head of the pack is almost on top of us!" he yelled into the mic between bursts from his MP7. He changed mags and fired thirty more rounds in a matter of seconds. The expelled brass danced on the roadway, tinkling like tiny wind chimes.

Gaines drove the buggy around so when Tice was finished he would have an unobstructed field of fire with the top mounted M249, and while Tice programmed the firing mechanism Gaines brought his suppressed MP7 into the fight. He was firing controlled three round bursts down range, dropping flesh eaters in their tracks. "Jesus, Mary and Joseph," Gaines exclaimed into his mic. The staggering amount of walking dead made his head swim and the stench emanating from them instantly made his eyes water. The undead procession lurched forward, seemingly unstoppable, shoulder-to-shoulder across the eight lanes of I-25. He shook his head in disbelief when he realized how far into the distance the ambling column reached.

Desantos looked at his watch. *One minute left.*

Cade had been kneeling next to the LSV squeezing off controlled three round bursts with his MP7. He had already burned through his fifth magazine and he could feel the heat radiating from the stubby weapon's barrel. The zombie corpses stacking up at both ends of the overpass made him wonder how in the hell they were going to get off of this death trap. *I guess we're going to see how off road capable these things really are,* he thought to himself.

"The device is armed," Tice alerted the team over the comms as he climbed back into the LSV.

"Thirty minutes... on my mark... three, two, one... *mark,*" Desantos said quickly over the comms.

Cade stopped shooting momentarily and when he heard Desantos say "mark" he started his own countdown timer. The big numbers on the face of his Suunto started rolling backwards at an alarming rate. It was sobering knowledge that when the readout hit zero the harnessed power of the atom would be unleashed and the mushroom cloud would bloom upwards, carrying radioactive soil roiling into the beautiful Colorado sky. As an afterthought he took note of the wind's direction. *West to East... the best case scenario.* Cade emptied his MP7 into the walkers, once again changed the magazine and then he clambered into the gunner's seat.

"*Let's go, go, go,*" Desantos bellowed as he powered the buggie into a half-cookie and gunned it towards the pile of bodies.

"Don't forget we have the second device onboard," Cade said to Desantos seconds before they went airborne. The LSV landed awkwardly on the other side but remained upright thanks to its racing suspension and wide wheelbase. Desantos fought to keep the speeding vehicle under control and pointed it south.

Cade ripped into the advancing dead with the M249, raking them head high, back and forth. He expended one hundred rounds with only four short pulls of the trigger while the brass cascaded from the weapon in a shiny bronze arc. He swiveled the smoking gun around and checked their six just in time to see the other two buggies take flight and clear the carrion wall.

The LSV unexpectedly skidded to a complete stop. "Z's twelve o'clock," said Desantos, concern evident in the tone of his voice.

When Cade faced forward, the scene before him turned his stomach. The intersection was teeming with walking dead--among them a dozen pre-school-aged kids. The undead four- and five-year-olds, still tethered together for their last eternal stroll, were already crawling onto the front of the LSV frantically trying to get to

Desantos. They were too close for Cade to engage them with the mounted gun so he let go of it and scrambled to bring his MP7 to bear.

The horrific scene unfolded two feet from him in slow motion. As Desantos reached for his MP7, one of the little creatures got a hold of his gun hand while a second zombie latched its teeth onto his forearm.

In a millisecond Cade's world was rocked. Starting with the girl in pigtails who was chewing on his friend's arm, he put a bullet into each preschooler's brain.

"They were just kids... like Sierra and Serena!" Desantos hollered as he clutched his bloody arm.

"Mike... take off your belt and use it as a tourniquet," Cade ordered.

Tracers from Lopez's M249 zipped inches from Cade's face. The bullets chewed into the encroaching zombies, expelling hunks of putrefied flesh and dermis into the air. He walked the fire along their ranks, granting Cade enough time to trade places with Desantos.

"Get out... you're gunning. Time for some payback," Cade said through clenched teeth as he climbed down.

Desantos was able to get out of the driver's seat on his own power, yet he required Cade's help to climb up into the gunner's seat.

"Strap in Cowboy," Cade said. He knew he had to keep talking to Desantos in order to keep the man from going into shock. He hoped that his friend was one of the infected the doctors called a slow burn because they still needed the time to set up the second device, arm the thing and get back to Springs. He got on the comms and alerted Ari about Desantos' condition and asked for an immediate extraction. Then Cade raised Springs on the comms and broke the bad news about Desantos and the upcoming emergency extraction. Together they decided that Gaines, Tice, Lopez, and Maddox would stay behind with the LSVs until Tice was done synching and arming the second bomb. Then the team would hitch a ride back to Springs with the Rangers onboard the Chinook, leaving the buggies behind.

***

Schriever AFB

Nash moved closer to the flat panel display. She was puzzled by the LSV's sudden stop and equally troubled, when, after a few flashes of gunfire, Desantos and Cade swapped places. Relief washed over her as all three vehicles started moving, zippered through the encroaching Z's and continued south on I-25. *One down, one to go,* she thought to herself.

***

I-25

The three LSVs tore ass along the Interstate which was virtually free of walkers--for now. Once they arrived at the south overpass, Tice and Gaines hopped out and immediately went to work. Together the two men removed the bomb components from the LSV and carried them to the sidewalk, finally setting the two heavy pieces next to the guardrail. The other two vehicles were parked, one at each end of the overpass, providing security as Tice worked diligently at assembling the device.

Cade swiveled his head and scanned the sky, looking for their ride back to the Air Force base. "Hold on Mike... the dust-off is inbound... you *are* going to make it..." Before Cade had finished reassuring the stricken operator, Jedi One-One was in a hover, directly overhead, blasting them with rotor wash. Suddenly from overhead, staccato bursts of hot lead belched from the Ghost's whirring minigun, raining death from above on the living dead.

"Jedi One-One on station," Ari's reassuring voice stated as the helo touched down.

With help from Gaines and Lopez, Cade strapped Desantos into the Ghost Hawk and then found a seat for himself. He removed his tactical helmet and donned a flight helmet so he could communicate with the flight crew.

"How fast can you get us to Schriever?" Cade asked Ari.

"Less than eight minutes. Hold on," Ari warned the occupants of Jedi One-One.

The helo banked violently and accelerated faster than it had ever been pushed. Fifty feet below the black helicopter a torrent of colorful vehicles with glints of glass and chrome thrown into the mix blazed by. Cade stared at the hypnotic stream with Doctor Fuentes' antiserum front and center on his mind, and although he had been a skeptic all along, for Desantos' sake he hoped that he was dead wrong.

Chapter 43
Outbreak - Day 9
Schriever AFB Infirmary
Colorado Springs, Colorado

With a hollow thud Jessica Hanson crashed the rickety hospital bed into the swinging door and with Pug's help they muscled it over the threshold and into the infirmary.

"Easy," Archie Stockton implored. He had awoken during the squeaky trip across the base, dismayed to learn that he was still strapped to the bed. "Refresh my memory... when are these coming off?" he said, nodding towards the leather wrist restraints.

"Sorry, you were asleep and I didn't want to wake you," Jessica said apologetically. "The cuffs were just a precautionary measure. Fuentes said I could remove them *only* if you woke up and were still *normal.*"

"Keep it down. Some of us are trying to get some rest. I've been standing around all day and I am bushed," Carl intoned, still face down on the massage table, unaware that the sheet covering his back was splotched technicolor red and yellow where fabric met raw flesh. "*Joking*... will someone please get me another book?"

"Who are *you*?" a bedridden man asked. Intravenous lines snaked from his right arm and a bedpan took up the real estate on the table by his head. Without allowing Jessica or Pug time to reply, he prattled on: "My name's William. I'm worried sick. I haven't seen my partner since yesterday. Can one of you check around and see if

Ted Keller is still alive... I hope those monsters didn't get him. *Please, Doctor?*"

The door swung shut, closing with a thud at the same instant Jessica Hanson's eyes rolled into the back of her head.

William's face registered shock as he watched the doctor's face track straight for the collapsible side rail on the wheeled bed as her limp body collapsed forward, and with a resounding crack hit square on, a fan of blood spraying his white sheets. Jessica Hanson came to rest face down on the floor. Two small entry wounds behind her ear wept blood, feeding the crimson puddle rapidly forming around her head.

One, two, look at the goo, the voice in Pug's head sang with a sad cadence.

Archie Stockton watched the smoking barrel hovering a foot above his head slowly track downward and come to rest on his forehead.

"*Hey Awwrchie!*" Pug teased the helpless man in his best Edith Bunker voice. "Whoever wants to *live* raise your hand?"

Archie Stockton's big biceps bulged as he gamely fought to free his arms from the restraints. The gunmetal brushed warm on his skin. It was the last sensation he would experience before death embraced him once again. The pistol coughed twice. *Three, four, alive no more.*

Carl played dead and watched the rivulets of red course across the floor, like a river's tributaries, inches in front of his downcast face.

"*Don't do it!*" William begged, stick thin arms reaching for the sky.

Do it. Do it. Do it. The voice was getting stronger, more forceful. Pug leveled the silenced .22 at the groveling man and pulled the trigger twice. The small subsonic bullets left pencil eraser-sized stars an inch apart on William's forehead. His body went limp and his left arm crashed down, catapulting the stainless steel bedpan across the room where it landed with a resonant clatter.

Five, six, hit the bricks.

Pug marched across the floor and yanked the hanging cotton room divider. It slinked open, running on the rails inset into the ceiling. The sound reminded Pug of a Slinky walking down a flight of stairs. He clinched his fist angrily. *I could never get one of those things to work,* he thought to himself. Then he saw the woman, wild eyed, her face bruised and battered. She was laid up in the last hospital bed. "And who might we have here?" he asked in a sing song voice. Glancing at the blue Air Force uniform hanging near the bed, Pug put two and two together. "Ahh, you're in the Air Force?"

The woman shakily nodded an affirmative.

"Thanks for your service," he said in an insincere monotone voice before the .22 chugged twice, sending two bullets into her left eye. *Seven, eight, I feel great,* the voice sang. "Now about that book you requested, my incapacitated friend. How about *To Kill a Mockingbird?*" Pug pressed the silencer to the back of Carl's head and squeezed the trigger two times in quick succession. *Nine, ten, you're dead my friend.*

The clear liquid poured from the bottle with throaty glugs as Pug skipped around the room, wetting every surface. *A Slinky, a Slinky such a wonderful toy...* He paused and stole one last look at his handy work, the five dead bodies in various death poses causing a pleasant chill to trace up his leg, and then he tossed the lit book of matches over his shoulder. The resulting whoosh said *mission accomplished* in his mind.

***

Schriever AFB Parade Grounds

"Raven, sweetie... I have a real bad tummy ache. I'm going over there to find a bathroom," Brook said, pointing to the Base Affairs building. And then holding her stomach she went on: "You run ahead and see if Carl needs anything."

"OK Mom," Raven said enthusiastically, fully grateful for the newfound responsibility and trust she had earned the last few days.

Brook made a mad dash for the toilet, wanting this to be just a bout of diarrhea. The pain felt entirely different--almost like *really* bad menstrual cramping. Then her sixth sense started to tingle and she began fearing the worst.

Chapter 44
Outbreak - Day 9
Schriever Air Force Base

Here I come to save the day. The voices repeated the mantra over and over as he rushed back to the research tent where he had met the sweet Doctor Hanson and the big lug Archie Stockton.

By the time he reached the puffed out tent, the fire engine's shrill sirens echoed among the prefab buildings. He stopped, thoroughly winded, and put his hands on his knees. He hadn't run this much since he escaped Las Vegas ten days ago. And before that probably some training hoops he had had to jump through at his last job in the *old* world. *That one was fun,* he thought, *shooting people and getting paid for it. Those two Blackwater rogues had to go and ruin it for all of us.*

He entered the *breathing* building quietly, silenced pistol tucked away in his waistband. Once inside, ventilation fans drowned out the sounds of the emergency vehicles responding to the conflagration at the infirmary.

The Alpha writhed on the gurney in the ante room, hungrily eyeing the piece of meat that had just walked through the door.

"I'll deal with you in a minute," Pug promised the squirming zombie who hissed back as if it understood every word.

Doctor Fuentes stood in front of a bank of computers watching multiple readouts on three different monitors. On the table next to him a centrifuge whirred rhythmically, honey-colored vials diffusing the stark sterile light.

SHAWN CHESSER

"*Ahem*," Pug cleared his throat rather dramatically.

Fuentes slowly turned at the waist with a half-eaten Oreo cookie clenched between his teeth. "Cam I helf you," came out along with a fine spray of chocolate crumbs.

Pug's eyebrows jumped an inch. "Tell me about the cure..."

Chapter 45
Outbreak – Day 9
Schriever Air Force Base

Ari finessed the screaming Ghost Hawk fifty feet off of the deck pushing two hundred and fifty-five knots. It had only been six minutes since Desantos' hasty exfil and now they were less than a minute out from Schriever. Ari radioed ahead that they had a WIA incoming, told them it was General Desantos and that they would be delivering him directly to the medical hangar where the quarantine area and research tent were housed.

Cade was staring, still transfixed on the ribbon of I-25 when the column of desert tan Bradleys and Hummers flashed by briefly under the port side.

"Ari... any idea what unit we just overflew?" Cade queried.

"19th Special Forces... man, have they been through the wringer... came through the Rockies from Utah earlier today."

"Then those are Major Beeson's boys down there... solid commander. He taught me how to shoot," Cade replied.

Desantos opened his eyes and said, "I thought *I* taught you how to shoot, Wyatt."

"Cowboy, you taught me everything I know... relax, we're almost home," Cade said as he tightened the belt around the infected arm. He noticed that not only was Desantos' forearm cold from the tourniquet site on down to his fingertips, but the rest of his extremities were cooling as well. *Not good,* he thought to himself worriedly.

"I'm cold... and hot at the same time," Desantos said making eye contact with Cade. "You *must* kill me before I turn."

"Roger that, Cowboy, you have my word," Cade said, feeling the emotions he had sequestered earlier punching holes in his resolve. "Don't worry... I'm not going to let the man on the pale horse take you."

Desantos closed his eyes and his head lolled back and forth as Ari reared the chopper's nose up and side slipped her around the tall hangar, almost belly landing the bird before the wheels had fully extended.

***

50th Space Wing Command

Freda Nash had watched the entire Bin Laden raid unfold in real time, and even when the helo went down she wasn't half as worried as she was now. At the time she had had no idea who was aboard the Stealth Hawk that day in May, but she knew that Desantos was in the Ghost Hawk right now, life hanging by a thread. The Keyhole Satellite tracking Jedi One-One steadily beamed the image to the flat panel in front of her.

Nash later learned that Mike Desantos was in fact onboard the Stealth Hawk along with SEAL Team Six when it went down and *had* survived the Bin Laden raid in Abbottabad, Pakistan. But she harbored a strong suspicion that her friend was not going to live to see another sunset.

Nash watched the ongoing mission on the second flat panel. The CH-47 pilot held the bird in a pinnacle hover above the overpass with the rear ramp yawning open, then the helo's back wheels gently touching the guard rail. It was one of the most difficult maneuvers to perform in the big dual rotor helo and the pilot was making it look easy.

She couldn't be sure but it appeared that the second nuclear device was wedged between the vehicles and the operators were trying to reach the hovering chopper on foot.

Z's were crowding the men from both ends of the overpass. Flashes winked from the guns wielded by the brave men she was praying for.

"Springs, this is Gaines. The device is armed and we are on the move. How copy?"

"Nash here. Good copy... Good job and God's speed boys."

On the other screen Jedi One-One was just crossing the west fence.

Worried, Nash broke protocol and tried to hail Ari. "Jedi One-One I need a sit rep. How is the General?"

She was greeted with silence.

**

Schriever Air Force Base Research Tent

"That's your story and you're sticking to it?" Pug asked, disbelief coating his words.

"This is all of the antiserum we could produce. This isn't Pfizer Laboratories," Fuentes said scathingly, sweeping his arms at the vinyl-walled tent.

"Good," Pug said as he swept the centrifuge still bristling with golden vials onto the rubberized floor. The machine bounced, shattering the test tubes into thousands of pieces and splashing the antiserum across the floor. Pug raised the silenced pistol and took a step closer to the wiry Doctor. "Any last words?"

Fuentes stood up straight and said, "If you destroy all that we have worked so hard to achieve... then I hope there is a special place in hell for you."

The flat-faced killer smirked as he shot Doctor Fuentes once through his open mouth and again in his right eye. *Eleven, twelve, I am going to hell.*

While Pug searched for something flammable to *"cleanse"* the area, he heard a distant helicopter and also sensed the tent vibrating around him. He found several bottles of isopropyl alcohol and began emptying the contents on the computers and medical equipment arranged around the inside of the tent. The immobilized zombie received a few extra splashes of the fast-drying liquid. Pug hurriedly lit another book of matches and tossed them onto the creature's chest, then stood transfixed as an ethereal blue flame danced around the monster and then raced down onto the floor following the trail of accelerant around the tent. Pug heard rapid footsteps approaching

SHAWN CHESSER

from the quarantine end of the hangar. He only had seconds to escape but he wanted to see the zombie burn. *Go. Go. Go!* the voices implored. He heeded their advice and trotted back to his civilian sleeping quarters. Along the way, mingled with the sounds of sirens and people running to and fro, he heard a female's voice say *"twelve minutes"* over the base wide PA system.

Chapter 46
Outbreak - Day 9
Schriever Air Force Base
Colorado Springs, Colorado

With Desantos' limp body draped over his shoulders in a fireman's carry, Cade trudged along the walk heading for the research tent. Out of necessity and fearing for his friend's life, Cade finally began seeing the glass as half full. *The antiserum had better work,* he said to himself, or *Fuentes is going to have some explaining to do.*

Cade rounded the corner, accidently dragging his friend's head through the waist high shrubs lining the walk. Desantos reacted by letting out a guttural moan.

"*Stop right where you are!*" a voice barked, echoing off of the towering hangar walls.

Cade stopped walking and looked up, trying to determine who was shouting at him.

Three men dressed in white cleanroom suits fully blocked the walkway with their guns drawn.

Cade swayed back and forth under Desantos' weight and said, "Put the guns down, I have an injured man here." Just then, he noticed that the doorway in the far distance behind the men was belching flames and smoke.

The men approached cautiously, eyes scanning ahead, with their guns held at the ready. Upon noticing the Captain's bars on Cade's ACUs and that he easily outranked all three of them, the clean suit trio stood down and pointed their weapons towards the ground.

"Captain, have you seen *anyone* running this way?" the nearest man called out.

"No, but you might want to follow these," Cade replied, gesturing to the wet boot prints leading off in the direction he had just come from. "Can one of you run ahead and alert Doctor Fuentes that General Desantos has been infected and needs the antiserum?"

"I'm sorry sir... but we're pretty certain the doctor is dead... the whole tent is involved and it is burning *hot*. The person responsible is still on the loose."

"How about the infirmary, is..." Cade searched his memory for the woman's name and it finally came to him. "Is Doctor Hanson around? I am *losing* this man," Cade sighed as he gently lowered Desantos' body to the cement walk.

"The infirmary went up in flames first, Sir. We can't find Doctor Hanson either. There is a good chance the same person started both fires."

Cade instantly lost his legs and crumbled to the ground when the soldier mentioned infirmary and fire in the same breath. He feared for his family's safety: Brook and the baby, Raven, Carl--they might have all been in there.

"*Whoever started those fires just signed my friend's death warrant and I want him to be held accountable!*" Cade bellowed at the soldiers, frothy spittle flying from his mouth. "*Go and find the motherfucker... and take him alive. That is a direct order!*"

"*Yes, Sir!*" the men shouted in unison, before they tore off following the trail of sticky antiserum.

Chapter 47
Outbreak - Day 9
Schriever AFB, 50th Space Wing

The Global Hawk continued to orbit ten miles from the stretch of I-25 soon to be reduced to one immense smoking crater, and hopefully with it a few hundred thousand living dead. If the two five-kiloton bombs did what they were designed to, Schriever wouldn't have to be abandoned.

Major Freda Nash watched the scrolling red digital clock counting down the final few minutes. She had just witnessed the Chinook carrying the remainder of the Delta team along with her longtime colleague Agent Tice cross over the outer edge of the blast danger zone. The helicopter was flying low level at maximum speed and only minutes from touching down. Both of the fires on the base were almost under control but the full extent of the loss of life wouldn't be known until the ashes were sifted through. Most troubling was the fact that she hadn't yet received an update on the General's condition.

***

Cade knelt on the ground and removed Mike's tactical helmet, then he wrapped his arms around his friend's muscular upper body and heaved him into a sitting position.

Desantos coughed violently, showering Cade's chest with saliva. Beads of sweat cascaded from his face and Cade noticed that his body had changed temperature yet again. Minutes ago he had felt cool to the touch--now he was super hot--almost too hot to touch.

Cade sighed, accepting the fact that his friend and mentor was going through the final stages prior to reanimation.

With his right hand cupping the back of Desantos' head, Cade drew his face near enough to whisper in the dying man's ear. "Remember our pact?" *No response.* "You took care of Brook... now I will do the same for Annie and the kids... to the best of my ability."

An unintelligible groan escaped Desantos' lips.

With his free hand Cade unsheathed the Gerber combat dagger. "I promised that I wouldn't let you become one of them... and I promise that your death will be avenged. I love you brother..." Cade slid the razor sharp seven-inch blade effortlessly between the vertebrae at the base of Mike's neck and pushed it deep into his brain. After a slight shudder, Mike "Cowboy" Desantos' final breath caressed the side of Cade's neck.

Cade stared at the rolling countdown on his Suunto until it reached zero. He didn't expect to hear the bomb blast immediately, but continued holding Desantos' lifeless body, with his friend's hot blood coursing down his forearms fully turning his blouse dark crimson.

Three minutes and twenty-eight seconds after his watch zeroed and a distant claxon started blaring, a low rumble many times louder than thunder reverberated over the base.

"We did it friend," Cade said and then he let the tears flow.

###

Thanks for reading *In Harm's Way*. Look for Book 4: *A Pound of Flesh*, the forthcoming novel in the *Surviving the Zombie Apocalypse* series in the Fall of 2012. Please contact me on Facebook.

SHAWN CHESSER

ABOUT THE AUTHOR

Shawn Chesser, a practicing father, has been a zombie fanatic for decades. He likes his creatures shambling, trudging and moaning. As for fast, agile, screaming specimens ... not so much. He lives in Portland, Oregon, with his wife, two kids and three fish. This is his third novel.

CUSTOMERS ALSO PURCHASED:

JOHN O'BRIEN
NEW WORLD
SERIES

JAMES N. COOK
SURVIVING THE DEAD
SERIES

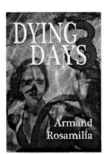

MARK TUFO
ZOMBIE FALLOUT
SERIES

ARMAND ROSAMILLIA
DYING DAYS
SERIES

HEATH STALLCUP
THE MONSTER
SQUAD

CPSIA information can be obtained at www.ICGtesting.com
Printed in the USA
LVOW07s1339141015

458243LV00021B/548/P

9 780991 377671